KINGDOM
COME

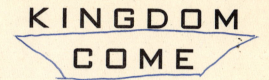

KINGDOM COME

A NOVEL

LARRY BURKETT
T. DAVIS BUNN

A JANET THOMA BOOK

THOMAS NELSON PUBLISHERS
Nashville

Published in Nashville, Tennessee, by Thomas Nelson, Inc.

Scripture quotations are from THE NEW KING JAMES VERSION. Copyright © 1979, 1980, 1982, 1990, Thomas Nelson, Inc.

This is a work of fiction. Any similarity to real life in the scenes, characters, timing, and events is merely coincidence.

Library of Congress Cataloging-in-Publication Data

Burkett, Larry.
    Kingdom come : a novel / Larry Burkett, T. Davis Bunn.
      p. cm.
    ISBN 0-7852-6770-0
    1. Christian fiction. I. Bunn, T. Davis, 1952-
    PS3552.U7243 K56 2001
    813/.54 21   LC Control Number: 00046572

Printed in the United States of America

1 2 3 4 5 6 QWD 05 04 03 02 01 00

This book, and others to come, would have never become a reality without the efforts of Janet Thoma. She is a great friend, a tireless worker, and most of all, a godly person. Janet is an editorial vice president for Thomas Nelson Publishers, and her behind-the-scenes efforts have birthed many great books.

We are grateful that she had the vision to introduce us to each other. This book is dedicated to our friend and colleague, Janet.

Now when He was asked by the Pharisees when the kingdom of God would come, He answered them and said, "The kingdom of God does not come with observation; nor will they say, 'See here!' or 'See there!' For indeed, the kingdom of God is within you."

LUKE 17:20–21

PART ONE

KINGDOM COME

ONE

Samuel Benjamin Atkins left the diner's air-conditioned shadows and paused to study the endless blue depths overhead. There was a taste of springtime freshness to the early May air, but he'd bet his bottom dollar that North Carolina summers were a long march of heat and high humidity. Not that he'd still be around. Not that he'd mind a few Carolina summers of his own, for that matter. Anything would be better than the stifling mugginess of another Washington August.

Back in his car, he drove a further thirty miles along the interstate before entering the Charlotte Turnpike. Twenty minutes later he was among the steel and glass towers of a bustling city. Ben Atkins took the Center City exit, stopped to ask directions from an old-timer drowsing in a downtown park, and shortly pulled up in front of the new city tower.

Windows down and tie loosened, he sat there a few moments to get his bearings. It was a habit bred through long experience, rolling into strange territory where every little detail helped to ensure his safety. Charlotte was a strange mishmash, one he had seen in several other eastern cities. High towers shouting wealth and newfound prosperity sprouted beside tired buildings with smoky glass and time-washed names. Overhead stretched enclosed walkways crowded with pretty ladies and grim-faced executives. Down below, the sidewalks

3

were nearly empty. A group of young black men loitered outside a Burger King. A few old men sat on park benches in what his wife used to call farmer's fancy dress——white shirt, light-colored slacks, thin socks, black shoes, bow tie, and straw hat with the brim bent up. A pair of policemen walked by, studiously ignored by the blacks, solemnly greeted by the old men. A trio of businesswomen bustled past his car, heads together in serious discussion, blind to all but their world of money and power. Behind them walked a family of five, the man and his son in dungarees and work-stained boots, the wife and daughters in matching print dresses. These were the kind of folks with whom he had always felt more comfortable, inhabitants of the farming world out beyond the city's reach.

Ben Atkins pulled into the multistory parking garage and took the tunnel over the street to the city tower. This was another modern oddity he had often seen but never grown accustomed to. The skyscraper housed the regional judicial system, precinct station, prosecutors, and five tightly sealed floors given over to the county lockup. Ben took the elevator to the floor reserved for federal offices, spoke to the receptionist, and was guided down a bland hallway. At its end stood double glass doors emblazoned with the seal of the Federal Bureau of Investigation. Inside, a second receptionist took his name and asked him to have a seat. He settled down and practiced what all law enforcement officers became experts at—waiting.

Ben Atkins was forty-two years old, six feet four, and 220 very solid pounds. The eight months in Washington had softened him some, but not much. The slight blurring to his craggy features was also touched by a fluorescent tan, but the leathery toughness carved by eighteen years of Wyoming wilderness remained for all to see. His grip was still iron hard, his eyes calm and far seeing, his voice quiet, his manner reserved. He had traversed the strange waters of bureaucracy and remained his own man.

"First time I've ever known anybody from Washington to show

up early." A lean, feisty man in his early thirties walked over. "Wayne Oates, senior resident agent. Welcome to Charlotte."

"Ben Atkins." He tested the grip as was expected, and gave the formal identification. "I've been appointed chief inspector, to determine whether your findings warrant moving on to a full criminal investigation."

"Good trip down?"

"Great. First time I've ever been in these parts. Wish I'd brought my fishing gear."

"Tell you what. Let's finish up this little ditty, then take a couple days off. I'll ferry you out to a place where the fish sit up and beg to be caught." The man's smile didn't touch his eyes, which were busy sizing Ben up. "You a lawyer or an accountant? Every headquarters man I've ever met is one or the other."

"I studied law," Ben said, not minding the inspection. "Never got much chance to use it. Spent most of my time out west. Wyoming, the Dakotas, a while in Arizona, but I didn't like that so much. Place is growing like a prairie fire, becoming a distant suburb of Los Angeles."

"You don't say." Wayne Oates gave Ben another up-and-down glance. "You must be tired as last Tuesday of Washington."

Ben thought he detected a slight envy beneath the words, which was hardly a surprise. An ambitious man would no doubt find the small Charlotte office stifling. "I don't pay those Washington folks enough mind to let them get under my skin."

Wayne Oates grasped his upper arm, then guided him through the gate by the reception desk. "I was worried Washington would send down some slope-headed, wet-nosed bureaucrat who couldn't find his own feet without some regulation manual."

"Your report made this situation sound pretty serious," Ben ventured.

"Tell you what," Wayne pushed open an office door and ushered Ben in before him, "why don't you sit yourself down over there. I'll wrangle up some coffee, then I'll show you what I've got. You can make up your own mind. How does that sound?"

Wayne departed and returned bearing two mugs of standard-issue coffee—too many hours on an overhot burner. Ben took his black and pretended to like it just fine. Wayne Oates was somewhere around five-ten with black, precisely trimmed hair. He bore a pock-marked face that spoke of living through some hard times. Raised on a farm, Ben guessed. Not much harder life than that. Wayne Oates wore his gray suit coat over a white shirt with a button-down collar and club tie. His feet were hidden inside wing tips that weighed in at about five pounds per shoe. His quiet, gray eyes remained fastened on Ben, giving nothing away. "How much do you know?" he asked.

"Why don't we begin with the assumption that I don't know anything at all. It'd be pretty close to the truth, anyway. I've never been down in this area before in my life." He sipped from his mug. "You raised on a farm?"

"Tobacco." The gray eyes blinked. "You?"

"No, my father was a steelworker. Born and raised in Pittsburgh. Left me with a hankering for wide open spaces. Liked what I saw of your area on the way down. Different from out west, but nice. Never seen such colors. Sky out west is a washed-out blue, and there aren't so many trees. Man could get attached to a place like this real fast." That was enough, he decided. *Let's get started, friend.*

Blank eyes regarded him a moment longer before Wayne Oates walked to a roll-down map covering a good portion of the side wall. "This is the southern half of central North Carolina. The region's called the Piedmont, and is mostly low-lying hills that run from the Coastal Plains region of the east to the Appalachians and Great Smoky Mountains west of here."

His hands circled the large concentration of roads and names at the map's bottom. "The largest metropolitan center is right here, around Charlotte. Outside of this area the region's mostly made up of towns under twenty thousand in population. The Piedmont has been one of the fastest growing areas of the nation since the early seventies. But there are still some places, like here." Wayne Oates pointed to an area two-thirds of the way up the right-hand side. "Regions that haven't seen much change for fifty years. Maybe more."

"Why's that?" Ben reached into his side pocket and pulled out notepad and pen. Not so much because he needed to write it down as he wanted to show how serious he was taking it all.

"Number of reasons. Location's bad, off the main roads. Companies tend to move near interstates, big cities, and airports. The region's hillier around there, with less level terrain available for development. Nearest technical school's fifty miles away, nearest university over a hundred. Also the people just aren't that interested in leaving the past behind. The towns are mostly small farming communities, a thousand or less in population. People around those parts are kind of set in their ways, not much concerned with keeping up with the rest of the world."

"That the area we're talking about, where your hand is?"

"That's it. Starts west of U.S. 64 here, goes northeast toward Jonesville. No state highways within twenty miles, as you can see. This ringed section in the middle here is Albany National Park. Fellow down at the university reckons it contains remnants of the world's oldest mountain range. Now they're just a trio of steep-sided hills. Old Indian territory, so they say. Locals claim the park itself used to be sacred land; only the chiefs and medicine men were allowed on those three hills. Haven't been any Indians in these parts for almost a hundred years."

Wayne Oates walked back and sat down behind his desk, his face and eyes and voice still as blank as a wall. "Area we're talking about is twenty-four miles long, eleven miles wide at the thickest point. Shaped kind of like a pregnant cigar, with the park at its center. The park itself is the smallest in the nation."

"Why include a state park in your figures?"

Wayne Oates stared at him silently, then went on as though Ben had never spoken. "Two hundred thousand acres, three thousand of which are inside the park. Two towns, one at each end. Five good-size lakes totaling forty-five hundred acres. The rest of the land is mostly given over to small holdings. North Carolina's traditionally been home to small farmers, except the old cotton area in the southeast. Hundred acres is a good-size farm around these parts, especially if you're growing tobacco. The rest of the acreage around here produces soybeans and corn, and some truck farmers raise fruit and vegetables. Nice area. Good people, or used to be. Some of the families down there have been working the same patch of land since before there even was a United States of America."

Ben tried again. "And now somebody's going around buying it up?" Maybe some strong-arm tactics. Still, that wouldn't make it a federal matter unless they could show organized crime was involved. But what would the Mafia want with a backwoods area of North Carolina?

"Far as we can figure, land started changing hands two years ago—"

"Two years?" Ben exclaimed, then instantly backed down. "Sorry, it just seems like a long time for somebody to be operating undetected in an area like that."

"I didn't say some*body*. This isn't the work of one big buyer." Wayne Oates's eyes turned to smoky ice. "We're not down here sitting on our hands, no matter what you folks up in Washington might think."

"No one said you were," Ben said quietly. It was an old story, this conflict between field offices and Washington, both thinking the other did nothing besides warm their chairs, produce paper, spend money, and fight to protect their jobs.

Wayne Oates remained unappeased. "If it was some*body*, we'd have wrapped this up long ago. Until last year it was just people moving in, others moving out."

Ben leaned back in his chair, crossed his arms, tried to keep his mind from jumping ahead.

"Back before last Christmas, the former sheriff paid us a visit. He'd just retired, and was right angry over the man they'd chosen to take his place. The two little towns in that area are called Douglas and Hamlin, total population about thirty-six hundred. Or was. The sheriff told us people he'd known all his life were picking up and leaving town—lock, stock, and barrel. Businesses were being bought up and changed beyond all recognition. Those were his exact words. *Beyond all recognition*."

"And you still don't know who they are?"

In reply, Wayne Oates unfolded a surveyor's map. "Land records show they started here and here." He pointed to north and south of the park. "They're the two least populated areas. Then it started spreading. Pretty slow at first, but like wildfire these past eighteen months." Wayne Oates ran a hand through his hair. "Local contractors've been going crazy up there. Near as we can figure, the building permits show some twenty-eight hundred new homes going up on the north side alone." He gave Ben a moment to take that in, then added, "The farms are changing too. Going from steady cash crops like tobacco and soy to vegetables, fruit, free-range animals. Lot of new construction there too. Silos, greenhouses, and three new packing and refrigeration plants."

Ben felt himself tightening down. This was something real, something big. His mind raced through possibilities and came back repeatedly to that hated word, *cult*. "Any new industry?"

"The area holds two textile companies and a furniture maker. Or it did. Then all of a sudden, after no new development for decades, the place just starts exploding. A couple of assembly operations, two huge distribution centers."

Ben Atkins inspected the map. "I thought you said there weren't any major roads out there."

"That's right. There aren't. And these people aren't building any new ones. All the community investment is going into new water and waste treatment, a medical clinic, underground cables—that sort of thing. Most of the new houses have generators and deepwater wells;

must cost a fortune. Everything's legal and aboveboard, right down to permits for a brand-new sewage system."

"And nobody's noticed anything until now?" Two years. The thought chilled him. Some revolutionary faction might have dug in and prepared for serious battle.

"Sure they did, but the contractors are out there making money hand over fist, so who's gonna say something and maybe kill the goose that's been laying the golden egg? One told me he'd been given a job to put up an apartment village four miles east of Douglas. That's the town on the area's western border there. Two hundred units, meeting hall, little shopping complex, sports areas. What happens, they agree to his price, his first price, then up it 10 percent, provided he finishes by the end of next month."

"What happens if somebody doesn't want to sell? There's got to be some people in a place like that who won't move, no matter what they're offered."

"Sure, there're some. Less than you might think, though. And the answer is, nothing. I checked on that first off. Some are old people who don't have anyplace else to go and don't care much about money. Some are the farming families I told you about. Two of the local pastors. Some of the townsfolk. Two, maybe three, hundred total. Out of close to five thousand. Far as I can make out, those who've stayed have been left pretty much alone. No harassment. None. Not of anybody who stayed, and not of any of the families I could find who've left. The retired sheriff said far as he knew everyone's been treated with the utmost courtesy. Those're his words. *Utmost courtesy.*"

Ben straightened his back, stretched as far as he could. He had a tendency to stiffen up if he leaned over like that too long. Too much time on horseback. "Any chance you could take me out and show me this setup?"

"You kidding?" Wayne Oates smiled grimly. "I wouldn't miss this for the world."

Ben Atkins sat in the car and watched the countryside unfold beneath a cloudless sky. Small holdings centered around trim farmhouses speckled the rolling hills. They left the interstate and passed through a town of slow-moving traffic, neat frame houses under vast shade trees, many pedestrians. A nice, homey, comfortable area. As far from the threat of a large and highly organized cult as Ben could imagine. But two decades in the West had taught him just how deceptive appearances could be. The most normal person could call an armed fortress home; the blankest face could hide a killer. He tried to keep himself from being charmed by the region and the day. But it was hard.

Wayne Oates had not spoken two words since the beginning of the trip. He drove as Ben expected he did everything, with calm deliberation and total concentration. Ben started to ask what he thought all this meant, but decided to wait. The man clearly wanted Ben to make up his own mind.

They turned off the highway onto a less traveled county road. A small road sign indicated the town of Douglas and the Albany National Park, nine miles. They entered a long stretch of pine forest that sloped down into a gentle valley. They passed several farms, crossed a swift-moving stream, drove up a steeper ridge, then crested a heavily wooded rise.

Instantly Ben Atkins gripped the dash and exclaimed, "What the blazes is that?"

"Take a wild guess," Wayne Oates replied.

The vista below was a swarm of activity. A cluster of new warehouses sat in the center of a chaotic storm of trucks, scrambling forklifts, and people. Beyond the warehouses rose monstrous piles of lumber, construction materials, coils of cable, and crates of goods under neatly pinned tarpaulins.

"It's one thing to hear about it, and another to see it," Wayne said.

But what held Ben's attention were the fences. Bordering the entire area, stretching out in both directions as far as Ben could see, was a pair of gleaming metal fences. A space fifteen feet wide had been cleared on both sides, cutting a straight swath through the forest to Ben's right.

Wayne drove slowly down the hill. The closer they got, the more Ben was clutched by both certainty and dread. The fences were the clearest possible indicator of something both sinister and major.

As though reading his mind, Wayne Oates began speaking. "Concrete-embedded steel posts, top-grade steel mesh, fifteen feet high, the inner fence topped by coiled razor wire."

"Regulation prison fencing," Ben said, the words almost a moan. "How far—"

"Right around the whole area. Both towns, the park, woodlands, everything."

They slowed as they passed the first fence. "They built the fences right up to either side of the roads," Wayne continued. "There aren't any four-lane highways around here, so the widest berth is about eighty feet. They put in those sliding steel gates you see there, steel slats set crossways for support, all the gates built up on little rubber tires."

"And not illegal so long as they're not closed," Ben said, almost to himself. He glanced over his shoulder. Standing just inside the inner fence were two young men. Nothing was said, no move made toward the car. Beyond the warehouses and trucks, all work had halted. Ben watched as people stepped around crates of machine parts and generators and pumps and bales to stare them down.

Ben shifted in his seat, freeing the gun holstered under his left arm. "Are they armed?"

"I haven't had any reason to search them. Not yet." Wayne released his double-handed grip on the wheel, pulled out his gun, cocked it, and set it on the seat between them. "But my guess is, to the teeth."

Ben had been involved in several raids on secret militias, and knew how easily the slightest confrontation could lead to violence. Even a friendly wave could result in gunfire. Everything became filtered through the militants' fog of inbred rage. "They recognize your car?"

"They do now. They pretty much ignored me until yesterday." He sped up and continued along what seemed like just another leafy country road. "I reckon they won't be ignoring us again, not ever."

"What happened yesterday?"

"The highway patrol arrested their leader." Wayne Oates sounded grimly satisfied. "He's waiting for us back at the county lockup."

"All right," Ben said. "I've seen enough."

"No sir, you haven't." He pulled up to a stop sign, then took the turn toward Douglas. "Not yet, anyway."

Ben felt an icy dread. "Don't tell me you've found an arms cache."

"Afraid not." Wayne Oates cast him a grim look. "What you're about to see is a whole lot worse."

***

Dottie Betham worked in the front room of the community center, surrounded by women and men ranging from their early teens to their eighties. It was astonishing just how much paperwork was required in dealing with the federal government. She had no experience with this sort of task. But only three of them had any previous contact with bureaucratic red tape, so they learned by doing. The atmosphere was not so much dour as grimly determined. People sat at their desks, ringed by a vast assortment of forms and files and computer printouts and tomes of state and federal regulations. Those who understood, taught. Those who didn't struggled forward as best they could. The arrest of their leader had only heightened what was already a quietly frantic search for answers.

Her own job was to coordinate compliance with the regulations required for a new apartment complex they were attempting to build with low-income supporting funds. The task required ninety-three forms—seventeen county, fifty-one state, twenty-five federal. Her former job as a freelance journalist had rendered her perfectly inadequate for the work. She was drowning in paper. But Dottie was also first cousin to the leader's now-deceased wife. Because she had known the leader longer than almost anyone else, and was one of the few single women in the community who approached the leader's age, most people assumed that the leader and she would soon wed. So Dottie was handed more responsibility than she wanted.

A teenage girl by the front window rose from her desk so fast her chair clattered over backward. "That FBI man is back!"

The room froze. An older woman at the chamber's center intoned, "Just get on with your work, everyone."

When no one moved, a stern man barked from the corner, "You heard what Paul told us at the meeting. Don't show them nothing untoward."

Reluctantly the cluster by the window broke up and returned to their desks and their papers. But the tension was heightened, and Dottie felt quiet and sullen rage charge the air.

Her desk was in the second row, facing toward the window and the front lawn. Dottie pretended to type at her computer while her attention remained caught by the two men climbing from the nondescript official car. One of them she had seen several times before—lean, thirtyish, blandly dangerous. The other man was a stranger. Taller, older, solid as a mountain, with the rawboned features of a cowboy. Broad shouldered and cleft chinned, a gaze as direct as a gun barrel. For reasons Dottie could not fathom, she shivered.

Dottie Betham dropped her head back to her work. It would be best for all of them if the authorities would just leave them alone. But she knew it was not going to happen. And for the thousandth time she regretted having ever stepped foot in this place.

The original town of Douglas was hard to spot, it had been so transformed in recent months. Ben Atkins halted by the front door of the new community center and gave the surroundings a slow sweep. The fire station was the only original structure that appeared unchanged, and even there stood three gleaming new hook and ladder trucks and a huge storage tank. The two old-timers seated by the station's open door returned his gaze with silent hostility. Even from this distance, across the street and the broad tree-lined lawn, Ben could feel their anger. His fingers itched and the holstered gun felt eager, as though ignited by unseen danger. Ben had drawn his gun in action fewer than a dozen times, and each time had left him feeling branded.

He forced himself to continue the inspection. A central lane, lined by shops and trees and awnings, ran straight north from where he stood. Everything was new or recently refurbished, spruced up and neat as a pin. Most of the buildings had recent additions, rising up where there was no room to expand outward. The only disturbance to the day's brilliant calm was the sound of construction from every point on the compass, and the knowledge that unseen eyes watched his every move. Unconsciously Ben shrugged his jacket and holster to a more comfortable angle. As long as they weren't aiming down the length of a rifle barrel, he could live with the hostile eyes.

Ben turned back to where Wayne Oates stood by the door to the community center, waiting and watching. Ben read the name on the door out loud: "Kingdom Come."

"That's the name they've given to this whole area," Wayne said. "Officially."

The news registered slowly. "They've legally incorporated their commune?"

In reply, Wayne opened the door and waved him inside. Though the hall was empty, the sense of being observed was far more intense. The pair took a half-step apart, the unconscious move of men trained never to offer a sniper a single target.

Ben asked softly, "You've been attacked here?"

"No assault, no direct threat, nothing I can base a charge on." Wayne led him down the central hall and out a rear door. "Not yet."

"Any sign of heavy arms?"

"None." Wayne walked down a covered path through a neatly manicured garden to a small back building. The glass door announced that the small structure housed the Kingdom Come police department. "But you saw all those tarps and trucks. They could be bringing in antitank missiles and land mines by the crate."

"What about the local cops?"

Wayne Oates halted by the door to the police headquarters to turn and offer a bleak smile. "We think alike."

"What's that supposed to mean?"

"The local cops," Wayne said, "were the first place I turned."

Ben followed Wayne inside. Some local police were all too willing to turn over sticky problems to federal agents, glad to have someone else to assign both impossible decisions and blame. Others fiercely resented what they saw as outside interference.

At first glance, the redbrick building's interior looked like any new small-town police station. The place smelled of fresh paint and frequent cleaning. The radio and computer terminals were all top quality. State and national flags draped from flagpoles by the back window.

The young man behind the desk was not a cop. Ben could not say how he knew, but he was certain nonetheless that the man was not trained as a police officer. He held the clear-eyed expression of someone who had never faced what life revealed to an officer of the law. The man was in his late twenties, talking on the phone and smiling easily. Then he spotted Wayne and sobered, his gaze clouding. He said merely, "I've got to go, Mrs. Blake. Yes, I'll have Hal stop by. No ma'am, he won't forget. All right, now. You take care."

He hung up the phone and rose to his feet. "What is it this time?"

Wayne Oates asked, "Is Officer Drew around?"

"He's out on patrol."

"Radio him and say two FBI officers would like to have a word."

"Hal Drew told you the last time not to bother him again."

Wayne leaned across the counter and gave his words a cold weight. "Call him. Now."

The young man flushed with easy anger. But he reached for the microphone and said, "Come in, Hal."

A languid voice said over the speaker, "Go."

"The FBI man is back."

"You don't say."

The angry gaze swiveled to Ben. "And he's brought a friend."

"Well, I guess it's our lucky day, then." The man's drawl held the easy cadence of Southern rural heritage. "I recollect telling that fellow Oates I was done talking to him."

"That's exactly what I said."

"Guess he don't listen too good. Well, you tell him to take a seat out back. I'll be coming in directly."

"Any idea when, exactly?"

"Directly, I said. Got me more important things to do right now than jawing with a man who never learned to keep his nose out of what's not any of his business."

"Roger that. Oh, and Mrs. Blake called."

"She seeing them imaginary fiends in masks again?"

"They climbed her trellis last night."

"I'll stop by on my way. Hal out."

Ben Atkins breathed around the tightness in his chest, and spoke for the first time. "I'd like to see your lockup."

The young man set down the microphone. "What for?"

"It's his right," Wayne Oates said, his voice softened with anger. "Open the connecting door while you still can."

The young man hit the button, and the fortified rear door buzzed open. "Help yourself. But there's nothing to see."

Ben walked back into the lockup. The eight cells and the central watch-station were as gleaming and fresh as the front office. And utterly empty. Ben surveyed the place, with the eight mattresses still in their plastic wrapping and the bars of soap untouched. "This their only jail?"

"It is now. The other one in Hamlin's been knocked down. And Sheriff Hal Drew is their only officer on duty. I guess you'll have to meet him some other time."

Ben felt the ache of coming battle. "They've taken over the local government. That's what you wanted me to see, isn't it?"

"One more stop," Wayne replied. "Then we're done."

⚏ ⚏

Wayne Oates ignored the elevator and headed for the back stairs of the community center. On the second floor he pushed through the door marked OFFICES and walked toward the suite at the front of the building. Ben glanced through open doors to either side, and saw busy people halting in their work to stare him down. The images clashed mightily. Ben had often come into conflict with militias and cults, had confronted their paranoia and their rage too often to count. Anyone who had worked the Western states' empty reaches as long as Ben had learned the signs and the dangers. Yet few such groups showed anything like this normal facade to the world, and fewer still operated within the existing bureaucratic framework. Either he was reading this community entirely wrong, or he was confronting a genuine nightmare.

Wayne entered the front office and was met by a cold-faced woman already on her feet behind her desk. "I'd like to speak to your mayor."

"What an interesting request," she responded with frigid vehemence. "Seeing as how you've locked him up on some trumped-up charge."

"What about your city manager?" Wayne pressed.

"Sorry, we're fresh out of hospitality today," she shot back.

"City councilman? Who is it that takes charge of things when your leader is away?"

"He's not away," she shot back, her clear-eyed anger remarkably similar to the young man's in the police station. "Our lawyers are on their way to Charlotte right now to arrange for his release."

Wayne hesitated, just a fraction of an instant, but long enough for Ben to realize this was news. Ben agreed. Only a well-oiled cult would have attorneys on hand, ready and willing to fend off lawmen. This was serious indeed.

Wayne Oates said, "It's usually in a community's best interest to cooperate with federal authorities."

"Not this town." She stabbed an angry finger toward the door. "Release Pastor Chuck, and we might have something to say to you. Now good day."

Ben waited until they were back in the car and driving out of Douglas to ask, "Who is this Pastor Chuck?"

Wayne Oates glanced at his watch, then placed a call on his pocket phone. "Jim? It's Wayne. We're on our way to meet Fran. I just got word they're sending attorneys down to spring the man. That's right. No, we don't have time. Fran is waiting for us, and you know—" He paused a moment. "Good. Talk to the judge and ask him to delay things just an hour or so, will you? Right. We'll hurry."

Ben paused long enough to inspect the pandemonium surrounding the warehouses and the long straight line of fencing. Then he repeated, "Who is Pastor Chuck?"

"As far as I can figure out," Wayne Oates replied, accelerating up the rise, "Reverend Charles Griffin is king of all he surveys."

THREE

Reverend Thurgood Innes sat at the head of the oval table and presented the elders of his Orlando church with an attentive face. In truth, he was seven hundred and seventeen miles away. The governing synod of the Reformed Church of America was scheduled to begin its annual congress in Richmond, Virginia, the next day. After serving seven years as an associate member, he had finally been elected to the RCA synod. He could scarcely wait to start his journey.

Thurgood Innes shifted impatiently in his chair and resisted the urge to glance at his watch. His elders were by and large a good and godly group, but my, could they wrangle. It had been the same with every church he had pastored—mix politics with money and religion, bake for several years, and the result was a weird concoction of tastes and directions and aims and voices. Some meetings, the only point of agreement was their *amen* to the opening prayer.

"I'm telling you, the church doesn't need new hymnals." That from Miller Kedrick, chief financial overseer and the church's largest donor. "We've still got six unopened boxes in the choir room. I checked before I came in."

"And I'm saying that these old choir books just don't do the trick any more." The music minister was a new fellow, only with the church eight months, straight out of seminary and a real find. But he was not accustomed to dealing with the Miller Kedricks of this world.

"We're having to print more than half the songs we sing each Sunday in the bulletin, and—"

"That's what we have the screen over the pulpit for, in case you haven't noticed."

"I know all about the screen. I happen to program it every Sunday, in case *you* haven't noticed."

Miller Kedrick grew tight rings of red about his neck, like angry gills. "Now you look here—"

"We can't put the bars of music in either the bulletin or on the screen. Which means people who want to harmonize can't, not unless they know the hymn backward and forward. And *that* limits us to all the old praise favorites." The music minister turned toward Thurgood for support. "I'm getting complaints from both sides, people who want different praise songs and others who want the music along with the words. We need those new hymnals."

Thurgood Innes was known as a mediator. The conversation had already passed the point where he would normally have intervened and oiled over the stormy waters. But the new music minister needed a chance to forge his own way among this group. Thurgood decided to remain silent a bit longer.

"We don't have the money!" Miller Kedrick was a bully, plain and simple. He was a huge contributor to the church and had a Midas touch with almost every one of his numerous business interests, including the church's own Caribbean outreach projects. But he tended to ramrod his opinions, and expected everyone to toe his line. "Fixing the atrium's leaky roof cleaned us out. You'll just have to wait."

"I have the money in my discretionary fund." The music minister tried not to sound smug, but it was hard. "We had planned to use it for a special youth concert, but if I need to, then I'll just have to spend it on the hymnals."

"Oh, I would hate to see that happen." This from the table's farthest end, a widow in her sixties, the church librarian. "Those concerts are a vital part of our youth ministry."

"They sure are." This from the youth pastor, a quiet young woman who went out of her way to avoid Miller Kedrick. She sat three seats down from the finance man now, and moved back farther in her seat to avoid his glare. "Every concert, we bus in several thousand kids who normally wouldn't step foot in a church. How much money are we talking about here?"

"Six thousand hymnals at four dollars and eight cents apiece. They're giving us a fifty percent discount."

"I can use part of my own discretionary fund to cover half the concert's expenses, if the church will spring for the rest," offered the youth minister. "We can charge a couple dollars more for the camp outing and make up most of it."

"Now just a minute here," Miller Kedrick growled. The red had risen to envelop his ears as well.

"Take five hundred dollars from my account if you have to," the librarian agreed.

"That won't be necessary." Thurgood Innes gave the music minister a quick little nod. Well done indeed. He liked a pastor who was able to stand up for what he believed in. Working in a church of this size at times required a thick skin. "I'm certain we can come up with most of the funds from the general budget."

"I just told you—" Miller sputtered.

"Let's have a look around and see what we turn up." Innes cast a single swift glance down the table, letting Miller know he had lost this round. "Now then. As you know, I'm off to Richmond. The national synod starts tomorrow. Is there any issue you feel I need to raise before the leaders of our denomination?"

He settled back and let them ramble. He already knew what he would be bringing to the synod table, which was almost nothing. His first meeting would be spent listening more than speaking. The synod was as fractious as his own elders, if not more so. The RCA denomination had gone through a very rocky decade and was now so divided there was even some talk of one faction forming a new group.

The problem was growth, plain and simple. Some of the RCA churches were undergoing an evangelical explosion. Others were not. Those with memberships in the thousands were becoming increasingly impatient with their more conservative-minded brethren. They wanted change, and they wanted a larger say. Within the synod, however, the staid older group held a slim majority.

Thurgood Innes pastored a church based in Orlando, one that had grown from several hundred to more than five thousand members in the past ten years. But he was known as someone who respected the old traditional ways. Thurgood was therefore seen as a linchpin, a man who could move comfortably within both camps. There was even talk of his taking the place of the outgoing president, who was scheduled to retire in a year. Thurgood Innes had no intention of upsetting the synod by spouting off during his first official conference. Not unless he had something that would justify . . .

His attention was snagged by a change in the conversation. The shift was so staggering it took him a moment to focus upon what was being said, for all around the room heads were nodding in agreement.

"I'm really worried about this," the music minister was saying.

"I haven't heard that much," Miller Kedrick said. "But what I have heard is bad."

"I know Chuck Griffin," the youth minister said. "I just can't believe he's involved in a cult."

Thurgood Innes eased himself forward, listening hard. He, too, had heard the rumors about Griffin, another RCA pastor.

"I don't know what else to call it," Miller Kedrick countered. "I've spoken with a supplier who works with several of the local construction companies up around Charlotte. He says they're in the process of building two thousand more units right as we speak."

The librarian asked, "Two thousand units of what?"

"Houses and apartments." This from the music minister. Agreeing now with Miller. "I had no idea it was growing that fast."

Thurgood sat up straighter. Neither had he.

"They've taken over the county government. Joined two old townships together and changed the name."

"To what?"

"Kingdom Come." Miller Kedrick snorted. "If that doesn't sound like some far-out cult, I don't know what does."

"Not only that," the librarian offered, "but I've heard from colleagues that there are spin-offs popping up all over the place."

"That's terrible." This from the quietest member of the elders, a lanky orange grower who had left the farmwork to his son and had concentrated on backing up Thurgood whenever and wherever he needed it. "If this got out, why, it'd hurt our good name something awful. They might as well tar and feather us all."

"It could positively destroy us as a denomination," the music minister solemnly agreed.

Thurgood Innes let out a breath he had not even been aware he had been holding. If this issue could unite his elders, then perhaps it would have the same effect within the synod. If so, whoever championed the cause would be a shoo-in for the presidency.

Perhaps he would need to speak after all.

FOUR

Ben Atkins mulled over what he had just seen as Agent Wayne Oates drove them back toward Charlotte. Where the two-lane highway joined the interstate, Wayne pulled into a diner's parking lot. Ben glanced back, staring down the long, straight blacktop. The old state road was cracked and tree-lined and utterly still. Ben watched as a strong spring wind touched the trees and scattered golden dollops of sunlight up and down the country road. He knew without any question that his world had been split in two; the part before discovering what lay down that deceptively peaceful lane, and whatever was now to come.

The diner was a flat building with garishly painted plywood walls and a low-slung motel extending out behind. A vast parking lot contained a dozen or so semis drawn from the rumbling stream on the neighboring four-lane road. Wayne threaded his way through the trucks and their thundering motors, his tires scrunching over gravel and rough pits in the concrete. Ben watched as a woman in her forties stepped down from a nondescript Jeep, dropped her cigarette onto the ground, and walked over. She wore jeans and a flannel shirt and scarred cowboy boots. Her hair was a mousy brown, her face as grim as her gaze.

She cast practiced glances fore and aft as she opened the back door to Wayne's car. She slid inside and demanded tensely, "Were you followed?"

"No."

"You're sure?"

"This isn't my first contact with an insert, Fran."

"All right. Drive around behind the motel. There's a slot by the garbage bins where you can hide in the brush and keep a lookout."

"What about your Jeep?"

"I used a different car around the commune. If they followed me to and from Charlotte, we're cooked. Drive."

Ben asked, "You're that certain the group is dangerous?"

She did not even look his way. "So who's this?"

"Agent down from Washington."

"You're sure?"

"Come on, Fran." Wayne swung the car in a tight circle, swiveled in his seat, and backed carefully in beside the Dumpsters. Despite the closed windows, the car was instantly awash with the smell of refuse. "This is Wayne Oates you're talking to. I wouldn't bring a perp out here. Don't get paranoid on me."

"Right." She reached into her shirt pocket, drew out a pack of cigarettes and a Bic lighter. She lit one and took a deep drag, then said with the smoke, "It doesn't really matter anyway. I'm all done in there."

"No you're not."

She flicked her hair back, revealing an angular face drawn tighter by perpetual unease. "I wasn't asking, Oates."

He put a little more pressure behind the words. "You're actually thinking of walking away from an ongoing investigation?"

"Not thinking. Doing." Another harsh drag. "My cover's blown."

"Are you sure?"

"Three nights running, they've brought a group around and prayed over me and my little lost soul."

Ben halted Wayne's further protest by placing a hand on the man's arm. He turned more fully and said, "I'm sorry, ma'am, I didn't catch your last name."

"Tottler."

"Ms. Tottler, I'd be most grateful if you could please tell me what you're so anxious about."

Eyes the color of her hair glinted through the cigarette smoke. "Does it show?"

"If you were wound up any tighter, you'd spin out of here like a Hubble gyroscope."

She smoked in silence for a moment, then said, "Nothing you can put your finger on. But a thousand little things."

"I understand."

"You're not just some headquarters 'crat, are you?"

"No ma'am. I've been in the field for over twenty years." Ben kept his tone easy, offering calm and strength to a woman clearly drained of all but nervous energy and fear. "Wyoming and Arizona mostly. A little time in the Dakotas and Montana, but I'm not partial to ten months of winter."

"You've worked with militia cults?"

"Several times."

"Take whatever you've experienced," Fran Totter said, her voice flattened by the smoke and the fatigue, "and multiply it a hundred times over."

Ben exchanged a glance with Wayne. "Did you find an arms cache?"

"No, and that was a mystery. I spent a lot of time looking around. A number of the homes were armed, but more in the way of hunting rifles than militia-type weapons." She was calmer now, her gaze not glinting quite so harshly. "But all the other signs were there. All power focused into the hands of one man."

"Charles Griffin, is that right?"

"That's the man. You met him?"

Wayne Oates replied, "Not yet. We're headed downtown from here. He's in detention."

"The man's a total mystery. You'll never meet a quieter, more soft-spoken guy."

"Describe him for me, please," Ben asked.

"Wispy character, maybe five-ten, a hundred and seventy pounds. Dark brown hair, green eyes, tends to dress casual. No distinguishing features other than a very soft voice." Ben's confusion must have shown, for she added, "Don't get me wrong. When that guy says jump, the whole lot of them are already in the air."

Ben nodded, then asked, "What else?"

Fran stabbed her cigarette out in the armrest ashtray. "You've seen the fence?"

"Yes. It goes all the way around the community?"

"It will soon enough. The completion date is next week." She looked at Wayne. "You tell him what they're doing with federal money?"

"Partly."

"They have filed all the proper forms and gained federal and state funding to build a new water filtration system, a sewage treatment plant, and a hospital. They're using their own money to set up a generating plant."

Ben could not help but show his dismay. "A cult so well organized that they're drawing on government funding?"

Wayne said, "Tell him about the kids."

Fran said, "They've emptied the schools."

Ben asked, "We can move on that, can't we?"

"I didn't say they had shut them down," Fran corrected him, fishing out another cigarette. She lit it, sucked so hard her cheeks turned to caverns. "They're open, but empty. Every kid in the place is officially registered for home-schooling."

Wayne added, "A lot of these country schools are structured along standard lines. The grammar school and high school are built side by side. Twelve grades together, makes for easier busing and watching the kids develop. Only nowadays there's not a single child in sight. Every classroom is empty. Last time I stopped by, the principal was dead drunk."

Ben mused aloud, "I can't believe we're facing a cult so large it can actually take over a pair of towns."

"Believe it," Fran said grimly. "I've been there for seventeen days now, and I haven't slept a wink the entire time. They've known I was an outsider from the start. Eyes followed me everywhere. Nobody said anything, but I was blown and they were waiting. Waiting and watching for the chance to take me down."

The thoughts were enough to push her out the door. "We're about finished here, aren't we?"

"Wait." Ben rose from the car with her. "How can you be so sure they meant you harm?"

"You go spend a couple of days in there," Fran replied, already pacing away. "See for yourself what it feels like to be stalked by eight thousand people."

He watched her stride off, saw the angry way she tossed her cigarette to one side, then followed the gesture with glances to every side. Reluctantly Ben allowed, "I just might have to do that."

The new Charlotte lockup followed the trend of many wealthy cities, housing the jail on security-isolated floors within the justice building. From outside, the building was just one more steel-and-glass temple dominating the burgeoning skyline. The courts were separated into municipal and county and state, with the lockup housed in the middle. The jail's central corridor stank of disinfectant and compressed humanity and rage. Metal doors and shouts and jangling keys and electronic buzzers and blaring televisions formed a din that was trapped behind the bulletproof windows and the solid steel walls. After the country's deceptive quiet, Ben found the familiar chaos almost comforting.

Wayne held the door open to the prison conference room and waited for him to enter. Ben hesitated, then decided, "I think I'll watch from next door."

"Suit yourself."

Ben stepped into the observation chamber and pulled a metal chair up close to the one-way mirror. He watched as a jailer brought in a slender man in his late forties, muffled within a one-piece yellow jail coverall. The man offered no resistance as the jailer linked his ankle chains through the catch bolted to the floor, then shackled his wrists to the steel table.

The jailer retreated to the door and said to Wayne, "Press this buzzer here when you're done. I'll be right outside."

"Thank you. Okay, sit down, Mr. Griffin," Wayne said,

The prisoner had a young man's easy features, save for the deep creases streaking out from his eyes and mouth. Otherwise he was fairly nondescript, giving Ben no immediate sense of fury or compacted danger. Through the speaker, Ben heard the man ask, "Is this the way you treat all your traffic offenders?"

"You have been accused of careless and reckless driving," Wayne Oates read from the folder opened before him. "And possibly driving while under the influence."

"Your breath and blood tests must have shown I hadn't been drinking."

Wayne replied, "There are a number of new designer drugs that are not immediately detectable."

"I do not drink, and I do not abuse drugs." The voice carried no hostility that Ben could hear. Almost no inflection at all. The man's tone was as wispy as his chin, slight and seemingly ineffective.

"And yet you left the road and rammed your truck into a tree."

"I was tired. I had been working almost three days straight. I must have fallen asleep."

"Right." Wayne flipped a page. "What had you been doing for those previous three days?"

"Too much." The man smiled thinly. "As a matter of fact, I need to thank you for the chance to get some uninterrupted sleep."

Wayne flipped the page. "We have received some alarming reports about your cult, Mr. Griffin."

"It is not a cult."

"Running a sect that opposes the rule of law is a felony, Mr. Griffin."

The pastor hesitated, then responded with, "'I am put here for the defense of the gospel. For me to live is Christ, and to die is gain.'"

"What is that, your cult's motto?"

"I told you, it's not a cult. And the words come from Philippians."

Ben strained to hear beyond the words, but could not discern anything that might suggest that here sat the leader of the largest cult in American history.

Oates persisted, "What can you tell me about all the activity—"

The jailer rapped hard on the door, then opened it with a clang. "Some visitors for the prisoner."

Angrily Wayne rose to his feet. "I didn't say—"

"It doesn't matter what you said." A pair of dark-suited men entered in a rush. The older man was tall and slender and African-American. He slapped a folded document down on the table. "The court has just ordered him to be set free." He spotted the chains and turned gray with rage. His voice sounded throttled as he demanded, "Get these things off him."

Wayne tried to hold to the offense. "And you are?"

"Phil Trilling. Reverend Chuck Griffin is my client," the older man snapped. "And as soon as I finish here, I'm going to have you brought up on civil charges."

The chained prisoner said, "It's all right, Phil."

"No, it's not. It's despicable." When the jailer still did not move, the man shouted, "Get these chains off my client *now!*"

Wayne waved the jailer forward. The lawyer grew increasingly choleric as the chains rattled through the catches on the floor and the table. "This is utterly *outrageous.* I'll have you before the judge tomorrow—"

"You're going to do nothing of the kind. Now let it go." The prisoner had not raised his voice, but the effect on the older man was astonishing. The attorney collapsed like a deflated balloon.

But Wayne did not back down. "It is a federal offense to maintain a private militia."

The lawyer gaped at Oates. "You're *insane.*"

"Let it go," the prisoner repeated. When he was sure the lawyer would remain silent, the prisoner turned to Wayne Oates. "May the Lord bless you and keep you. May He make His light to shine upon you."

Wayne Oates's expression tightened further. "We'll be watching you."

"Come on, Chuck," Phil Trilling said. "Let's get out of here."

FIVE

That following morning, the Charlotte FBI office was both muted and tense. Ben felt as though he was seated at the vortex of a massive storm. They had faxed their preliminary report to FBI headquarters the previous evening. Five telephone conversations then ensued, moving up the regulation ladder step by step as alarm bells sounded. Waking people up, lighting fires, raising the levels of dread and adrenaline all night long.

Like most FBI regional offices, glass-fronted cubicles encircled a large central chamber. Wayne had the slats down over his internal window, but they were not completely angled shut, as if Wayne was uncertain whether he wanted his colleagues to observe the coming conference call from Washington.

"Who do you think will be involved?" Wayne asked.

Ben swiveled around from surveying the sunlit vista beyond the tall external windows. Wayne's face was made leaner, the pockmarks deeper, by the previous day's experiences and the coming parley. Ben asked, "Have you ever been involved in something this big?"

"Not on the front line."

"A potential head-banger like this case, we'll have ten, maybe twelve people clustered around a seventh-floor conference table." Ben leaned back, set one boot on the corner of the desk. He might have grown accustomed to the toneless gray or navy suits required by head office, but if he didn't have on his Tony Llama lizard-skins, he didn't feel dressed. "There will be a resident specialist on cult psychology. Somebody else who's been tracking commune development and militias. Glorified pencil pushers who couldn't find the trigger on their gun without a map and a guide. But they won't matter. Not today."

"Why not?"

"Because they'll be cowed to silence by the heavyweights."

Wayne shifted, making the standard-issue chair squeak nervously. "Evan will sit in?"

Evan Hawkins was the division head, four levels above Wayne and the next above Ben. "My guess is, Evan would rise from his deathbed for this call. Have you ever met him?"

"Once."

"Evan is all right in my book." Ben was glad for the chatter to fill the elongated moments. "He spent twelve years based in the FBI's San Francisco office, three more in Dallas. He's ambitious, yes. Guys who aren't ambitious don't last long in the shark-infested waters of Washington. But Evan has never forgotten what it means to be a field officer."

When Ben halted there, Wayne pressed quietly, "Who else?"

"Well, now, that's the question, isn't it?" He felt the acid of bureaucratic indigestion rise in his throat. "My guess is Theron Head."

Wayne froze. "You're kidding me."

"Take a look at what we're facing here. The largest cult in America's history, two hundred thousand acres and maybe fifteen thousand residents. That makes what, six thousand able-bodied men? That's not a militia. That's a career maker."

"I've heard stories about Theron Head."

"Sure you have." Ben knew he should stop there, but found that nerves gave a life of their own to his tongue. "Around headquarters, he's known as the Toad. You'd understand if you ever worked with him. He's this small guy, maybe five-five and weighs about as much as a wet breeze. Very quiet, very mild looking. But looks are deceptive. He doesn't talk much, but when he does it usually means his career goes up one notch and somebody else's slides down. He's spent his entire working life in Washington, made it to the number-three slot in the Bureau, and as far as he's concerned, he's only gotten started."

"You don't like him."

"I don't like Washington." Ben resisted the sudden urge to describe Theron Head as a pencil-neck bureaucrat with the morals of a pit viper. After all, the man was his boss. "I never knew how good we have it in the field offices until I landed—"

He was halted by the phone ringing. "Here we go," Ben said.

Wayne picked up the receiver. "Oates." He listened, then said, "Yes sir, right here beside me. Right. Just a moment." He hit the loud-speaker and settled back. "All right, sir."

"Ben, you hear me all right?"

"Just fine, Evan."

"We've got a basic group of players here with me. And Theron's decided he needs to sit in."

Ben pointed his finger like a gun and fired off a round at Wayne. His voice bureaucrat-bland, he said, "Good morning, Mr. Head."

Evan Hawkins marched straight on, as of course Theron Head would not bother with anything so superfluous as a polite greeting. "Ben, we just want to make sure we're on the same wavelength here. You agree with Wayne Oates that we're talking about a dangerous fringe element the size of a fair-size town?"

"I've been here too short a time to say anything about danger or threat for certain," Ben replied. That was another thing about Washington he disliked, the hurry-up-and-wait mode, pressuring field agents to make snap judgments, which were then left dangling until the decision was reached by safe consensus. "But whatever it is, it's big."

"And neither of you saw anything at Kingdom Come that sug-gested the presence of a standing militia?"

"Nothing except the fence." And the eyes. Ben recalled the gazes that met him as they passed the warehouses, and shifted as he had the previous day in the car seat. "That fence is the most amazing thing I've ever seen. Regulation prison issue. Ran out in both directions for miles, supposedly all the way around the compound."

"We've done some quick checking up here. And everything points toward some careful inroads into the state and county treasuries. Massive projects either completed or headed that way." A shuffling of paper, then, "Water treatment, hospital, sewer system, low-income housing, solar panels, and diesel power generators for their very own substation."

"And the community center," Wayne reminded them. "And the warehouses."

The discussion drifted in predictable circles, going over the points raised in Ben and Wayne's report, then moving to analysis of other cults. The number of doomsday cults had been steadily rising for years. The nation's angriest, most rage-filled government haters were finding strength in numbers, holing up in isolated areas and priming for action. The former head of a California FBI field office was counted among their leaders, at great embarrassment to the agency. Authorities were increasingly on the alert for cults using the Internet as a secret gathering point from which to organize a major terrorist strike. As a result, the FBI had spent hundreds of thousands of man-hours developing contingency plans against numerous worst-case scenarios. The question was not *if,* but rather *when* and *how* and *where.*

Generally the FBI separated paramilitary groups into two distinct categories. The larger by far comprised those who were more mouth than menace, the frustrated and the lost and the enraged who consider any organized authority their enemy. The smaller category, however, comprised those classed as *agents provocateurs*, firebrands who stirred up the antigovernment infantries and gave shape to the rage of others. This category contained those actually planning one action or another. Seldom did a month pass without someone being brought up on charges. Three days previously, a group had been arrested for hoarding firearms and bomb-making equipment and for drawing up plans to destroy power plants in northern California. The FBI currently estimated that nearly two hundred armed cults existed within the United States. Thankfully, very few held more than a dozen members.

Which was why their current discussion returned again and again to the staggering numbers within Kingdom Come. That and the speed at which it seemed to be growing.

Evan continued, "We've been doing a quick-and-dirty on the leader, Charles Griffin. He pastored a church in Indianapolis. The one that was shot up three years ago."

"I remember that." Ben Atkins leaned forward. "Some maniac walked into a church service and started blasting away."

"That's the one. Griffin resigned soon after and disappeared."

The overly bland voice of Deputy Director Theron Head was instantly recognizable. "Mr. Oates, tell me everything you can about the leader."

Wayne sat up straighter in his chair. "I've only met him that one time, sir."

"Describe him and the encounter. Don't leave anything out."

Wayne gave it his best shot, his voice as regulation gray as his tie. When he was done, the silence held long and tight. Finally Theron rumbled, "When you met the leader at the prison, you ordered him shackled to the table and the floor?"

"Yes sir."

"Why is that?"

Wayne swallowed. "I wanted to provoke a reaction. I felt like we'd let them operate in the clear for too long. I was hoping we could make them show their true colors if we humiliated their leader."

A long pause, then, "Good thinking, Mr. Oates."

"Thank you, sir," Wayne replied weakly.

Ben felt it necessary to point out, "We've had no indication of anything sinister."

"We can't afford another fiasco like the one in Waco," Theron snapped. "We must flush these perpetrators out immediately."

"They have broken no laws, and no one has been forced from their homes," Ben Atkins reminded them. "We have nothing whatsoever to indicate a criminal plot."

There was a moment's astonished silence. Then Theron Head said, "Which is why I want you to infiltrate their movement, Mr. Atkins."

"Kingdom Come has already identified me as a federal agent."

"Not necessarily a bad thing. As Mr. Oates wisely pointed out, we need to provoke a response."

"What about Fran Tottler?"

It was Evan who replied. "She called in saying she was taking a leave of absence, and then vanished. We can't raise her."

"Another reason why we cannot let this wait a day longer," Theron Head continued. "You should move into her place today. This afternoon."

"But sir—"

"That was not a request, Mr. Atkins." A hand came down on the unseen table. "All right. That's enough for now. Good day, everyone."

There were quiet murmurs around the conference room, but as Wayne reached to cut the connection, Evan's voice came over the speaker. "Ben, pick up the phone."

He did as he was ordered. "Yes?"

"Hang on a second." Clearly Evan was waiting until the conference room emptied. Then he demanded, "Mind telling me what you were thinking, arguing with Theron like that?"

"It seems to me that we're jumping to unfounded conclusions here."

"There are times to speak your mind and times to stay quiet. You got them mixed up pretty bad."

"We have no concrete evidence that the group is planning anything sinister," he repeated.

"Oh, come off it, Ben! Agent Tottler has come back with everything we need!"

"I still think—"

"And I'm telling you it doesn't matter what you think. All you've done here is sign your own death warrant!" Evan Hawkins slammed down the phone.

Ben settled the receiver down, looked at Wayne, and said quietly, "I hate Washington. I really do."

SIX

Dottie Betham walked back from the community center wondering what on earth had brought her to Kingdom Come. Even more baffling was what forced her to stay. The tree-lined streets and the old-timey air of a contented evening mocked her. As did the cheery greetings cast all about her, people glad to be here and happy to salute their new neighbors. Dottie passed one cluster after another, all speaking of how their beloved Pastor Chuck had been released and was now back resting at home. The construction saws were quiet now, the banging hammers and the grinding motors and the overloud talking of the construction workers all put away for another night. Birdsong had taken its place, and the sky was cast with a feathery lace of burnished gold set within an endless realm of blue. The May evening was redolent with the scent of blooming dogwood and magnolia. Everything in Kingdom Come seemed satisfied with life and the future ahead, except her.

She entered the door of her apartment just in time to hear the phone ring. The sound was so startling that she dropped her bag of groceries in her haste to rush over. "Hello?"

"Dottie? Dottie Betham?"

She recognized the voice instantly. "Ed! How *are* you?"

"Me?" Ed Starling was current affairs editor at *Newsday*, one of the nation's top weekly newsmagazines. "My number-one writer goes flying off to never-never land, leaving me in the clutch—how do you expect me to be?"

She did not care that her laugh sounded shrill with frantic relief. Nor did it matter that Ed Starling always talked like that. It was his way of buttering up writers before applying the thumbscrews over pay. "If I'm that good, how come you never offered me a permanent job?"

"Because I know you wouldn't accept it." He spoke so fast, Dottie was tempted to believe he had actually given it thought. "You love your independence too much. You've done, what, four hundred articles for every magazine under the sun, interviewing presidents one week and cooking snails in France the next."

The number was more like five hundred, but the rest was true. Dottie Betham had earned an enviable reputation as someone who could be dropped into the thick of things and trusted to send out fifteen hundred words on time, and right in line with the editor's desired viewpoint.

"Never mind me," Starling continued. "The question is, how are you?"

"I wish I knew." She hated the way she sounded, petulant as a teenager. But she could not help it. Being connected to the outside world left her ready to sob with relief. "I thought I'd come down here to North Carolina and have some time to relax. But all I seem to do is dwell on my mistakes."

"Tell me about it. That's what I hate about vacations. Soon as I catch up on my sleep, I have waking nightmares. I've decided that's why people go off on these action-packed holidays. Travel fifteen thousand miles in nine days and dive the Great Barrier Reef. It's the only way they can escape looking in that old vacation mirror and seeing how their lives are going straight down the tubes."

"Maybe I should do an article on it," Dottie suggested, only half kidding. "How people design vacations to run away from themselves."

"Maybe, but not now. I'm not after a new topic, I'm fishing for a writer. You."

She sat down in one of the stiff-backed dining chairs. Dottie had rehearsed this moment a thousand times in her mind. Particularly late at night, when the desire to return to the treadmill was greatest. How she had come to realize that her finest asset was also her greatest weakness. Her ability to change gears was based upon a talent to keep the entire world at arm's length. It had protected her from being hurt too much by life, but it had also left her bereft and lonely and so empty the nights threatened to swallow her whole. No matter how painful the days at Kingdom Come might be, with the frustrating work and the isolation from all she held dear, no matter how hard the nights were, Dottie was convinced that if she walked away now she would be turning her back on her last chance to ever really care deeply for anything, most especially herself.

Even so, the desire to return to the frenetic life-as-usual, the competition, and the sense of *belonging* left her clenching the receiver so hard her hand shook. "What's up?"

"What's up, she asks, as if she wasn't sitting on top of the gold mine as we speak." When Dottie did not rise to the bait, he demanded querulously, "You're still living with that cult, aren't you?"

"I'm here in Kingdom Come, yes. But I told you when I came down here, it's not a cult."

"Fine, fine, whatever. The thing is, how did you know?"

"Know what?"

"Don't give me that. I'm the editor. I'm supposed to be the one with the nose for the next big thing. And now I'm scooped by one of my own writers?"

Dottie turned and stared at her reflection in the parlor mirror. Her brown hair was chopped to a practical length, which only seemed to accent the horsy angle to her nose and chin, and the worried cast to her eyes. This was not the face of a happy woman. She sighed and turned away. She had never much cared for her looks. "You're not making sense, Ed."

"I'm talking about the cult!"

"I told you—"

"Cult, commune, whatever. All of a sudden, I'm hearing these little comments popping up. How so-and-so is moving down, or has a friend who's talking about it, or a wife wants it and the husband doesn't. How many people are moved in?"

"Somewhere around nine thousand."

"Nine thousand is a big number, Dottie. Nine thousand is news. And I thought you were going there on vacation."

"I was."

But the words were spoken so weakly he could easily rush over them. "I want to tie you up with an exclusive retainer. Whatever you write, we get first dibs. That all right with you?"

"Ed, I'm not sure—"

"Don't tell me you've already signed with somebody else." The words were a moan, the aggrieved editor planning for battle. "After all the breaks I've given you. All the leads I could've easily fed to a more seasoned writer. This is the way you repay me?"

"Stop it, Ed." She took a breath. "First of all, I'm not sure there's a story."

"Not yet. But you were right to go down. Something this big is going to attract controversy. Not to mention the rumors about off-shoots. Is that true?"

This surprised her. News of other communities had only started being mentioned during the past few weeks. "How did you hear about this?"

"I was right, wasn't I?" The editor's voice rose a full octave, like a hunting dog on the scent of prey. "This is *news*. This is *tomorrow*."

"Ed, it's not—"

"I know, I know, you're seeking but you're not finding. But

believe me, your instincts were right. There's something brewing, something major. A commune this big is going to bring down all sorts of pressure."

She could not deny it, not when the pastor and everyone else was predicting the same thing. "Maybe."

"*Maybes* are for runners-up. Certainties are for the headliners. Are you with me on this?"

She sighed, wishing the way forward was clearer. "I suppose I am."

"Don't worry, we'll treat you right. I'll have the contract in tomorrow's mail. Stay in touch, Dottie. And let me know everything you hear."

Ed was brusque, he was pushy, he was irritating, he was brutal in contract negotiations. But he was also the best in the trade when it came to sniffing out breaking stories. Ed Starling was why *Newsday* remained on top of the heap, scooping more leads and Pulitzers than all the other weekly newsmagazines combined. Among freelance journalists, working for Ed Starling was a badge of honor. Being placed on open-ended retainer by *Newsday* was a scoop in itself.

Dottie Betham turned in her seat, inspected the tanned features staring back at her, and wondered why all she felt was defeat.

⌑ ⌑

The ruling synod of the Reformed Church of America traditionally held its annual conferences in hotels that dated from the nation's earliest days. Critics within the RCA said it was because the majority of synod members felt more comfortable with cobwebs and fables of past grandeur rather than with tomorrow's challenges. Reverend Thurgood Innes thought there was probably some truth to that, but as he nodded his thanks to the uniformed bellhop who held the door for him, he found he did not care. He treaded the length of the Persian carpet, crossing the marble-pillared lobby beneath the trio of crystal chandeliers, and decided a few days in goose-down comfort would suit him just fine.

The newly refurbished Richmond Renaissance dated from the era of mint juleps and hoop skirts and carriages pulled by four-in-hands. The lobby had a discreet corner whose brass-framed sign announced it was reserved for smokers; the fragrance of Cuba's best and the equally rich tones of moneyed Southerners spiced the lobby with wealth and power. Thurgood Innes gave the receptionist a grand smile, loving everything about this place.

"Thurgood, Thurgood, Thurgood. What a delight it is to welcome you, my boy." The synod president was a grand old man of the denomination, pastoring a church founded seventeen years before the Revolutionary War. "I can't tell you how pleased I am with your election."

"Thank you, sir. The honor is humbling." Thurgood felt genuine warmth toward the distinguished rector. He was one of the few conservatives who felt he could learn newer and better ways from the more evangelical churches. "I remain indebted to you for your support."

"Nonsense. Couldn't think of a better man to have join us, and I mean that sincerely."

Thurgood felt a presence at his elbow, and said, "I believe you have met my senior elder, Miller Kedrick."

"Certainly, certainly. An honor, sir." The president shook hands briefly. "I can only wish my own church had been able to match your success with the outreach projects."

"Business is business," Miller Kedrick replied in his customary bark. "You want a success, run it like one. Put a bunch of namby-pamby old maids in charge, and a shop selling gold at ten cents on the dollar would go under."

"Miller, please," Thurgood murmured.

"All I'm saying," Miller said, more loudly now that he smelled opposition. "There's only one rule to making money, and that is, Do whatever it takes. Teaching that to a church committee is like getting a goat to dance."

"No doubt it would do us all good to remember this wisdom," the president intoned, smiling at Thurgood's embarrassment. "Now if you will excuse us, Mr. Kedrick, I wish to have a private word with our newest board member."

Thurgood allowed the president to draw them away before starting in with, "I can't tell you how sorry—"

"Don't give it another thought. What is his background?"

"Oh, Miller has a hand in just about everything. Construction, mostly. He almost went under about eight years ago. That was just after I arrived in Orlando. He had started a huge housing development out near Disney, and one of his backers suddenly pulled out. His wife left him at the same time. Apparently the two blows left him permanently bitter. It was also about then that he became so involved with church activities."

"Here, let's claim this corner for our own, shall we?" The president waited until Thurgood had settled onto a leather settee, which was so soft it felt like solidified butter. "Actually, Miller Kedrick is not the reason I wanted to have a word." He hesitated a long moment, clearly uncertain how to continue. "I assume you've heard about Charles Griffin."

Thurgood felt the lobby's tumult fade into the background. "Rumors only."

"They're not rumors, I'm sorry to say. Do you know him well?"

"Hardly at all. I've met him a few times. He seems like a nice enough fellow."

"If you had asked me a month ago, I would have said that Chuck is as solid as they come. He's a graduate of my own alma mater, and I recommended him to his first church." The president's face creased downward. "Thurgood, I can't tell you how distressing I find this. Especially now."

"Sorry, I don't follow you."

"The synod is facing its greatest challenge in our two-hundred-year history. The larger churches like your own are clamoring for a greater say in our affairs, and rightly so. But you know the difficulty I've had in bringing our more conservative members around." He twisted his hands together, the work-hardened fingers looking like pale, gnarled roots. "I dread the prospect of someone standing up at our opening session, pointing at Chuck Griffin's development, and predicting that this is the direction all our larger churches are headed."

Thurgood realized with a start that the synod president was waiting for him to offer advice. He hesitated a moment, wondering if he should suggest that the exact opposite might happen, that this could be a rallying issue. As he waited, he realized that this might be the opening he was seeking.

"What if," he said slowly, "we beat them to the punch?"

"What are you talking about?"

"You could use your opening remarks to speak on this."

"No, not me. My first speech must strike a positive note and speak of a future where we are united and moving forward together." It was the president's turn to pause. "You, on the other hand, could bring this up for me."

Seeing an advantage, Thurgood played hard to get. "I don't know if that would be wise."

"You have a solid reputation with both sides. The progressives see your numbers and your successful outreach programs."

"They're Miller's programs, not mine."

The president impatiently waved that aside. "The conservatives see you as a man who respects their desire to maintain our heritage. I could invite you, as our newest member, to stand and say a few words. You could speak of this heritage, and simply question the move to extreme measures, and use Chuck Griffin as an example. I could ask a conservative member to address it again tomorrow in our first working session."

Of course this was where the man had been headed all along. "I'm not sure if this makes for a proper introduction to the synod."

But the president had already moved on. "The size of this thing is staggering. I've just received word from a trusted ally on the ground. Kingdom Come now has over six thousand families living inside their community."

"What?"

"And that is a conservative estimate. The place is growing at the rate of over a dozen new families every day. Think on that, Thurgood. That's over three hundred families a *month*."

Which meant his own church's growth paled in comparison. "How do you want this handled?"

"Short and simple." the president said. "Chuck Griffin lost his wife several years back, as you know, and then there was that horrid shooting incident. You can simply say that you are concerned that Chuck's tragedies might have affected his judgment. Be that as it may, the synod must maintain standards for the entire denomination."

Six thousand families. "Whatever you want."

The president reached over and patted Thurgood's knee. "I knew I could count on you."

SEVEN

Ben Atkins woke to the sound of hammering. He required a long moment to recall where he was—the bedroom of Agent Fran Tottler's apartment inside the community known as Kingdom Come. As he rolled from the bed, he wondered what on earth had caused him to argue with Theron Head.

The previous afternoon Ben had left the FBI office, checked out of his downtown motel, and driven his rental car back to the community. Charlotte's rush-hour snarl had slowed his progress to a crawl, not that he had minded. It had meant that he had crested the final rise under cover of night. Ben had pulled the car to one side of the empty road and stood peering down at the fence. It glinted silver and mysterious in the moonlight, snaking in both directions as far as he could see. He had remained there, studying the terrain, searching for sentries on patrol. But the night was untouched by movement. A pair of hawks had cried from farther down the ridge. A truck had rumbled up the rise beside him, tested its brakes with a harsh sigh, then took the road down and through the fence. Ben had stood and watched as the warehouse loading-door cranked open and light splashed into the night. He had heard laughter and easy talk, someone complaining loud enough for him to catch most of the words, how they were missing dinner because the driver couldn't read his watch. He had walked back to his car and started down the hill. He had followed Wayne

Oates's directions to the apartment formerly used by Fran Tottler, their missing insert. He had slept with chairs rammed tight against the front and back doors, and his pistol under his pillow.

That morning he drank his second cup of coffee by the back window, watching as workers scurried to complete another set of apartments identical to his own. Ben had worked construction all through college, and he knew hustle when he saw it. Either those guys were making double overtime, or somebody was driving them with a whip.

His apartment was a standard one-bedroom modular design, with furniture to match. Everything had the look of IKEA Swedish-modern, functional and boring. Ben took time to search for anything out of the ordinary—bugging equipment, camera hookups for monitoring newcomers, books on cult doctrine. He found nothing. He dressed slowly, hating the fact that he had no choice but to go outside, uninformed of what dangers he might face, and with no one but himself to blame.

As he was locking his front door, yet another mystery occurred to him: Why were there no watchtowers? He stood with the key halfway into his lock, visualizing how the long fence had glinted in the moonlight. Any border that long, particularly where it went through forests, needed a series of tall sentry posts within sighting distance of one another. Otherwise the fence was purely cosmetic. But why would anyone go to the trouble and expense of erecting a structure like that without plans to keep people out? Or was it to keep them in?

"Don't tell me yours doesn't work either."

Ben jerked upright. "Excuse me?"

"Half the locks in this unit had to be replaced." The ready smile the woman offered slipped away as he turned to face her. "Oh. It's you."

"Afraid so."

"I saw you the other day at the community center."

It did not help at all to realize she was as disconcerted by their encounter as he was. "I see," Ben replied.

She offered a nervous hand. "Dottie Betham."

"Ben Atkins."

"You're with the FBI also?"

He turned his wince into a nod. "That's right."

"Do you have a card?"

Ben hesitated, but saw no reason not to hand one over.

She inspected the card with its embossed federal logo, and said, "I met the woman, your colleague. Her name is Fran, isn't that right?"

"Fran Tottler." No reason to deny information they already had. "She's gone."

"And you're her replacement." She grimaced, almost a smile, and her face became softer and far more attractive. "And I'm prattling."

"To be honest, I'm surprised you're talking with me at all."

"Oh, they knew you'd be coming."

Ben did not bother to mask his surprise. "You don't say."

"Well, not you personally. Somebody. The authorities couldn't just let something this big slip by."

"No."

"Some of the people you'll meet would just as soon ride you out on a rail."

"Tarred and feathered besides, I imagine."

The smile grew momentarily genuine. "A distinct minority."

"What a relief." Ben leaned against the wall, taking in this chatty woman. Dottie Betham was not the least bit what he would expect for a cult follower. She had the lean, angular face of a forthright and independent woman. She was dressed in a no-nonsense sweater and slacks and pointy-toed, lace-up walking boots. Hardly what would pass for a uniform. Ben asked, "So what brings you here?"

"I wish I knew." The smile slipped away. "I had all sorts of notions when I arrived, but now . . ."

He pretended to a casual interest. "Now?"

Intelligent gray eyes focused hard. "Right now I'm talking to an outsider, and I'm late for work."

"Work?"

"Good-bye, Federal Agent Atkins." She slipped by him. "Whatever it is you're looking for, you won't find it here."

—✠——✠—

Ben strolled down to the center of what had until recently been a sleepy village far beyond the reach of modern times. Now he was surrounded by bustle and preparations and building. One storefront after another was being stripped down and expanded. He spotted the remnants of a Piggly Wiggly, a Rose's Five and Dime, a dress shop, an electronics repair shop, and a funeral home. All were undergoing major renovations. Eyes followed him everywhere. Ben observed hostile gazes at every turn, and understood what Fran Tottler had meant by "being stalked."

Ben noticed a familiar striped pole and crossed the street. He was relieved to find that the quaint barbershop remained the same. He started to enter, drawn by the elderly faces and the hopes they might be prone to gab. But as he reached for the knob, his attention was caught by the sound of a furious argument coming from next door.

Ben took a hesitant step toward the neighboring entrance and tried to peer through the window. But the blinds were drawn against the morning sun, the sunlight so bright he could not even read the name upon the glass. Up close the noise was a verbal barrage, one step away from violence. Ben's heart rate shifted into high gear as he sidled toward the door. The sidewalk was empty now, as though everyone had ducked under cover.

He found himself recalling another time under a drier, hotter sun. A July some eight years ago, perhaps nine now. Ben had been breaking in a new partner, on their first inspection of a supposed militia. They had scrambled up a rise on their bellies, peered through the underbrush, and observed a strange rite of rising hatred. Thirty or so men had been shouting and haranguing one another in the center of a dusty square, gradually building to a crescendo of aggression. The young agent beside Ben had chosen the worst possible moment to sneeze. One of the group down below had spotted them, and automatic fire had erupted all around them. They had been lucky to escape with their lives.

With his left hand Ben gripped the door handle and turned sideways, offering whatever guarded the interior the smallest possible target. His right hand reached under his jacket and slipped the safety off his revolver. One steadying breath, then he pushed the door open.

The cheery little door-chime mocked both him and the bedlam Ben found within.

He found himself standing at the entrance to a village diner. Three tables and a booth seemed ready to come to blows, which was amazing, seeing as how the youngest guest appeared over sixty. But faces were red, hands closed to fists, voices so strident the words seemed torn from their throats. So many people were yelling he could scarcely make out what was being said.

The lone waitress leaned against the counter, eyeing the battle with a worried gaze. A beefy man in a cook's peaked paper cap peered through the kitchen window and shouted his own opinions. Ben slipped the safety back on his pistol and forced his chest to unlock. He eased himself onto the stool closest to the door, ready to leap into action. He struggled to make sense of the words, but it was beyond him.

A man's voice rose above the general din, clear enough for the entire sentence to be audible. "Reverend Calhoon says he's got the date down pat, came to him last night in the bath. The Master's coming back the end of next week!"

"Which is exactly what you told us *last* week," a woman shrilled back.

"If Calhoon knows so much," shouted another, "why is it we don't hear a word about it from Pastor Chuck?"

"On account of him not listening good!" The man wheeled back to the narrow-faced woman in tortoise-rimmed spectacles and shouted, "Reverend Calhoon says the Teacher didn't come 'cause we didn't pray hard enough!"

"Oh, stuff and nonsense. Horace, you're a fool, and that pastor of yours is a *distilled* fool!"

The heavyset man was dressed in shirt and suspenders with a tie almost lost beneath his heavy jowls. His face was beet red with the strain of bellowing. "Don't you dare call him that. Don't you *dare!*"

"You know full well what the Scriptures say about the Second Coming." The woman was so stringy her hands scrabbled across the linoleum table like bird's talons. "A fool I said and a fool I meant! Anybody else would heed the Master's orders not to predict the day nor the hour, and *certainly* not the *week*."

Ben felt assaulted both by their fury and by his own sickening after-effects of adrenaline rush. He stared at the surrounding faces, but could not put a lock on what he was seeing. Rage, certainly. But danger?

"That's all fine and good for the likes of you smarmy folk. But I'm counting the days, yessir, counting the *days!* Why?" The beefy man rose as much as the dinette counter allowed. "Because I know my place is set at the table. Not like some people who're gonna be left guessing on the Judgment Day!"

All the voices rose together at that point. To Ben's left the cook shouted something to the effect that anybody in their right mind would be preparing for the call. And somebody else said something to do with seasons and signs. But piecing the words together was like trying to listen to a tune in a hurricane. Doctrine, Ben decided. It had to be something cultish to get these people so riled.

Behind him, the door slammed shut so hard the chime broke and clanked across the floor. A new voice shrieked, *"Quiet!"*

Everyone turned around, including Ben. Dottie Betham stood with hands on hips, eyeing the room like a schoolteacher staring down an unruly class. "I could hear you clear down the other end of the block!"

"This biddy accused Reverend—"

"I said be *quiet*, Horace." Dottie took one step into the diner. "In case any of you haven't noticed, we've got ourselves a visitor here today. From the FBI!" She jabbed one finger toward Ben, then swiveled back to the smoldering man with the foghorn of a voice. "And you've been warned twice that I know of not to carry on with your opinions."

"They're not *opinions*. I've got every right—"

"That's where you're wrong. You've got no right at all. You've been warned, Horace. You know what the next step is?" When the man just sat and glowered, Dottie went on, "You'll be brought up before the elders and churched. And if that doesn't work, you'll be expelled." She swiveled around to face the stringy older woman. "And you stop egging him on, Clarice!"

The narrow-faced woman tried for huffiness. "I never—"

"Oh, stow it." Dottie Betham marched over to the counter. "Give me two coffees to go."

"All right, Dottie."

Dottie glared at the waitress. "I can't believe you let them go on in here."

The waitress snapped the lid on the first cup. "Like I've got any choice."

"Stuff and nonsense." Dottie scowled through the alcove at the chef. "If you'd just toss them out once, they'd be tame as little lambs."

The waitress snapped on the second lid and passed over the cups. "He's as bad as the rest of them."

"I don't want to hear about it." She set down a dollar bill and passed Ben with a scathing glare.

Despite her hostility, Ben forced himself to rise and follow her from the diner. Whatever answer he was seeking, it certainly would not be found in that strange group. Ben caught up with Dottie halfway down the block. Dottie greeted him with, "Don't you dare start. I've got a good head of steam that I'd just love a reason to work off."

He fell into step beside her. Decided to try just one comment. "You really cleared the decks back there."

"Which is just one symptom of my problem here." Her anger bit the words off neat and precise. "Everyone assumes I'm here because I'm intended to be Pastor Chuck's next wife. Which means I speak with an authority that's not my own."

"Charles Griffin?" He took her silence as assent. "Intended by whom?"

For some reason, the question shook her. "You must think we're a bunch of opinionated fools."

"I haven't any idea at all," Ben replied honestly, "what to think of any of this."

"Horace is a born troublemaker. He doesn't belong here, far as I'm concerned. But the rest of them in there are good people. The salt of the earth, when they're not riled."

"Something sure got under their skin."

She stopped and turned to face him. "Before you go jumping to the wrong conclusions, Mister Smarmy FBI Agent, try fitting this on for size. You receive what you think is a call from God. Something so powerful you are willing to cast aside your life, your work, everything you've spent a lifetime building up. You pick up stakes, you come rushing down here because you are absolutely positive this move is *divinely intended*. Now then. Wouldn't something that shakes the fundamental concepts of this new world, something that challenges the purpose behind your being brought here, wouldn't that make you angry?"

"Is that what brought you here, feeling like it was intended?"

"I . . ." Dottie halted and gave her head an angry shake. "This is not about me, Mister Agent. And it never will be."

Ben watched her long-legged stride move away from him, surprised to find himself wishing that it was.

EIGHT

The Reformed Church of America's ruling synod met in the Richmond hotel's finest ballroom, at tables arranged in a square and draped in rich red velvet. Behind each member's chair sat one or two trusted elders, there to assist the member and report back to the home churches. Beyond them sat observers from a number of other churches. Most of the observers came with grievances or issues they wished the synod to act upon.

The previous evening's opening session had gone extremely well. Thurgood Innes had spoken at the personal behest of the synod president. His comments had been well-rounded, respectful, concerned. By unanimous vote, the morning meeting's agenda had been altered so that the Kingdom Come issue was the first item for consideration.

Again Innes found himself seated to the right of the president, there to walk the synod toward the desired decision. This was a vital piece of maneuvering, as the matter had found such resonance among members that the president wanted to use it as the basis upon which a harmonious tone was set for the entire conference.

There was only one holdout. Reverend Lloyd Bowick, a respected member of the conservative branch from New Hampshire. Up until that moment, Innes had considered him a valued ally. Now he was ready to throttle the fool.

"I caution my brethren against drawing any hasty conclusion," the old pastor intoned for the third time. "Charles Griffin is a good man and an able pastor. I am certain when we reach the bottom of this we will find nothing untoward, certainly nothing so scandalous as a cult."

A younger member observed, "Anybody who's been through losing his wife and then having his church shot up could go off the deep end."

"Not Chuck Griffin," the old man insisted. "I counseled him after his wife's tragic demise. The man might have become somewhat aloof, yes, I'll give you that. But he managed his affairs well enough, and his parishioners remained highly satisfied with him as a pastor. I know, because I have asked."

A voice from the table's other end demanded, "Then how can you explain him just up and leaving his church in Indiana like he did? I heard he didn't even wait for a replacement, just packed up his belongings and left to start this commune thing of his."

Another voice said, "I just can't get over the way this thing of his is growing. What were those numbers again, Thurgood?"

Innes shuffled through his notes, pretending to need to search out the information. He was enormously pleased there was no need for him to be the voice of opposition. "Apparently there are upward of six thousand new families within the compound, and they are increasing at the rate of over seventy-five families a week."

"I haven't visited the community, so I can't explain it," Reverend Bowick admitted. "But there is one possibility we haven't considered."

"And that is?"

"That God's hand is upon Pastor Griffin's work."

The old man waited through the murmuring and head shaking, then said in a firm voice, "Think on this, gentlemen. God calls us from the unexpected direction. It is one of His most enduring traits. What if Chuck Griffin really was saved from that attack on his church by a miracle? You know this is what his parishioners claim, that God's hand was upon that day, and the prayer revival that followed. What if the Lord's intention was to establish Chuck as an earthly beacon? What if Kingdom Come is a community set apart by the Lord's decree?"

Their respect for the old man kept them from objecting too swiftly. Finally one of his own conservative allies growled, "Oh come now, Lloyd. Do you really think we're faced with an old-fashioned awakening?"

"I don't know." The elder statesman's voice did not rise, yet his entire body shook with the fervor burning in his gaze. "But woe betide us if we condemn the Lord's anointed servant." He raised one trembling hand toward the ceiling. "Woe betide us!"

There was a moment's uncertain silence, then one of the most conservative members snorted quietly. Farther along the table, a leader of a huge evangelical church rolled his eyes and began tapping his pencil impatiently. Other eyes tracked these two responses. Nothing needed to be said. A silent consensus had been reached.

Thurgood turned back to Reverend Bowick in time to watch the pastor lose his zealous fire and become an uncertain old man. The president shot him a glance. Thurgood nodded in agreement. But before he could speak, one of the younger members suggested, "Maybe we should have Chuck Griffin come to Richmond and explain to us himself what this Kingdom Come is all about."

Thurgood lowered his head, shuffled his papers, and said in a guarded tone, "I'm not certain that's possible." He turned to the president and asked in a voice supposedly for their leader alone, "Do you know if he's out of jail yet?"

"Chuck is in *prison*?"

The president's gaze gleamed with approval, but all he said was, "I believe the authorities released him yesterday."

Someone asked why he had been jailed, but Thurgood's response was drowned out in the rising tumult. The president rose to his feet and said loud enough to carry, "All those in favor of inviting Charles Griffin to explain to the synod his present activities, say aye."

"Aye!"

"It is unanimous." He banged his gavel. "This meeting will take a thirty-minute recess."

As the room noisily began to empty, the president turned from his chair and briefly settled his hand upon Thurgood's shoulder. "Well done, Thurgood. I knew I could count on you. Very well done indeed."

Thurgood basked in the president's praise, until Lloyd Bowick caught his eye. The New Hampshire pastor did not glare. Thurgood could have shaken off anger like water off a duck's back. This was different. The old reverend looked at him with genuine sadness. The scrutiny seemed to reveal the potent mixture of Thurgood's motives.

Angrily Thurgood turned away, only to be confronted by Miller Kedrick. His chief elder was glaring across the table at the old man. "Addle-headed troublemaker," the businessman growled. "Ought to be kicked off the synod and sent straight to the asylum."

The vehemence was peculiar, even for Miller. "He has the right to express his opinion."

"Not over this guy. Anybody who backs this Chuck Griffin idiot deserves the worst."

Thurgood Innes wanted to agree. But something in Miller's face left him unsettled. At this proximity, the scars of a hard-fought scrabble up the corporate mountain were evident. Miller's eyes held a beady squint from years of taking aim at enemies. Discolored splotches marred his cheeks and the left side of his nose. His lips were compressed so tightly they almost disappeared. The man was far from attractive. He had the saggy bulk of an aging weightlifter. Thurgood realized he had never seen Miller Kedrick come even close to smiling.

Thurgood found himself asking, "What is it about Chuck that gets under your skin so?"

The question jerked Miller around. "You're asking me?"

Thurgood forced himself to meet Miller's gaze. "That's right, I am. What has you so concerned about the church?"

"Incredible. You don't get it. Not at all." Miller bolted from his chair as though pneumatically ejected. "This isn't about the *church*."

"Of course it's—"

"Baloney." He stuck a finger the size of a short stogie in Thurgood's face and bit off the words. "This is about two things and two things only. It's about *money*. And it's about *power*."

Angrily Thurgood swiped the hand away. "I don't know what you're talking about."

"You will," Miller Kedrick sneered, and turned away. "You mark my words."

NINE

"Apparently this Kingdom Come cult is as well-financed as they come." Evan Hawkins, Ben's boss, sounded as worried as Ben could ever recall hearing. "Two very wealthy individuals evidently have donated the commune all their money. One is a big local landowner; his daughter and their family attended this Griffin fellow's church up in Indiana. The other is Gloria Parks. The name ring a bell?"

"Sure." Gloria Parks was the only daughter of Sam Parks, founder of a worldwide discount shopping center. "She's donated everything?"

"Enough, anyway. The local guy has two textile factories, both outside Hamlin. Parks has apparently almost completed construction of a new distribution facility just off the local road."

"I've seen the warehouses."

"Imagine they'd be hard to miss. Going to be over a half-million square feet when they're done. You know what that means, don't you?"

"Not just money," Ben said. "Employment."

Evan Hawkins's chair creaked over the phone line. Ben knew the man's habit of leaning back and setting his size thirteen wing tips on the windowsill. "This ranks right up there at the top of our worst-case scenarios. A cult so big it actually takes over a local government. Enough business and income to become self-sustaining, to provide employment to all who want to work. I'm telling you, this has got the front office jumping like popcorn on the fire."

67

"I'm still not sure," Ben said slowly, "that we're facing a cult."

"Don't you start," Evan warned. "I'd have thought your last drenching would have warned you off swimming against the tide."

"I'm just after the facts here."

"If you're wise, you'll keep your head low and follow the party line."

Ben bit down on his retort. He could not explain his unease over the FBI's heightened concerns, not even to himself. "What's next?"

"You know how these things go. We're still in the talk-talk phase. But my guess is, when they act it'll be on several fronts. Probably cut off municipal funds and connections, for a start. We'll also obtain lists of the people involved—we're expecting your help on that. See what skeletons we can uncover. Somebody will pressure the two local banks to close down 'temporarily.' And we're talking about sending in the IRS to conduct on-site audits on all the community leaders and businesses."

It was the expected response. Such things had been worked out on paper and discussed for years, ever since the anti-government militias began growing in force and numbers. Even so, Ben felt it necessary to say, "I've spent a day going around. And I haven't seen a single weapon. Or any indication of a militia in training."

"Which doesn't mean a thing." Evan was growing increasingly impatient. "Come on, Ben. You know how big an area we're talking about."

"Huge."

"With a fence around the whole shindig. They could hide an entire artillery brigade and we'd never know." When Ben did not respond, Evan's voice hardened. "You're walking out on a limb. Don't go handing Theron Head a saw."

"I'm not planning—" He halted at the sound of someone knocking on his door. "Hang on a second."

Ben walked over, carrying the mobile phone with him. He opened the door to find himself staring out at a pinch-faced Dottie Betham. "Hello."

"I've been sent to collect you." Her voice was as tight as her gaze.

"Excuse me?"

"There's a community dinner and meeting tonight. We want you to come. That's what you're here for, isn't it, to inspect us?"

"Mind if I ask who's behind the invitation?"

"Chuck Griffin." She crossed her arms. "Well?"

"Give me a moment, please." Ben turned around, raised the phone to his ear, said quietly, "You heard?"

"The grand high pooh-bah himself sent for you?" Evan's tension heightened. "Let's hope it's not an invitation to your own hanging."

"Sending a woman to invite me to dinner doesn't strike me as a reason for a red alert, Evan."

"Where's your gun?"

"Slung right under my arm."

"Good. Keep the safety off. Take the phone. Code it for emergency dialing. The first sign of trouble, hit the switch. Call me in any case by midnight. Otherwise we'll send in the troops." Evan was the one who sounded strangled. "I've got a bad feeling about you going in there alone. Very bad."

———※——※———

As she walked alongside the federal agent, Dottie wondered what this rawboned man must be thinking. Ben Atkins observed everything, missed nothing. And gave nothing away. His face was angled like a stone carving of a bird of prey. Nothing seemed to faze him, not the friendly greetings cast her way, nor the hostility that blanketed faces as they turned toward him. She wanted to apologize, but could not explain why. These people belonged here; he did not. Yet she found herself drawn to the man, as well as to the depths and the mystery that walked with him.

Ben must have felt her eyes, for he turned and offered a slight smile. "Penny for your thoughts."

"I was just wondering the same thing. What are *you* thinking?"

Ben was silent a long moment, as though even this innocuous statement required careful consideration. "I was thinking," he finally replied, "how I can't find anything threatening about this place or these people."

The words halted her. "Is that what you're looking for?"

"Shouldn't I be?"

"No, you shouldn't." She found the familiar heat rising. It seemed this man had the ability to rile her with a raised eyebrow. "Now you listen up. I may not agree with everything that's going on around here. But I do know these are fine people, and they deserve better than what you're giving them."

"What am I giving them, Dottie?"

"Suspicion," she shot back.

He cocked his head to one side. The afternoon sunlight glinted off what looked like an invisible band pressed along the hairline above his ear. Dottie realized it must have come from years of wearing a hat. She asked, "Are you a cowboy?"

He smiled for the first time. Not a polite lifting of the edges of his mouth. A grin that poked dimples into both cheeks and drew comfortable lines out from his eyes and cheeks. And suddenly Ben Atkins not only looked human, but incredibly handsome. "What makes you say that?"

"You've got a band around your hair, like you've been wearing a Stetson all your life."

"You are one observant lady." He ran a self-conscious hand down the hairline. "I've spent a lot of time in the saddle, and I love range riding better than just about anything. But I've never roped a cow in my life."

A passing car slowed, and the window rolled down. A woman from the community center called over, "You all right there, Dottie?"

"Fine, thanks."

The woman and her three companions gave Ben a cold look before driving on. Ben watched the car vanish into the afternoon shadows, his smile now a distant memory, then inquired, "Any idea why your leader wants to see me?"

She bristled. "Chuck is not my *leader*. And this is not a *cult*."

Ben gave her a long look, then admitted, "I almost believe you."

She realized the flow of cars and people was thinning out. "We'd better get a move on, or we won't find a seat."

As they continued down the tree-shaded sidewalk, Ben continued, "It's been my sad duty to deal with eight militias and three doomsday cults. You get to know the signs. This place doesn't fit the mold."

"Because it's neither of those."

He glanced down, then away, and asked in an overly calm voice, "Does Kingdom Come have a standing militia, Dottie?"

"Of course it doesn't!" Anger pressed her to walk faster. "But you're not going to believe a thing I say, are you?"

"I'd like to."

Beyond the quiet, inbred caution, she caught a hint of something else. Something that sounded almost like sadness. "Why don't you, then? Believe me, I mean."

He walked on in silence, until they turned a corner and the community center came into view. "Back a ways you said you didn't agree with a lot of what these people stood for. What did you mean?"

She flushed, but not in anger. "That's a very personal question."

"I'm just trying to get a handle on things. I don't know any other way to do that but watch and listen and ask."

"Would you be willing to answer my questions in return?"

"Anything." Without hesitation. "It's the least I can do."

Dottie halted beyond the listening range of the clusters of people encircling the main entrance. She searched his face, trying to come up with something unexpected. "Are you married?"

He jerked his head back a fraction, but recovered swiftly. "I was," he answered. "My wife died four years ago."

"I'm sorry."

"It's all right, Dottie." He took a long breath. "Gwen was a school-teacher. We were married nineteen years, most of them good. Very good. Got married when I was eighteen and she was seventeen. One boy. He graduated from law school last year, just getting started in Sioux Falls."

"You don't look old enough to have a son who's a lawyer."

"Thank you, Dottie." He reached up, as though unconsciously searching for the brim of his Stetson to adjust it against the westering sun. "Is it my turn to ask now?"

"Yes." And it was also her turn to breathe hard. "Most of these people are here because they feel called. I know that doesn't make any sense to you, and I can't help that. But they do. If you want to know them at all, you're just going to have to accept the truth of this."

"Do you?"

"Do I feel called, or do I accept it?"

He crossed his arms. "Both, I guess."

"The answer is yes, I do accept it, in *them*. But no, I don't feel called." Coming then to the crux of the issue. "I came because Chuck invited me. I was suffering from a severe case of burnout. My life seemed a mess. Chuck's wife was both my cousin and my very best friend. More like the older sister I never had. After Elvie passed on, I would talk with Chuck every week. It was a way to try to stay close to Elvie, and Chuck is just a great listener. I told Chuck about my . . . problem. He said I should visit Kingdom Come and take some time off."

"Has it helped? Being down here, I mean."

She opened her mouth, then clamped it shut. It was too easy talking to this man. He drew out things she knew she was later going to regret having said. "Let's go inside," she said brusquely.

TEN

Ben Atkins entered the hall knowing he should expect danger, and wishing he did not feel so disarmed. The place reminded him of town gatherings he had found throughout the Midwest, people who knew each other so well they could guess what would be said long before their mouths opened. People who remembered habits back three generations and more, who spoke of one another with such easy familiarity that almost anything could be forgiven, or almost every slight turned into a reason for revenge. Only these people, if he understood things correctly, had only been together less than two years. It did not fit. Nothing did.

The community center's main floor had not one but two great halls, separated by what appeared to be sliding walls. Which meant that even larger gatherings than this could be accommodated. The place reminded Ben of big-city convention centers, with its high ceilings and industrial carpeting and professional lighting and silent air-conditioning. A stream of people came and went through rear doors, lading trestle tables with washtubs of ice and colas and huge steaming tureens of food. Everyone seemed to be either helping or eating. It was not a cafeteria line so much as a vast clan gathering, people visiting from table to table, laughter echoing off the distant walls, everyone talking at once.

Dottie Betham led him to free seats at one of the tables and deposited him. Ben greeted the others with an ease he did not feel. No one said anything, but he knew he was not welcome. He sat and ate food he did not want, and continued to study the room.

All the eyes that met his were hostile. But none seemed dangerous. And no one he could see was armed. He kept wishing he could find something, anything, that would signal precisely what it was he found here. Something he could take back to the chair warmers in Washington and say, here, this is exactly what we're facing. Good or bad. What he wanted most of all was simply to *know*.

A bell sounded, one loud gong, and everyone rose. The chattering did not cease, nor the laughter. Everyone moved together toward the second hall, where row after row of folding chairs sat facing a broad stage. Upon the stage was a long table with fourteen chairs, filled with twelve men and two women. Two of the men were black, one of the women either Hispanic or Arab. The center chair was taken by Charles Griffin.

Dottie walked ahead of Ben, allowing a cluster of women to draw her slightly apart. Ben observed her sloped shoulders and bowed head, and knew she was ashamed to be seen with him, no matter what their leader might have requested. He slowed and allowed people to surge around him, until Dottie became lost in the crowd.

He chose a seat in the hall's back left corner. Ben sat and stood with the others as the assembly sang and prayed through the opening. Once more he was struck by the utter normalcy of it all. He could have been attending a weekly church service or a clan reunion. People raised their hands toward the ceiling, swayed, stood with eyes closed, or did nothing at all. There was none of the disciplined tension, none of the fear and repressed fury he had witnessed in every other cult he had investigated.

The business portion of the meeting began, and Ben realized this was a weekly event. There was no roll call, no making sure that everyone was present. Instead, people came and went in easy liberty, listening to discussions over water treatment and lawn care and waste pickup and housing and a variety of ordinary issues. Ben listened and grew increasingly confused.

What was more, Charles Griffin said nothing at all.

The fourteen people on the stage did far more listening than speaking, as one committee member after another approached the center-aisle microphone and gave his report. Most of the business was about something referred to as the Gathering. From what he heard, Ben surmised the Gathering, whatever it was, was going to be big. There were reports on buses and traffic and housing and tents and bedding and food and the arena and electronics and music . . . on and on. All the organizers were urged to speak swiftly and sit back down. The panel chairman did not seem to be Chuck at all. A bespectacled man sat beside the pastor, a rotund older man with a strong Southern accent—Georgia or Florida Panhandle was Ben's guess. Ben made a mental note of the name when it was spoken by several people, Reverend Paul Caldwell, and assumed he must be Reverend Griffin's number two.

When the chairman threw open the floor to other business, someone demanded to know how Chuck's recent imprisonment affected things. The chairman called for order as people turned to glare in Ben's direction.

Ben tensed when Chuck rose from his seat and stared over the assembly to where Ben sat. For the first time that evening, Ben felt the heat of uncertainty. He watched as Chuck signaled to someone on the front row. A young woman came up and listened and then turned and pointed back toward Ben. Chuck said something more. The young woman looked at the pastor in utter astonishment.

Then a familiar face rose and started toward the microphone stationed in the central aisle. Ben recognized the dark-skinned man as one of the lawyers who had come and sprung Chuck Griffin from the Charlotte lockup. The attorney began without preamble. "We've received word from some friends in Washington."

The rotund elder interrupted, "Start with your name, please."

"Phil Trilling, acting attorney for the community." The man had skin the color of sourwood honey, delicate features, and feather-strokes of silver in his tightly curled hair. And a very impatient air as he spoke. "As most of you are aware by now, the authorities have taken notice of us."

The young woman who had been speaking with Chuck Griffin slipped by the attorney and walked straight toward Ben. Many of the assembly turned with her approach, including Trilling. The lawyer continued. "We can't say for certain yet, but there's a good chance they're going to come down on us hard."

A voice called from the assembly, "Can you give us specifics?"

"Not yet. Just educated guesses. Theirs, not mine."

The young woman arrived at Ben's row. Her face was set in angry lines as she bent over and said, "Come with me."

Ben hesitated, then asked, "Can I ask where?"

"Pastor Chuck asked me. Just come, okay?"

Reluctantly Ben rose and followed her down the central aisle. A ripple of comment followed his passage. The lawyer watched him with a cold, courtroom gaze and said, "The FBI has us under investigation, as everybody knows, or should. They trumped up charges to arrest and detain Pastor Chuck. But it doesn't look like it's going to stop there." He waited then until Ben was up close, then pressed angrily, "Will it, Agent Atkins?"

A thousand sets of eyes stabbed him in the back as he continued toward the stage. He wanted to flee, but for some reason felt locked into this dangerous parade up the central aisle. The closer he got to where Charles Griffin stood and awaited him, the tighter his entire being locked down, ready for attack.

The attorney continued to chase Ben with the words, "They'll probably try to close our banks, just like we've talked about. So if you haven't been stocking up on coins and currency, best do so now. And those of you who work in the community offices, don't be surprised if all of a sudden you find your work with the state and federal authorities grinding to a halt. Other than that, it's hard to tell just what they'll throw at us—maybe mass IRS audits, maybe attempts to arrest and harass us outside the compound. It's up to all of us to keep a sharp eye out and report anything . . ."

Trilling's voice trailed off as Charles Griffin walked across the stage, waving Ben toward the side stairs. Ben condemned himself for being caught and trapped so, but still found himself drawn forward. Obeying the pastor's invitation, Ben climbed the stairs and stepped onto the stage. He could hear the murmuring rise behind him as Charles greeted him with an outstretched hand and a warm smile.

Ben felt utterly off balance as Charles Griffin said, "Welcome, brother. It's good to have you join us tonight."

"Thank you." Despite the sensation of naked vulnerability, what struck Ben hardest was how this was the first time Charles had spoken all night, and he did so now with a warmth that seemed astonishingly genuine.

The pastor was not a large man. His slender frame stood two inches below six feet. His face was lean in the way of an overstressed doctor, cheeks slightly hollow, eyes rimmed by fatigue. The impression of gentle weariness, which Ben had noticed through the prison one-way window, was only heightened by this closer inspection. As was the shame he felt over how they had mistreated this man.

But the shock grew stronger as Charles reached up and placed a hand upon Ben's shoulder, and drew him over to stand in front of the stage's microphone. He turned Ben so that they faced the assembly together. In a voice that carried to the very back of the chamber, Charles announced, "The Lord has spoken to me. He has said that I am to call this man my friend."

From his place in the central aisle, the lawyer gaped open-mouthed at the two of them. Up and down the rows, people stood and rocked and chattered in amazement.

Charles Griffin then cut off the microphone, turned back toward Ben, and said in a voice intended only for him, "You should consider the possibility that you have been brought here for a far higher purpose than you suppose."

Ben had once heard a colleague describe a meeting with the attorney general, where the agent-in-charge had botched an important investigation. The AG had called the man in and blistered the paint off the walls with her anger. The agent had told Ben that he had felt as though he had been punched in his soul. Ben had never fully understood what the man had meant until now.

There was no fire to Charles Griffin, not in his gaze nor in his voice. The pastor merely patted Ben's arm, gave his warm smile, and said, "The only way you will know your true destiny is if you learn to call upon the Lord your God."

He then turned and nodded toward the chairman. The rotund pastor seemed to find nothing at all disturbing about the exchange. He merely approached the podium, turned the microphone back on, and said, "Thank you, Brother Trilling. If there is no further business, this meeting is now adjourned."

All around where Dottie Betham was seated, she could see faces sharing her own consternation. If anything, Chuck Griffin was seen as being far too silent, too calm, too reserved for a good leader. None of the people here questioned the fact that God had anointed him as a prophet. But there was growing debate over him as *leader*. He preferred silence to speech, shadows to limelight. It was only because so many of the community elders bowed to his leadership that the challenges had been muted, the criticism never raised in meetings.

To have this quiet, reserved man draw an FBI agent up to the elders' stage and declare him a divinely welcome guest was staggering.

Clearly, a number of those around Dottie shared this sentiment.

Most meetings ended on a happy note, sometimes with singing, other times with breaking into clusters of friends who carried the discussions back for cake and coffee. Tonight, however, the talk was tumultuous. Confused. Doubting.

Faces tracked Ben Atkins's progress down the center aisle. Dottie studied the people nearby and saw anger, perplexity, malice. No matter what the pastor might say, this was the same federal authority that had been behind the pastor's arrest. The authority that now threatened to upset the life they were trying to build.

She observed how Ben grew increasingly grim in his march down the center aisle. He deflected the open hostility with a stone-faced rigor.

A woman seated in front of Dottie turned around. She was a bespectacled, heavyset Southerner in her early fifties, someone Dottie knew vaguely from one meeting or another. Her husband was supervisor of one of the warehouses, and she was a physical therapist or something to do with kids. Tonight she wore a shapeless pastel blue frock and a saccharine smile. Her cat-eye glasses glinted in the overhead lights as she continued to watch Ben's passage. Then she said to Dottie, "Now that your pastor friend is out of prison, I guess you won't have so much time to spend with the policeman there."

Dottie could scarcely believe her ears. "I beg your pardon?"

"Everybody is talking, honey." She reached across the back of her chair and patted Dottie's knee. "You best mind your p's and q's, is all I'm saying. Take care of the home fires and let the policeman be."

The woman's pudgy features bore the sort of superior smirk that masked almost everything and represented a lot of what had driven Dottie from church in her teenage years. But Dottie was not a teenager anymore, and she was used to fighting her own battles. Dottie reached forward and gave the woman's shoulder a little pat in return. "Are you absolutely certain," Dottie asked sweetly, "you have any business poking your nose into my affairs?"

Before the woman could respond, Dottie rose and slid through the aisle. "Ben!"

A hundred faces turned with his. She walked over and said, "Welcome to Kingdom Come."

"I've been shot at, stalked by real live Indians, even took down a drug lord all by my lonesome. Once I even got hunted by a pack of wolves," Ben replied. He scratched his head. "I've been attacked by men with staffs and steel-toed boots. I've sat through dozens of stake-outs. I've worked my way through four, maybe five, hundred cases. But I don't think I've ever been caught so unaware as right now. I feel like I just took a two-by-four on the chin."

Dottie had to smile. Ben's honesty was about the most disarming trait she had ever found in a man. "You sound to me like a man in need of dessert."

ELEVEN

Charles Griffin sat on his back porch, watching the last faint traces of day enclose his world and wondering how the prophets of old managed to stay sane.

For once, however, it was not problems within the burgeoning community that occupied his mind. Two more pressing items blocked out all else. The first was the telephone call that had just come through. Lloyd Bowick was a pastor and dear friend who was also serving on the Reformed Church of America's ruling synod. He had formally invited Chuck down to address the synod, and warned him that he was becoming the object of growing concern.

The second was his recent release from the Charlotte lockup. Chuck could not get over how horrible prison had been. He had taken five showers the night of his return, and still carried the stench embedded in his skin. Even now his ankles and wrists felt raw from the shackles. The apostle Paul had spoken with such eloquence about his own captivity, both in prison and under house arrest in Rome. Chuck Griffin had found neither inspiration nor closeness to God during his own time behind bars. The despair and the noise and the reeking, close-packed humanity had left him utterly unable to pray. He had always considered Paul to be a stronger man than himself. Now he knew it for certain.

Which only made his present circumstances that much more bizarre.

God's call for him to come to North Carolina and establish this community had been unequivocal. Had the majestic hand written the command in blazing letters on the sky, it could not have been clearer. But just as with Moses, Chuck found himself repeatedly wondering if maybe God should have chosen a better man. No matter that the weak were better able to focus upon God's strength. That sounded fine from the pulpit, but it held a faint hint of the ridiculous when seen from his perspective. A hundred times a day he was being accosted by people needing answers he could not give. Telling them to pray, or to wait upon the Lord, only went so far. He was not the man for the job, and never would be.

Chuck found himself longing for his wife, something he rarely did these days. It led to self-pity and wishing for a time that was lost now to the realm of memories. But the truth was, Elvie would have known what to do about the coming meeting with the synod. He could hear her now, chiding him for worrying over what he couldn't control and for doubting God's direction. He missed the freedom to tell her exactly what he felt, something a pastor could do with very few people. Days like this, with the glorious sunset lost behind a veil of fears and troubles, he found it hard to forgive God for taking her like He did. One moment all had been fine; the next, he had been battered by the impossibilities of life.

Chuck and Elvie had wed his first year of seminary. They had been married twenty-four years. At the time of her death, their two wonderful kids had just been starting out on their own. He and Elvie had just begun making breathless plans for a life as a couple, when suddenly she was gone.

She had complained of pains occasionally, aches running down her left arm and in her chest. But it was nothing they ever thought was serious, especially since the pains never lasted very long. Then one morning while making breakfast she had burned her hand on the stove, and the shock had been enough to cause a heart attack. The both of them forty-seven years old, him seated there at the kitchen table watching and arguing over whether they should go to Rome and Jerusalem and Paris or buy a new car, and then nothing. No future, no life ahead, nothing together except a rush to the hospital in the back of an ambulance, arriving too late to even say good-bye properly. Twenty-four years of married life was a long time only when there was a tomorrow. With a wife as fine as Elvie, and with her gone now and him seated there alone, twenty-four years was barely long enough to make a decent start.

Seated now on the back porch of a home so new it still smelled of paint and sawdust, surrounded by the strangeness of a thousand fresh starts, he could almost see the power of God's plans behind it all. Almost, but not quite, because Chuck found it hard to believe a gentle God would have robbed him of Elvie. No matter how vital the need to strip him of all connections to a life now gone. No matter how important the task ahead. Elvie had defined love for him. Some people spoke of how they could hold a newborn baby and see the face of creation. Not him. For Chuck Griffin, his clearest image of God's power had always been watching the face of his sleeping wife in the growing light of a new dawn. But such dawns were gone, as were all the hopes they once contained.

✕ ✕

Now, night was a gentle shawl of warm rustlings and starlight and feather-light strokes of wind. Moonlight painted the few tendrils of clouds with softest silver. It was his third Carolina spring, and still Chuck was unused to how gently the seasons came, how mild the nights. A night bird cried from the forest beyond his back garden, the sound a beckoning urge to remember other things. Harder things still than the loss of Elvie. The reason for his coming here. And the moment that had sparked it all.

Indiana springtimes were gray and wet, or at least so they seemed from this distance. At least that particular April day had been gray. And cold. A bitter wind had been blowing down from Canada, and people had rushed from their cars to the church. He could still remember how he had sat at his desk, waiting for the time to go to his pulpit and lead another service. It seemed as though everything about that fateful day was etched deep in his mind, engraved with the force of another unexpected blow.

Chuck always preferred to be alone the half-hour or so before a service. Be it a marriage or a funeral or a Wednesday night service like that one. If there was a guest speaker, like they had that day, he would politely insist that the visitors make themselves comfortable in the conference room next door. The following week their church was to host a regional gathering of pastors and seminarians. One of the national figures, the pastor of a church with over ten thousand members, had agreed to come early and preach. That night their little church was almost bursting at the seams.

Which meant that when the gunman appeared in the back doorway, there was nowhere for anyone to run.

The speaker had just risen to his feet. Then the chamber's rear doors slammed open with the force of an explosion. The speaker froze midway to the podium. Just stood there, the Bible in one hand, his finger holding the place. Then the man at the back of the chamber had shouted something vile. Chuck had no idea what the man had said. Nor did it really matter. Every vestige of his attention had become focused upon the madness in the man's gaze.

Time slowed to a glutinous crawl as the man whipped open his tattered raincoat to reveal the pump-action shotgun.

The assailant lifted his weapon and then fired one shot without aiming, straight over the heads of the people to his left, blasting out the side stained-glass window. Another shout of spittle and rage and senseless, maddened words, then he had pointed the shotgun up and blasted a hole in the roof.

The congregation had parted clean as the Red Sea, spilling down onto the floor, everyone piling away from the central aisle and the man with his gun. The man roared a guffaw of pure insane power. And aimed his gun straight at the heart of the guest speaker.

Chuck had not hesitated, not an instant. He catapulted from his seat as though propelled by the congregation's screams and their horror-struck faces. He leapt from the stage, vaulting over the flower arrangement. He raced down the central aisle. He had not said a single thing. Not a word. But his mind had cried two thoughts over and over, as the attacker's maddened gaze had fastened upon him. The first thought was, *Elvie!* The second was, *I'm coming!*

The attacker shifted his gun a fraction, and Chuck found himself staring into a barrel big and black as death. He opened his arms to embrace the coming blow, not so much racing toward the attacker as fleeing all the empty days both behind and ahead.

The man's gaze looked as dark as the gun barrel. Strange how Chuck had time to see and register that, but it was true. Chuck looked straight into the man's eyes and saw the dark emptiness of a man no longer there. The attacker had roared something else, and still Chuck heard nothing but the lunacy of a man able to shatter the sanctity of a prayer service. Then the man's entire arm and shoulder and chest clenched as he fired. And the gun's detonation drowned out the attacker's demented howl.

Chuck saw the flame and the smoke. He faltered and wrapped his arms around his chest, but not from pain.

All he felt was wind.

There was a quiet whoosh, a warm breath, then nothing.

He stopped. He had no choice. The chamber was filled with a shouting, wailing din.

The attacker stared at him, his mouth open, a great gaping maw in the middle of his scraggly beard. His wide eyes were seeing and yet not there at all, glazed with the frenzy of all that should have remained beyond the bounds of their holy sanctuary. The mouth formed sounds that were not words, or perhaps the words were lost in the surrounding chaos.

The madman gripped the gun, not with his hands but rather with his entire being, cocking the gun and aiming so that Chuck was staring at the barrel's black mouth, which was ready to consume him.

The barrel spouted flames and thunder yet again. Chuck's body convulsed against a blow that did not come. And for a second time Chuck felt the warm breath pass to either side.

There was nothing left to do but walk forward and rip the gun from the man's astonished grip.

The weapon was hot with all that had missed him. The smoke was acrid, a stench of what he had battled his entire life to keep at bay, from himself and his family and his flock.

The man stared at him, a fiend defeated by forces beyond his ken. Then he was lost beneath a pile of bodies, men and boys leaping from the pews to either side, wrestling him to the ground. The madman was shouting then, words that still made no sense even though Chuck was listening with all his might, struggling to understand what had just happened. But the words were no clearer than the impressions tumbling through his mind.

The police had swiftly arrived. The newspeople came soon after, alerted by astonished reports the police had not even bothered to mask in their initial radioed accounts. Newspapers around the nation had carried the same picture, the photograph taken by the police reporter. The picture had shown Chuck standing in the aisle holding the madman's shotgun. He had looked impossibly calm, his hair in place and his tie drawn up neatly to his collar. All about him, to every side, was carnage. The photograph showed him silhouetted by destruction. The altar flowers were ripped to shreds. The pulpit was blasted and splintered. The cross upon the back wall was caught in a halo of bullet holes. In the foggy background, the famous preacher, a man who had spent countless nights in the White House counseling three different presidents, stared at Chuck with dumbfounded shock. The same expression was mirrored on all the parishioners who surrounded Chuck. The photograph had captured their trauma perfectly, with dozens of hands reaching out and yet none touching him. The only calm person was Chuck, who stood and met the photographer with a gaze dark and brooding.

The image reflected his most naked moment, and Chuck hated it. Upon their arrival in Kingdom Come, his secretary had wanted to enlarge it and put it in the community center's front hall. He had been forced to confess just how much he despised it, which had hurt her and surprised everyone. But he could do nothing about the hundreds of photos kept by others, displayed in front rooms and used as a badge of pride, their way of claiming they had been there at the beginning.

Every time he saw that picture, Chuck relived the moment. He could not stop himself from recalling his suicidal rush toward the attacker. Nor could he protect himself from the honest knowledge that he had not been intent upon protecting his flock, as all supposed. Every time he saw that picture, he recalled anew how he had rushed toward that attacker in a frantic embrace of death and reunion with his beloved Elvie.

His desire to leave it all behind had been a hunger so great it shamed him now, the secret desires of his darkest shadows brought into brilliant light.

Over and over in the hours and days that followed, Chuck found himself coming back to one crystal-clear image. One he had mentioned to nobody.

What Chuck had never confessed to another was how, as the madman had been wrestled to the floor, he had felt the wind a third time. Which was why he had remained standing, alone and isolated even as the police had rushed in and the picture had been captured for all time. For the third wind had spoken to him, a voice as powerful as the moment, and as gentle.

Warm it had felt, blowing like a caress, gentling his forehead and his heart. It had been the touch of a mother comforting a feverish child, a wife soothing a panicked mate. The wind had been a kiss of life, a perfumed fragrance so perfect that he had been scalded by his own selfish desires. To miss his departed wife had been righteous only so long as it was balanced against his desire to serve. To seek to join her had been so wrong it left him feeling encased in the filth of someone else's grave. Yet the wind had assured him, letting him know with utter certainty he was forgiven, long before the voice had spoken. In fact, it was not the words that had rocked him, so much as the impression they had carried.

The wind had whispered to his soul only two words: *Not yet.*

But what had struck Chuck with the force of a blow to his very soul, and that which remained with him still, had been the message beyond the words. The message of eternal *purpose.*

Three days after the church shooting, the meeting of pastors and seminarians had started on schedule because Chuck fiercely insisted they continue as planned. Only it was a local gathering no longer. News of his miraculous deliverance had ignited something very deep within the church community. Something visceral. Pastors from every denomination had come, and from every state in the nation. The newspeople had lingered for the first day only, until the message of redemption and repentance had rattled their objective cages. No one was the least bit sorry to see them go. Something else was intended here. By that time it was the one point upon which all could agree.

Numerous times each day, Chuck was asked to go up front. To

take control, to lead, to direct. To speak. To pray. But he declined. People came from all over, there to see the church with their own eyes, to pray or listen or sing or just sit for a while. Food was prepared by unknown hands. The meeting started when people arrived and ended when all were tired—always after midnight. People rose and spoke when they felt called. They stopped glancing at Chuck for permission because he refused to respond. He sat and listened when he felt like it, or he knelt and prayed, or he stood and walked the church's halls. People offered him greetings and shook his hand and tried to engage him in conversation, but something either in his gaze or within his mantle of silence left them subdued and distanced. By the third day, he was left pretty much alone.

And still they came.

Nothing in the church's history prepared them for the visitors. From as far away as England and the Philippines and Australia and Romania and New Zealand and South Africa and Brazil, they came. Homes were opened to total strangers. Hotel bills were paid for those without money. Most had no real reason for coming, except that they had seen the picture of Chuck Griffin standing there with the shotgun in his hands, staring at the camera with his Lazarus gaze, and somehow they knew they had to come. They *had* to.

By the fifth day Chuck was beyond the point of needing to ask any further for forgiveness. He had repented as best he knew how, and had even come to see that despite his agony there was a sense of purpose behind his losing Elvie. He could look back now and see how the distancing had begun with her funeral. Up until the attack, he realized, he had been just marking time, going through the motions, attached to nothing and no one.

On the morning of the meeting's sixth day, Chuck entered the sanctuary with a deep sense of conviction that the Lord was going to ask him to lead his church somewhere new. Somewhere so bizarrely different from their present direction that a total divorce from so-called normal life had been required. Chuck sat in what had become his customary pew, midway up the left side, and stared at the carnage around him. The only change from the night of the attack was that the flowers had been removed and the stained-glass window had been covered by a plastic tarp. Only now Chuck did not see an attack. He saw a *beginning*.

To what, he had no idea.

For the first time since the conference had started, Chuck found himself focusing upon the speakers. Perhaps this was the way of all harsh shocks, he reflected. Perhaps a time of internal reflection was required. He had no point of reference. To his point of view, however, it seemed as though he had spent the previous five days coming to see God's design in these brutal events with a clarity of perception he had not known since losing Elvie's wise counsel. He knew God's hand was at work—if not in the actions, then at least in giving them purpose. He had been confronted with his own selfish will, and he had repented. There was nothing left to him on this earth with meaning save his two adult children and his church and his God. It was time to place first things first, and seek the purpose behind the mystery.

The first speaker that morning was an ancient warrior of the Word, a retired pastor from Peachtree City, Georgia. Paul Caldwell was his name, a rotund little man with a strong Georgia drawl and an opera singer's way of gesturing. He flung his arms open wide, and chanted in a voice too big for his little body. Reverend Paul Caldwell's accent was broad and country-Southern. But his message was clear as the morning light. The church of today was under attack. The world was set upon a path utterly opposed to God's holy design. Believers needed to heed the call to repentance and revival.

Chuck did not know he had risen until he found himself walking forward. A great murmuring tension filled the chamber, packed as it was at ten o'clock on a weekday morning. Chuck did not falter, though for a moment he wanted to. There was a sense of being guided by the same hand that had breathed upon him that fateful night. His responsibility at that moment, his challenge, was to go as he was being led.

As Chuck climbed the side stairs, the retired pastor adjusted his spectacles with a hand that shook slightly. The crowd shifted and swayed and spoke with a single voice, like waves rolling in from a holy sea. The pastor did not leave the pulpit, but rather stepped forward and embraced Chuck. Chuck felt in the man's solid arms a sense of being welcomed by the church and the holy clan.

Chuck turned to face the congregation, most of whom were by then on their feet. The older man remained there at Chuck's side, his arm resting in benediction upon Chuck's shoulder. Chuck looked out over the chamber filled with friends and strangers, family all. And spoke for the first time in six long days. "Let us pray."

"Come, oh come, great and holy Lord," Chuck intoned, speaking words that seemed gifted to him from somewhere beyond. "We beseech Thee, Spirit of life, breath of our souls. Speak to us, King Jesus. Ignite this gathering with your holy fire."

And then he spoke no more.

The wind returned, and this time it did not touch his heart alone. Whenever Chuck heard others speak of that momentous day, they referred to the experience as entering a holy hurricane.

TWELVE

Later that evening, Ben entered the apartment to the sound of the ringing phone. His boss, Evan Hawkins, was furious. "Do you realize what I've been going through for the past five hours?"

"Sorry." Ben kneaded his forehead. The truth was, he had forgotten. The time with Dottie had not been comfortable, seated in the same diner where he had witnessed the quarrel, feeling all eyes on them, picking at a chocolate cream pie he didn't want. Neither of them had been reluctant to rise and leave the hostile surveillance behind. "I got caught up."

"I've been sitting here worrying that the next sound I'd hear was the official notice of your demise!"

Ben kicked off his boots, carried the phone over to the sofa, and sank down. "Evan, how long have you known me?"

"What does that have to do with—"

"We've worked together on and off for sixteen years, isn't that right? Long enough for you to trust my instincts."

There was a longish pause, then, "What are you saying?"

"There is no danger here, Evan. None."

"I suppose you've got some solid evidence to back this up?"

"No. And that's the problem."

"It sure is."

"I've got a thousand things I could point to and say, this is why I think what I do."

"But you can't tell me what I want to hear. Which is that you've searched out a militia. Or found their arms cache."

"It's only my first day. But my best guess is, there isn't one to find." He loosened the knot of his tie and tossed it aside. "I've observed none of the signs typical of cults. And you know I've seen my share."

"Give me a for instance."

Dottie's invitation to join her for dessert in front of the crowd sprang to Ben's mind. His being called to the stage was next. Ben discarded them both. "Their leader's arrest hasn't been used as an excuse to foment a stronger hatred for the local authorities. The clan is not ordered to bind together more tightly. There's no great suspicion shown for anyone new. Instead, when one of their guys stood up and started talking about our plans to go after the banks and bring in the IRS—"

Evan exploded, "They know about that?"

"They know everything. But that's not the point."

"They've got a mole in our organization?"

"Evan, listen to what I'm saying here. When this source started warning them that we were going to shut the faucet to state and federal funding, the pastor—" Ben halted, caught once more by the feeling of being thunderstruck by Chuck's announcement.

"Who, the leader?"

Ben shook himself. "He is and he isn't. The leader, I mean. They've got this group of fourteen people who act as a sort of council. That's another thing. I haven't found any of the angry passion or magnetic personality we'd expect in a cult leader."

"Okay, okay, so what did the leader do?"

"He welcomed me. He told the entire assembly to treat me as their friend."

That silenced Evan completely.

"Listen," Ben went on. "I want you to come down and see this for yourself."

"Maybe I should." Speaking even slower now. "What about the reports of the other insert, Fran Totter, and the agent on the ground, Wayne Oates?"

"I can't answer for anybody but myself," Ben replied. "But my gut tells me this is not a crisis situation. This is something else entirely."

"What, then?"

"I wish I knew."

⚒ ⚒

The following morning, acting Agent-in-Charge Wayne Oates sat in the corner office. Their former top agent had retired eleven months before. Since then, Wayne Oates had run the Charlotte operation and tried not to let his hunger show. He had a lot of experience hiding what he felt and thought. It was as much a part of his background as the red Piedmont clay. Ambition was one of the many things a Carolina farm boy could not afford. He had learned at a very early age never to let on that his dreams rose beyond the horizon of ninety-seven acres of tobacco and soybeans.

According to office scuttlebutt, Washington had not appointed a new AIC because of budget pressures. As subtly as possible, allies were passing on news that Washington meant to shut the Charlotte office down. Wayne was not surprised. Charlotte was one of the small regional offices, left intact mainly because the city was growing so rapidly. There were few problems that justified their presence, however. Almost everything could be handled by special agents dispatched from the agency's principal office in Raleigh. Wayne was not fighting the closure so much as hoping to turn it to his advantage. Handling a large crisis on the scale of this Kingdom Come operation could mean reassignment to a place full of action and the chance to advance.

His phone rang just as he was completing the daily reports from his six special agents and was handing out assignments. "Oates."

A male voice intoned, "Hold, please, for Theron Head."

Wayne waved the last two agents from his office and carried his phone over to the window. He kept his back to the office, hiding the sudden tension that gripped him. He heard a pair of clicks, then, "Mr. Oates?"

"Good morning, Mr. Head. Nice to—"

"I've received an alarming report about Ben Atkins and his insertion into the cult. Are you in the loop here?"

Wayne struggled to bring himself up to speed. "No sir. I'm not."

"He had a telephone meeting with Evan Hawkins last night." The man's voice resembled a computer-generated drone. Toneless and impossibly bland. "Apparently the man had the gall to insist that there is no danger at Kingdom Come. That we should disassociate ourselves."

Wayne felt a flush of anger creep up from his collar. "That's crazy."

"I'm glad to hear we feel the same about this, Mr. Oates. Very glad."

Wayne fought to concentrate. But it was difficult. That some no-account deskbound Washington agent would waltz in and with less than two days on the ground conclude that all of Wayne's warnings were groundless was not just infuriating. Such a finding threatened to derail all his carefully laid plans. "It's not true. It can't be."

"Of course it's not true. But there are certain powers in Washington who would prefer not to have a problem so large that it would whip the press into a frenzy. They are desperate to hear whatever this Atkins fellow wants to feed them. What's more, they are terrified they might be called upon to act within the spotlight of national attention." A pause, then, "What do you say to that, Mr. Oates?"

"They're nuts." Nervously Wayne swiped at his forehead. "They think they can bury their heads in the bureaucratic sand and this will go away all by itself? They're crazy as loons."

"I quite agree." Theron paused to cough. Then, "I have had a careful look at your records, Mr. Oates. What I have read tells me that you are a fine agent. What I have *surmised* is that you are also an ambitious one."

Wayne felt his gut gripping tight. "Very."

"That is good, Mr. Oates. I assume you know of my personal cadre?"

"Yes." Theron Head's team was the stuff of legends. Not since the days of Herbert Hoover had the organization known such a tightly knit unit. It was almost a force within a force. With each step that Theron Head made up the bureaucratic ladder, he pulled his allies up along with him. The underlings were fiercely loyal and extremely secretive.

"How would you like to join their ranks?"

"There's not a single solitary thing," Wayne replied tensely, "I'd like more."

"The sort of response I like. Fine, then. I will be in touch, Mr. Oates."

The phone went dead. Wayne stood at the window staring out at the overcast morning, seeing neither the heavy cloud covering nor the throngs of morning rush-hour pedestrians. His vision was filled with the thrill of watching his future unfold.

THIRTEEN

It was not until the taxi pulled up in front of the downtown Richmond hotel that Chuck Griffin regretted his decision to travel alone. The elders of Kingdom Come had all wanted to come, but Chuck had clearly sensed that he was to make this journey by himself. Yet what had felt fine in the comfort of his community now seemed rash and reckless.

Chuck had previously attended three meetings of the Reformed Church of America's general synod. Once as a student, representing his seminary. Once as assistant to the head pastor of his first church, who was making a report to the committee. And once on his own, representing a group of middle America churches seeking help on a new joint project. He had always found the synod imposing, yet warm. Most of the members he not only admired but genuinely revered. He had always loved being a part of a denomination that could trace its heritage back to the American colonies. His honor's thesis at seminary had been on the role the RCA had played in the American Revolution. Attending a synod had always before been an event of great joy and anticipation.

Not now.

He stepped from the taxi and stood looking up at the impressive stone building with its uniformed bellhops. The brass doors swung open, wafting the rich odors of tobacco and power from within.

Chuck hesitated, wondering if it was too late to call back down and ask for someone to join him.

"Reverend Griffin?"

"Yes."

A fresh-faced young man offered a hand. "I've been sent to bring you inside. They're waiting for you, sir."

"They are?"

"Yes sir." The man's smile was strained, the look in his eyes very worried. "To be honest, all they've done so far this morning is mark time."

Chuck swallowed. "Lead on, then."

They marched through the plush lobby and took the stairs up one flight. Chuck's footfalls were masked by carpet so fine it looked hand groomed. His heartbeat sounded so loud in his own ears, he was surprised the people they passed did not notice.

The young man halted before tall, mahogany double doors and pointed Chuck toward a single seat. "If you wouldn't mind waiting here a moment, sir, I'll let them know you've arrived."

"Yes. Of course. Fine." Chuck sank into the chair and forced himself to remain upright and steady, at least externally. He wanted to pray. He would give anything to have things return to how they had been and how he had once thought they would always remain. But the prayer would not come.

"Chuck? Are you all right?"

He raised his head and looked up at Lloyd Bowick, the elderly church statesman. Chuck demanded softly, "Why am I here?"

The man offered no comfort whatsoever. Not in words, nor in the concern that draped about his features and bowed his shoulders. "Come on, son. They're waiting."

Chuck forced himself up and through the doorway. He faltered momentarily as he entered the chamber and saw the ring of grim faces. Row after row of observers flanked the synod, all of them dark suited, all of them somber and stern. The elderly pastor guided him into a chair at the head of the square table, alone and isolated.

Chuck sat facing the entire gathering, feeling yet again that a lifetime's worth of imperfections were on display. To have been brought to this position, he could not help but worry that he had somehow missed God's will in all this. He shook with fear, not over what was to come, but rather over the prospect of having listened to the wrong voice.

"Thank you for coming, Reverend Griffin." It was not the president who spoke, but rather a man to the president's right. The gentleman was vaguely familiar, but in his addled state Chuck could not put a name to the face. The synod spokesman asked, "Could you tell us what precisely is going on within this place called Kingdom Come?"

Chuck opened his mouth, but nothing came. He swallowed, and managed to say, "All my life, I have dreamed of nothing more than being a Reformed Church pastor."

A ripple of disquiet was unleashed by his words. A man from farther along the synod table leaned forward and asked, "Is it true that your group is growing at the pace of nearly a hundred families a week?"

"Y-yes." Even speaking the simplest word was a struggle.

"What precisely is behind this growth?"

"Revival," Chuck managed, though he had to force the word out, as though a power he could not identify did not wish him to speak.

The spokesman's shoulders hunched. "How many of your newcomers are already members of other Reformed Churches?"

Before Chuck could respond, one of the other members stiffened and demanded, "He is siphoning members away from our own churches?"

"Apparently it is not just members, but funds as well. Several churches in my area are reporting a marked drop in both attendance and donations."

There was a growing murmur in the ranks behind the synod, but Chuck caught only one word. *Scandalous.* He wanted to speak, to explain that he sought to recruit no one at all. Rather, from the start people had seemed drawn to the community by a hand greater than any church or pastor. He had a hundred things he wanted to say, descriptions of the miracles and the way people were pulling together, the sense of a new clan being formed, of a truly great beginning. But the words did not come. It was more powerful even than his inability to pray in the hallway. His mouth felt clamped shut, the words held down so tightly it was hard for him to even form them in his mind.

A heavyset man pushed through the side doors, thunking the doors hard against the wall. The entire gathering turned and watched as the man marched over and slapped a page down on the table in front of the synod spokesman, who frowned as he read. It was in this moment of silence that Chuck recalled the spokesman's name. Thurgood Innes, pastor of a huge church in Orlando, and newest appointee to the ruling synod.

Reverend Innes raised his eyes to meet Chuck's own gaze. "Pastor Griffin, could you tell us, have you granted other denominations permission to build churches within this compound of yours?"

Chuck wanted to respond that it was neither a compound nor his. But the tightly enforced silence gradually was coalescing into something more. He became enveloped in the only answer he could have found to this dilemma. A peace surrounded him, so great it granted him not just ease, but wisdom.

"Is it also true," Thurgood Innes asked, lifting the page, "that you have granted the Catholic church license to erect a parish church?" He granted time for the synod to murmur their disquiet, then pressed on, "Have you also permitted two Hispanic congregations to establish new churches? And a Korean church?"

Chuck wanted to counter by asking them how he, a mortal man and a sinner, could override what he felt was God's guidance. How he was not inviting anyone, yet people were coming from all over, and if they wished to have their own places of worship, why should he object? But Chuck could not respond in any way to the tumult rising around the table. He was captured by the distinct sense of watching something of which he was no longer a part. It did not matter that these were good people, striving to serve God, within a denomination whose heritage he cherished and called his own. The force that enveloped him also *claimed* him. He was called not to serve the synod, but God.

Chuck rose from his seat, and said the only words that were there for him to say. "I beg you all, come and see the revival for yourselves."

FOURTEEN

The next morning, almost in answer to Ben's silent musing over what to do with his day, the phone rang and Evan Hawkins announced, "I've decided to make a flying visit."

"Great," Ben replied, wishing he truly felt that way. "When?"

"I'm calling from the plane. Caught the red-eye from National. I arrive in Charlotte in less than an hour. Don't worry about meeting me. I'll rent a car and drive up to Kingdom Come."

"There's supposed to be a traffic problem today. Something about a gathering here this weekend."

"Gathering of what?"

"No idea."

"And you think you know enough to advise us that there's no danger?" Evan huffed at him from thirty-thousand feet. "Never mind. I'll call you from the car."

It was only after Ben hung up that he wondered why Evan Hawkins had not ordered Wayne Oates from the Charlotte office to drive him up. He stared out the front window, looking beyond the balcony and railing to where the sky was painted a fresh china blue. He couldn't help but ponder over what made Evan leave Washington on such short notice.

His position granted him sight of the slender shadow that slipped by his window and stopped to knock upon his door. Ben walked over and said to Dottie, "You're just in time for coffee."

"I can't, I've got to pack." Her face had the same pinched expression as the previous day. "I just stopped by to say that I've gotten another message from Chuck."

Ben pushed the door open and backed away. Dottie hesitated a moment, then stepped inside. Ben said, "You know, he could always call me himself."

"Exactly what I told him." Dottie Betham looked around. "These apartments look like pre-fab motel rooms. We've even got the same plastic flower arrangements and the same bad art."

"Sure you don't have time for a cup?"

"Yes, all right." She followed him over to the stools by the kitchen counter. "Though I shouldn't complain. The rate they're throwing them up, it's amazing the floors aren't crooked."

Ben fished another mug from the shelf. "I've been wondering how Fran Tottler managed to get a place here."

"That was the woman's name?" She watched him pour the mug full. "Black is fine, thanks."

"Haven't met many ladies who prefer their java black."

"It comes with the profession. In most newsrooms, you either drink it black or get used to powdered milk and sweetener, which I positively loathe."

Ben Atkins stared down at her. Today she wore an open-necked blouse with an Aztec design, fawn-colored cotton slacks, and sturdy walking shoes. Her hair was cut in a style as direct and efficient as her speech. Her features bore the tanned and lean look of someone who loved the outdoors, a fact that left him wishing they could for once have a normal conversation. "You were saying about these apartments?"

She sipped, then nodded her approval. "Anyone can come here and request assignment to these temporary accommodations. The rent starts off very low and rises every week. After a month at least one person in each apartment is expected to have a job within the community."

"I haven't paid a thing."

"Then come Monday or Tuesday you'll be visited by a very sweet old lady who will ask you to settle up or leave."

"How long have you been here?"

"Five weeks. Too long." She jutted her chin up, an impatient gesture that spilled her brown hair back off her forehead. "I came here hoping to take time out from the normal stress and strains, but it hasn't worked out that way."

Ben leaned both elbows on the counter. "Why not?"

"A lot of reasons." Expelling the words with a harsh sigh. "Mostly because Kingdom Come is not what I expected." A long hesitation, then she added, "Or maybe it's where I belong."

"I know that feeling," Ben said slowly. "All too well."

"You haven't been here long enough to know that for certain."

"Not here. Washington." Ben freshened his own cup. "Like I told you, my wife died four years ago. Last year I realized I was pretty much just marking time out in Arizona. Going through the motions, trying to cover over the hole in my life. So I accepted a post at FBI headquarters in Washington. What a mistake that was."

"Washington doesn't suit you?"

"I've never been one for big cities." He turned back to find her studying him with a frankness that left him willing to confess. "I'd hoped that the work would be interesting enough to make up for living inside a hive. And it is, as long as I'm on a case. But the bureaucratic hoops you've got to jump through drive me right up the wall."

Dottie cocked her head to one side, allowing the hair to spill down, gracing her cheek with a soft veil that turned her young, vulnerable, intensely interested. "Are all agents this easy to talk to?"

He had to smile. "My mouth gets me in trouble all the time. But I'm too set in my ways to change, and I've never found anything that suits me better than honesty."

She studied him a long moment, then said, "I almost forgot why I came by. Chuck asks if you will come to the Gathering tonight."

"Wouldn't miss it. Won't you be there?"

Her look turned wry. "I've been given a commission by *Newsday*. I'm being paid to go."

"So why are you leaving, Dottie?"

"I'm not. I'm just giving up the apartment for the weekend. The local sheriff is a friend. They've offered me a room for the weekend. We're having a serious overflow problem, and if half as many people show up as predicted, they'll be sleeping in their cars. I hate to do that to a kid." She rose from her stool. "They said to tell you there's an extra room you can take if you'd like."

There were a thousand reasons not to go stay with a local sheriff, but none seemed valid at that moment. "Glad to help."

"Thanks. I'll let the organizers know they can use your apartment." Dottie started for the door, then halted and half turned and said quietly, "I envy you, Ben Atkins."

"Me?"

But she did not say anything more, just opened the door and slipped into the shimmering light of another brilliant day.

He started to follow her, only to be drawn back by the ringing phone. "Atkins."

It was his boss, Evan Hawkins. "I'll be there in fifteen minutes."

"That's not possible."

"I'll tell you what's not possible." There was a heightened tension to Evan's voice, and a noisy thrumming in the background. "I'm flying over a traffic jam ten miles long. There wasn't a rental car to be had for love or money. I've caught a lift from the police traffic chopper. What did you call this meeting of theirs?"

"A Gathering."

"Looks like a cross between an emergency evac and a rock concert. The pilot needs to know where to set down this bird."

Ben was already reaching for his jacket and his keys and his gun.

"There's a series of warehouses just inside the fence, and they're sur-rounded by a parking lot. I'll meet you there."

Evan Hawkins was taller than Ben by a good three inches. He stooped as he rushed under the chopper's rotor blade, holding his suit coat and tie down flat. He straightened and glared through his mirrored aviator shades as he walked over and declared, "You've got two hours."

Ben offered his hand. "Mind telling me why you didn't inform the Charlotte office about your trip?"

Evan was utterly bald and had the cadaverous features of an aging jogger. His dark gray suit flapped about his frame as he walked around to the passenger side. He said across the car, "You already know."

Ben slipped behind the wheel of his car and punched up the air conditioner. The late May day was not hot so much as muggy. He guessed, "Theron Head has pulled this Oates character into his camp."

"You're a smart guy, Ben. Tough and levelheaded as they come. There's nobody I'd rather have doing the groundwork on a crucial case." Evan shook his head. "But what possessed you to argue with Theron, I'll never understand."

"Just calling them as they lay."

"This isn't the Boy Scouts, and they aren't giving out merit badges for honesty," Evan snapped. "We're in the majors, and you're about to get sent down. You've never come up against Head's cadre, have you?"

Ben put the car into gear and eased to the edge of the parking lot. There he halted once more. Traffic crawled through the gates in a con-tinuous line that backed up over the ridge and out of sight. A pair of young men with walkie-talkies, police traffic batons, and orange vests stood and directed the cars in alternate directions. "Take a look here, will you?"

But Evan was not listening. "Theron's team is the tightest, most vindictive group I've ever come across. Ambitious, spiteful, as secretive as Hoover's old clan. Which is why I'm telling you I don't have any choice. I'm washing my hands of you, Ben."

The words resonated so strongly, it felt to Ben as though his entire body had suddenly become one great bell. Sounding out a signal he did not understand. "What?"

"You've got one way out. One. You've got to do a complete about-face. Get down on your hands and knees and go crawling to Theron, tell him how wrong you've been, how dangerous this all is."

Ben slid the gearshift back into park. "What if I can convince you there's nothing sinister about this place and these people?"

"You're not listening!" A flush crawled out of Evan's collar and crept up past his ears, splotching his bald head. "Either you sign on with the powers that be or you can kiss your career good-bye!"

"What if I—"

"I heard you the first time." Evan swiped a nervous hand over his eyes and up across his head. "Ben, I've got a kid in her last year of high school and another one at Georgetown. I have no desire to finish my career marking time in Fairbanks. It's cold up there. Time moves very slow. I know. I've heard all about it from the last guy who crossed Theron Head."

Ben waited until he was certain Evan had finished. "You just said we've got two hours. Let me show you around."

"I'm here because I'm hoping we can locate something to convince *you*."

"I am convinced," Ben replied quietly. "And growing more so with every passing hour."

Evan shook his head. "Crazy," he muttered. "I never thought I'd stand by and watch you shoot yourself in the foot. Never."

"Just take a look around, will you?" Ben pointed through the front windshield. "I've done undercover work at two militias. Raided almost a dozen others, kept active files on I don't know how many more. There are certain traits you find. You know them as well as I do. They shut themselves off. They feed on insularity. They rage against authority. Any encroachment on their territory is used as an excuse to counterattack."

Evan released an explosive sigh, swiveled around to the front, swiped an impatient hand down his tie. "So?"

"So *look*. You've just swooped down out of the sky, we're sitting here in a car they've already tied to an FBI agent, and how much attention is being paid to us?"

"For all you know, they've got a pair of snipers sitting in that forest across the road, taking a bead on us as we speak."

Ben started to object, then changed course. "And the traffic."

"What about it?"

"You said yourself it's bumper to bumper from here to Charlotte. Do you see any resentment, any rage? Even the traffic wardens are friendly. Those people are *smiling*, Evan."

This time the Washington man took a longer look before saying, "They're outsiders."

"Sure they are. But what is bringing them to Kingdom Come?"

"That's why we sent you in here. To find out what's behind it all." Evan chopped the air between them. "Look, we both know there's never been a cult this size before. The rulebook's already been tossed out the window."

"And I told you," Ben repeated, "I don't think this is a cult."

"Then what . . ." Evan halted in mid-flow as traffic parted directly in front of them to permit a sheriff's car with flashing lights to pass through. "Want to tell me what's going on?"

"I don't have any idea." Ben watched as the car pulled up directly in front of them and a heavyset man in his fifties pried himself out from behind the wheel. The sheriff walked over and waited as Ben rolled down his window.

Up close the man smelled of Old Spice and leather polish. "Hot enough for you folks?"

Ben recognized the voice as belonging to the policeman on the other end of the radio. "Can I help you?"

"Looks to me like it's the other way around." He stuck a beefy hand through the window. "Hal Drew."

"Ben Atkins. This is Evan Hawkins."

"Nice to meet you." He leaned over far enough to study Evan. "You down from Washington?"

"Mr. Hawkins is deputy assistant director of the FBI's criminal investigative unit."

"Well, sir, you're welcome." He patted the windowsill, his wedding ring tapping on the metal. "Why don't we slip into my car? We'll get around easier if I can flash the lights from time to time."

Without waiting for a response, the officer turned and walked back to his patrol car. Evan demanded, "Did you arrange this?"

"I've never spoken to the guy before."

"Then how do we get rid of him?"

"It may not be a bad idea to make an initial survey with his help," Ben pointed out. "You can see the traffic."

"Help us?" Evan gave him a tight grimace. "Ben, you are well and truly lost."

Before Ben could respond, Evan slid from the car, slammed his door, and stalked over to the police car. He opened the rear door, inspected it carefully, then stood and waited. Ben joined him and offered, "You can ride up front."

In reply, Evan leaned over and asked the sheriff, "Don't you see any need for a dividing grill in your car, officer?"

"Haven't made but one arrest since I took this job; must be close on seven months now," Hal replied easily. "Most of the people I ferry in that backseat would be right offended if I sealed them off."

Evan remained bent over, his features taut. "Where's your weapon?"

That turned Hal Drew around. He met Evan's gaze and replied calmly, "In my desk drawer. Where it belongs."

Evan turned to stare at Ben, who had nothing to add. The assistant director shook his head and slid in, banging his door shut. Once Ben was inside, Evan demanded, "I want to know what's behind this offer of yours."

"Just doing what Chuck asked," Hal answered comfortably. "Treating this fellow here as a friend."

Evan looked from one to the other. "Who?"

"Reverend Chuck Griffin," Ben quietly reminded Evan. "The community leader."

"The leader has spoken about you personally?"

"I told you about this last night, Evan."

"Brought the lawman up front, told the assembly he was our new best friend. Set a lot of people back to the beginning of last week, that did." The policeman restarted his car, then asked, "Where to?"

Evan barked from the backseat, "I'd like to check out your arsenal."

The hand reaching for the gearshift froze in midair. "Come again?"

"Your arms cache. Make sure there aren't any heavy arms or illegal weapons." Evan leaned forward. "You have a problem with that?"

"I sure to goodness do." But the officer was grinning. "Since we don't have anything that comes close. Unless of course you want to check out old man Patterson's vintage flintlocks. He's got them stacked like cordwood in his back shed."

"What about your militia's training ground?" Evan jabbed with his words, sparring now, trying to raise a response. "Is that off-limits as well?"

But the policeman kept grinning as he turned to Ben and said, "I think maybe the chopper pilot took a wrong turn somewhere."

"Why don't you just drive us around," Ben suggested. "Show us what you think we ought to see."

"Now you're talking sense." Hal Drew slapped the car into gear, turned on the siren, and drove around the crawling traffic.

An hour later, Ben was even more convinced that whatever was going on here, it was neither illegal nor threatening. Evan had remained grimly morose, speaking in monosyllables, peering out the side window, giving no indication he was listening at all.

Sheriff Hal Drew had completed two circuits of the entire community, moving against the traffic flow where possible, and using his siren where not. The traffic wardens had all greeted him with grins and waves and halted vehicles. On the first route, they had traversed the outer border, taking in the massive warehouses, fifteen new construction projects, the water treatment plant, the skeleton of the new hospital, a second community center, and the recently completed four-hundred room dormitory housing. On the second circuit he had taken the inner route, showing them around the two towns, the tent city erected for the Gathering, the RV campsite now filled to overflowing, and the mobile kitchens. He had kept up a running commentary, speaking in tones of quiet pride about the growth, the people, the way newcomers kept fitting together and forming a clan.

The towns of Douglas and Hamlin anchored the opposite ends of the compound, with the park stationed directly in the middle. Because Douglas had the community center, it had become the focus of activity and greater growth. Hamlin remained a quieter place, even with the onslaught of Gathering visitors. Although the towns' closest borders were only six miles apart, the park's steep-sided hills were not paved, so all traffic was required to make the circuitous drive to the north or south.

Well-tended farms dotted the remaining countryside. Most of these homes sported large open porches and collections of weather-beaten rockers. Ancient groves of hardwood trees nestled alongside, offering shade and winter windbreaks. Not even the new greenhouses and silos glinting in the sunlight could detract from the region's charm.

Hal Drew spoke with pride about the community's move toward self-sufficiency in agriculture, pointing out greenhouses and storage bins with an openness that only drove Evan further into his seat.

Outside Hamlin, Hal Drew pulled off the inner road and entered a forested area. The blacktop gave way to gravel as it started up a steep rise. "This is now park territory."

Evan spoke for the first time since beginning the tour. "You're moving outside your zone, aren't you?"

"Well, yes and no. This park is so small it doesn't have a permanent guard on duty. When I arrived here, I found a letter from the National Parks Service asking if we could include the region in our regular patrols." The gravel road gave way to a rutted path. "Somebody from the front office has been talking with the service. The park fellows want to hand it over to us, turn it into a local protected area."

Ben swiveled in his seat, but Evan refused to turn from the side window and meet his gaze. "You don't say."

"It's too far off the beaten track to bring in many visitors," the sheriff continued, "and too small to justify them watching over it. They'd be happy to have us treat it as a local preserve."

Evan muttered, "It doesn't mean a thing."

The car bounced hard over a deep rut, then stopped. "Looks like we'd best walk from here. You fellows mind a little hike?"

Ben rose from the car and was instantly surrounded by the sweet scent of pines and honeysuckle. He took a deep breath, then said, "This is great."

"You ain't seen nothing yet." Hal started up the rise, following the trail. "I guess you could say this is as close as we come to a secret project."

That was enough to draw Evan up the slope behind him. "How many people live inside your commune, Officer?"

"The name is Hal." The man's excess poundage was showing now in huffing breaths. "Counting those who've stayed on, we're within shouting distance of fifteen thousand, and growing faster than any-body can keep tally. But it's not a commune."

"How many officers on patrol duty?"

"Just myself, full time. Got a couple of assistants, then a lot of unpaid wardens like them you've seen today."

"One policeman for a commune of fifteen thousand people?" Evan Hawkins was openly scoffing now. "You're saying the militia is actually responsible for keeping order, is that right?"

Hal now halted and gave Evan the first hard look of the day. "Mister, you don't know a fraction of what you *think* you do."

Evan braced himself for more, but instead Hal just turned and started back up the rise. As he climbed he said, "I've got seven retired deputies and policemen I can call on. Four more highway patrols who take care of monitoring the streets at night."

This halted Evan in his tracks. "You allow outside law enforce-ment officers access?"

Hal crested the rise, huffed a pair of deep breaths, then replied, "You're here, aren't you?"

Ben clambered up to stand alongside Hal. He stared down the ridge's other side, and had to say, "Good grief."

"Yeah, she's something, ain't she?"

Evan hurried up to join them. "What on earth?"

"Got to hand it to the front office folks, they played the park people like pros." Hal's good humor was restored by what he sur-veyed. "Told 'em we'd take over care of the preserve only if they'd give us the permits to build this. Then we had to get started before the for-mal permission arrived. It was either that or not have it ready for the Gathering. Close run thing, just the same."

Down below them stretched the largest outdoor theater Ben had ever seen. It brought to mind pictures he had seen of the amphithe-aters of Greece. Only this one was set within a natural valley whose tight sides were now lined with hundreds of rows of wooden benches bolted straight into the natural rock. Where possible, the forest had been left intact to provide leafy windbreaks for the vast stage. A huge grassy bowl stretched across the valley floor.

As they watched, lights flickered on, off, then on again. A hearty cheer drifted up on the windless air. The stage was framed by a latticework of professional lighting and an enormous sound system. A voice rumbled, "Testing, testing, one, two." There was a momentary crackling, then again, "Testing, testing, well, just praise God."

"Amen," Hal said, grinning hugely. "I say, amen."

Evan Hawkins turned his back to the valley and the cheering workers and declared flatly, "I've seen enough."

———— ⊱ ⊰ ————

The chopper was revved and ready for takeoff by the time they halted in the warehouse parking lot. The same line of automobiles snarled up the rise. Young children scampered alongside many cars, pointing at the police helicopter and shouting words that got lost in the rotor's noise. As soon as Hal stopped the car, Evan was out and moving. Ashamed by the way his boss was acting, Ben turned toward Hal, but the policeman waved him easily away. "Go see to the chief honcho. We'll talk later."

"Right." Ben hustled over to where Evan stood by Ben's own car. "You see what I mean?"

"Come on, Ben!" Evan's bark was harsh enough to draw the cords out on his neck. "You know as well as I do that we saw exactly what he wanted us to see. Or you should."

"And I'm convinced there's nothing dangerous here to see!"

"Then you're finished." Evan whipped off his mirror shades, revealing a furious gaze. "And I'm not going to go down with you. You understand what I'm saying?"

"Absolutely. That you're making a terrible mistake."

"You don't know that!"

Ben found his own anger rising. "I'll tell you what I *know*. I know you're taking a coward's way out."

"Watch your language, mister!"

"You haven't seen a single solitary thing that justifies your attitude!"

Evan's chin jutted out. "Give me a hundred men I can *trust*, and in just one day of scoping this place we'd find something. You mark my words."

"Funny," Ben shot back. "I seem to recall somewhere we were assigned responsibility to uphold the law, not break it!"

Evan raised one fist, forced himself to unlock the clench enough to point one finger at Ben's face. "I'm done here. With you, with this charade. Finished. I'm washing my hands."

Ben felt as though the chopper's blades punched the air, buffeting him. "Fine."

Evan's gaze widened. "That's all you have to say?"

"What else am I supposed to tell you? That I'll bend to your threats? That I'll kowtow to the party line just because Theron Head demands it?" Ben shook his head. "It goes against everything that brought me into the service in the first place."

"You don't know what you're up against!" Evan Hawkins swiped the hand down. "I'm wasting my breath. You've gotten hooked. You're joining the cult."

"As I live and breathe, it's not a cult," Ben declared, but he was speaking to empty air. Evan had already wheeled about and stomped toward the chopper. He opened the side door, climbed in, shut the door behind him, fitted on the headset, then used both hands to order the pilot away.

Ben Atkins stood and watched the chopper rise. The wind whipped and the dust scalded his face and hands. Still he stood, until the roar had diminished to a distant thrumming. He knew he was listening to his own career fade as well. And wondered why he felt nothing at all.

FIFTEEN

Friday afternoon, the synod of the Reformed Church of America gathered with a funereal grimness. One after another, the members filed in, pausing to shake Thurgood Innes's hand. Every member but one offered him personal thanks for his handling of this difficult, tragic affair. All the while, Thurgood was forced to ignore a knowing smirk painted upon his senior elder's face. As the president called the meeting to order, Miller Kedrick caught Thurgood's eye and mouthed the words, *I told you so.*

Just as Thurgood was lowering himself into the chair beside the president, Lloyd Bowick entered the chamber. He walked over to Thurgood, drawing him back to his feet. Ten years earlier, the senior statesman had been passed over for synod president. It had been the second synod meeting Thurgood had ever attended. He found himself recalling how the pastor who had nominated Lloyd had described him as a spokesman for God, a man firmly cast in the mold of a preacher of old. Unfortunately for Lloyd, the description had not gained him the support of the younger members, who were already seeking to cast the past aside. So the current president was elected as a compromise candidate. And Thurgood had never forgotten the lesson.

The statesman had a lion's mane of silver-white hair, a seamed face, and eyes that probed deeply. "What if you're wrong, brother?"

Thurgood found himself both uncertain and uncomfortable with himself, as though his suit had been tailored for someone else. "I haven't done a thing except—"

"What if this young man, Chuck Griffin, is doing nothing more than following a call of God?"

From behind him, Miller Kedrick snorted his derision. The statesman turned and studied Miller. The businessman was unable to hold the old pastor's gaze. Miller dropped his eyes to the floor and tugged angrily at his tie.

Then the statesman turned back to Thurgood. Lloyd Bowick said not a word, but Thurgood found himself being painted with the same brush as his elder. He had to force himself not to turn away. But the eyes of the synod were upon him. This moment would be remembered, he was certain. It was essential that he hold to his calm demeanor, no matter how shaken he might feel inside.

Lloyd demanded, "What if God has called these people to establish a point from which a nationwide revival might begin?"

"If that's the case," a voice grated from the table's other side, "why on earth did they surround the place with prison fencing?"

Another irritated member demanded, "What do you expect us to do while they drain our churches of members and money, just sit on our hands?"

Gratefully Thurgood turned from the statesman. "What's that?"

"I received a call last night from my number two." It was one of the younger pastors, a firebrand with a magnetic presence at the pulpit. "From the sound of things, over a hundred of my congregation is driving to Chuck's commune for the weekend."

"There's some kind of meeting going on," another man agreed. "One of my own deacons has organized three buses. I just learned of it yesterday or I'd have jumped on it with both feet."

"If what I heard is true," still another said, "half the churches in my diocese are sending groups."

"A Gathering, that's what they're calling it."

"Huge, from the sounds of things."

"Where are they putting people up? That's what I'd like to know. This Kingdom Come place is supposed to be out in the middle of nowhere."

"One thing is for certain. Wherever they're staying, it's our churches that are paying for it."

"How do you know that?"

"Stands to reason. Where else is a new church going to get the financing, except siphoning it out of our coffers?"

The president used his water glass as a gavel and thumped the table. "Let's please have some order here. Take your seats, everyone."

As he lowered himself, Thurgood glanced back at the statesman. But Lloyd Bowick was no longer a threat to anyone. The power he had shown was gone, as was the piercing gaze. He merely seemed old now. And confused. As though the argument had blown out his heart's light.

The president turned to Thurgood. "Reverend Innes, you've handled this matter so far, perhaps you'd be so good as to continue."

Suddenly all he wanted was to have this over and done with. "It seems to me that further discussion on the future of Charles Griffin is unnecessary. Minds are made up. So I open the floor to formal motions."

"We've talked this over," the youngest synod member said. "I'm putting forward the motion." He indicated the man seated to his right, one of the old-style conservatives. "Frank Jones here is seconding it. We have no choice but to give Charles Griffin the strongest possible censure."

"No," Lloyd groaned. "You can't."

The young pastor ignored him. "We therefore move to remove Charles Griffin and this cult of his from our denomination."

"Second," the man beside him said.

"I'm telling you, with God as my witness, Kingdom Come is not a cult," Lloyd Bowick pleaded.

Thurgood found his eye caught by Miller Kedrick, the only person in the chamber who was smiling. The expression looked positively evil. He dragged his gaze back to the meeting and said, "All in favor?" He counted swiftly. It was unanimous, save for Lloyd Bowick's lone dissension. "The ayes carry the motion."

Once more the president thumped his glass down. "We will adjourn for fifteen minutes. When we return, let us please leave this tragic incident behind us and move on to other business."

Thurgood Innes remained where he was, smitten by rising confusion and the sudden worry that he had just made a terrible error. But before he could search out the reason, a meaty hand landed on his shoulder. Miller Kedrick rasped directly into his ear, "Didn't I tell you? Money and power. They heard Griffin was tapping into their numbers and their pockets, and they panicked." The hand rose and fell, and to Thurgood it felt as though the businessman was driving a stake into his shoulder. "Play your cards right, and they'll be electing you top dog at the next meeting."

SIXTEEN

Late that afternoon, Ben Atkins sat on the porch beside Sheriff Hal Drew. Hal's wife, Mavis, had shooed Ben out of the kitchen when he had gone in to help, insisting there was nothing for him to do except wait for dinner. Dottie was rushing around somewhere inside, answering phone calls and coordinating something to do with the Gathering.

The house dated back to the twenties, white clapboard with a wraparound porch. The roof was steeply canted, such that from the street the smaller second story seemed to slide down to the porch's roofline like an oversize arrowhead. Ben sat in a hickory rocker that creaked a pleasant cadence to the gathering dusk. Hal's police radio was set on the porch railing, turned down so low the scratchy voices were scarcely a murmur. But Ben knew from long experience that the sheriff's ears were tuned not to the words but rather to any possible alarm. The radio was so quiet it hardly competed with the cicadas singing from the sweet-scented hedges that lined the narrow front yard.

Hal Drew had formerly been a sheriff around Winston-Salem. He had also served as deputy chief of a small-town police force in the Appalachian foothills. This much Ben had learned since following Dottie from the apartment building. Ben's one-bedroom apartment now harbored two families with a grand total of seven children. Ben rocked and watched the constant stream of people flowing by on the street. The air was filled with the excited chatter of people headed for a celebration. Children, adults, old people, all ages and shapes and colors. The only vehicles were electric buses and golf carts, ferrying in additional visitors.

Ben was both grateful for the time to sit and reflect, and deeply disturbed as well. He felt as though he was being gently torn in two. One side of his being was utterly content with the night and his position here, rocking beside a quiet country gentleman, waiting for dinner, feeling as much at home as he had since his wife's death. The other part of him, however, was frantic with worry. He could feel the fretful thoughts scurrying about his mind. He still could not believe he had risked his career over this particular case. The FBI was his *life*. Like most successful agents, Ben had never wanted to be anything else.

And yet here he was, facing the worst threat to his career in his twenty-one years with the agency, and part of him felt there was nothing to worry about.

That in itself left him so confused he could scarcely put two thoughts together.

Dottie Betham hurried through the front door, knotting a scarf around her neck. "I'm late. They need me over at the tent kitchen. Will you and Mavis be coming tonight?"

Hal nodded in time to his rocking. "I imagine we'll mosey on over directly."

Ben asked her, "Can I do anything?"

"Just don't put off your arrival too long or you won't find a seat." Dottie stepped from the porch and joined the throng moving along the street.

Hal seemed amused by the flow of people. "Who in their right mind would've thought we'd see the likes in Hamlin."

Ben searched for something that would confirm there was nothing dangerous about this Gathering, and reassure him he had done the right thing in putting his career on the line. But all he could come up with was, "You lived here long?"

"Yes, this is home. Mavis's sister attended Chuck Griffin's church up in Indiana. We were up visiting when he shared his vision."

"You don't mind all these folks invading your town?"

"They're not invading." Hal had the easy cadence of the country born. "They're welcome. This is their place now, much as it ever was mine."

"What makes you say that?"

Hal inspected him a moment, then answered with a question of his own. "Are you a believing man, Ben?"

"I used to think I was." The words came unbidden, drawn by the night and the people and whatever it was that brought them all together. "But my wife died about four years ago, and I guess I just let things slip."

"Easy to do."

Ben examined the man's comment for reproach, and found none. "My wife was active in the church. I suppose it was hard going back because everything there reminded me of her."

Hal's clear gaze glowed in the dimming light. "Must have been a shock, Preacher Griffin pulling you up on stage like that."

"Shock doesn't begin to describe it," Ben agreed.

"Like getting kicked by a tame mule," Hal suggested.

"I tell you," Ben replied. "If he had shot me in the foot with my own gun, I don't think I'd have been any more surprised."

Mavis Drew appeared in the doorway, waited for them to stop laughing, then said, "If you two jokers are about done here, supper's getting cold on the table."

Hal followed his wife inside. "You take the seat at the head there. Not every day we've got ourselves a real, live FBI agent to table."

Ben unfolded his napkin and confessed, "I'm still having trouble accepting that you're welcoming me into your house."

"What's important is, you've been anointed by the preacher himself," Mavis said. She had a prim way about her, the starched apron bordered with smocking and every gray hair in place. She folded her hands in her lap and said, "Mr. Atkins, why don't you bless this food?"

Ben stumbled through the words, the first prayer he had spoken in years. When he raised his gaze, it was to meet a quick little wink from Hal Drew. "Help yourself to the potatoes, Ben, and pass them on."

"Anyway, I can't thank you both enough for putting me up like this."

"Rooms're just going to waste," Mavis Drew replied. "Ever since our girl moved out to Kansas City with her brood, we don't hardly have grandchildren around here anymore."

"Only every other weekend is all," Hal said. "Our son has a hardware store up Asheville way. Talking about getting their own place here as well."

"They were beside themselves about not making it down this weekend," Mavis added. "Our boy and girl and their families, all of them. Just sick. Now you help yourself to some more of that roast beef, sir. Big man like you needs to eat more than what you've got on your plate."

Ben did as he was told, and took his first bite. "This is wonderful, Mrs. Drew."

"I'm Mavis to everyone I meet, and certainly to everybody who sets foot in my home." But she was pleased with his response. "I don't suppose a man on the move gets much home cooking."

"It's one of the things I miss about being married," Ben agreed. "One of many."

"Ben here's been a widower for four years," Hal said. "Lived his life out in Wyoming mostly. Been in Washington just a few months."

"If the man wants me to know his life story, he can tell me himself. Pass our guest the gravy bowl, Hal."

Ben said between bites, "I'm amazed at how easy you folks seem to be adjusting to this change."

"The Lord's hand is upon this," Mavis said matter-of-factly. "It's our task to follow and serve and wait for His holy day."

"Ben might not understand what you're going on about, Mother.

He's not been at church for a while," Hal explained. "Ever since his wife passed on he's let things slip."

Ben expected to receive the sharp edge of her tongue. But Mavis gave him a look of pure sympathy. "I've heard often enough how losing a spouse is worse than losing an arm."

"Felt like the heart was cut out of my chest while it was still beating," Ben agreed. He found his eyes smarting from the power of memories surfacing with the woman's commiseration. "For a while the whole world looked like it had been washed gray."

"That's as may be." Mavis Drew set down her fork. "But it's past now. Clearest sign you could have asked for is how the pastor invited you up front. You hear what I'm saying, sir?"

"Yes."

"That's good, on account of how I'm not in the habit of repeating what's important." Her tone was still soft, but the look in her eye was grave. Ben was certain Mavis Drew had raised herself two well-behaved children. The old lady continued, "The Lord has a plan for you, sir. I've known Preacher Griffin for quite some time now. And if I can say one thing for certain about the gentleman, it's that he doesn't waste his words, especially not when they have to do with the Lord's message."

"You can take that to the bank," Hal agreed.

"Your job is to get yourself down on your knees and ask the Lord to show you what's what." Mavis picked up her fork. "Now there's too much talking and too little eating. Everybody get to their business before it all grows cold."

⚒ ⚒

The half-mile walk from the Drews' home to the open theater took Ben through a brand-new tent city. Both sides of the road were lined with camps and piles of bedding and soup kitchens and emergency clinics and portable facilities. As he passed the weather-beaten sign announcing the park's entrance, fields opened to either side; all were filled with people and activity. At that moment, there came a great booming noise from up ahead, a wave of music that washed down over the street and the field and the throngs. The people around him responded with a cheer and sped forward. Ben watched as everyone in the tent areas dropped whatever they were doing and hurried to catch up.

Where the final rise grew steep, he helped a puffing lady push a teen in a wheelchair up the bumpy road. They crested the rise and were pressed impatiently forward by people coming up behind. Ben accepted the woman's thanks and stepped off the road to get a longer look.

The valley was filled to overflowing. Yet Ben found himself more convinced than ever that there was nothing deceitful about this gathering, nor dangerous. A choir in scarlet robes sang and swayed upon the stage, while behind them words to the song were displayed upon a giant screen. A dozen musicians played to the right of the chorus. The stage was ringed by folding chairs, before which stood many people Ben recognized from the platform at the community meeting. The crowd was huge. Ben stood at the valley-theater's perimeter and watched them sing and wave their hands and shout and clap, and felt in his gut that Washington was making a terrible mistake. One he could not permit himself to be a part of.

The decision propelled him along the rim of the valley-theater. Clusters of teens had claimed the high ground, some dancing and singing along with the music, others laughing and talking, still more holding hands and praying. The more Ben saw, the more convinced he was that here, in this place, all was truly well.

It was almost impossible for an agent studying a possible case to identify signs that all was healthy and safe and routine. The process of a criminal investigation was like a doctor searching for a disease. Such inquiries began with the *presumption of wrongdoing*. Ben continued along the valley's border, and saw this more clearly than ever before. By beginning an examination, the agency had already decided something was wrong, and now was simply looking for signs to *confirm* its diagnosis.

Which meant that any evidence Ben found to the contrary would be dismissed. In the minds of his Washington bosses, the fact that he had discovered neither illegal arms nor a militia only meant he had not looked hard enough. That he had been duped. That he was not doing his job.

Across the valley from where he walked, the leading edge of a rotund moon peeked out amid the highest trees. A murmur of delight rustled through the vast gathering, for the moon seemed impossibly large, poised as it was upon the ridgeline. The ruddy orange lip grew in size, competing with the stage and the music and the wash of stars overhead for attention. Ben watched as parents picked up young children and pointed at the sky, directing attention to a wonder that most of the world would consider too mundane, too everyday to deserve any notice at all. Even this strengthened his conviction that here in this place, at this time, these people were a danger to no one.

The song ended, and the same rotund little pastor Ben had seen at the community meeting approached the central microphone. "In the name of Jesus our King, welcome, one and all." Reverend Caldwell paused as wave after wave of cheering rose from the throng. Ben halted where he was. The pastor turned to the people seated along the stage's back rim, sharing smiles and head shakes, all of them clearly taken aback by the magnitude of what they were facing.

Finally the reverend turned back and held his hands up for silence. "A few odds and ends of housekeeping duties before we get started." He adjusted his spectacles and added, "You can think of me as the apostolic janitor if you like.

"Any trash you bring, take with you. Everybody helping out here is a volunteer, and we're all pretty much overwhelmed by what is happening. So if you've got a free hand, pitch in. If you see something that needs doing, especially when it comes to keeping the place tidy, do it yourselves.

"We know there must be folks out there with no place to stay. Behind the stage here there's a long table with a lot of pretty ladies doing their level best to match heads with pillows. Thank the good Lord, it looks like we're gonna have good weather this weekend." He waited through more applause, then went on, "Okay now, listen up because this next item is very important. A lot of you latecomers left your cars and were bused in. The problem is, some people left their vehicles right smack-dab in the middle of the road. We can't have that, folks. The Douglas road is our only way to bring in supplies and more bedding from Charlotte. So we're gonna have to tow the cars off, and you're gonna have to pay. I'm sorry, but that's just the way it is. Now if you'll look to the left of our stage, see that trio of electric buses? They're here to cart those who don't want to hoof it into Gastonia and pay to collect their cars. You can pull your cars over to the side of the road and get a ride back. Don't worry about missing the fun; it looks like we're going to be here awhile."

He turned to his seated brethren and exchanged a few words. Then back to the mike with, "We'd like to ask you in wheelchairs to move away from the stage, please. That's it, just form a row over there in front of the first regular seats. Fine. This big grassy bowl here is going to become our prayer center. Anybody wanting to join with us in prayer, step on down here. And please keep all the aisles between the arena's seats clear, folks. That's required by the fire code. Now, is that about all?" He looked back, received affirmative nods, then turned and said, "Any questions or messages, come to the table out behind the stage. My name is Reverend Paul Caldwell, and any of the people you see up here will be happy to help you out. Okay then, if you people will bow your heads, let's have a moment of prayer."

Ben stood where he was, watching as thousands upon thousands of people lowered their heads and waited. The old reverend gripped the Bible with both hands and began, "We're here, Lord. You've called us and we've come. We join as one and speak with one heart. You are our Father, our Abba, our sovereign God."

Still holding the Bible in one hand, the pastor stretched out his arms in benediction over the Gathering. "We have people from all over, Father. We have a temple cradled by Your blessed creation. We have music. We have pastors. What we need now, dear Lord, is Your blessed Spirit. Breathe upon us, Father. Ignite our hearts and this Gathering with Your Presence."

He waited a long moment. The night was impossibly silent. Impossible that so many people could keep so still that the valley itself seemed to hold its breath. Not a single baby cried, not a rustle of wind, not a whisper. Finally the pastor lowered his arms, and finished with, "In Jesus' precious name do we pray. Amen."

The band and the choir launched into another hymn, one Ben recognized from bygone days, "Come, Thou Fount of Every Blessing." It had been a favorite of his wife's, one he had often heard her sing in the kitchen when he managed to make it home for dinner. As he stood and listened to the music swell up from the valley below, two clusters of teens to either side chimed in, singing in close harmony. His certitude strengthened, and yet with it came an overwhelming agitation. What was he to do? How on earth could he convince an agency bent on finding evidence of criminal activity that these people were innocent?

Ben found himself drawn to a tree stump at the edge of the next clearing. He sat and stared out over the Gathering. He listened to the people sing of another assembly, one where all believers were rescued from danger and brought before the heavenly throne, where flaming tongues sang of His redeeming love. Ben recalled the words of Mavis Drew and her quietly fervent urge for him to pray. For some reason, this reflection eased his inner tumult until it almost seemed a proper part of the night. Perhaps this had been necessary, this worry and confusion, as it brought him to the point where he would willingly listen to someone suggest the illogical.

Ben found himself seeing clearly, perhaps for the first time, how he had allowed prayer to become so unfamiliar. Since his wife's passage and his son's departure for university, lowering his head in prayer had only heightened his sense of loneliness. Though Ben had never formed the thoughts, he recognized now that he had often felt as though everyone had abandoned him, even God.

Ben felt a sudden need to pray that was so strong it burned like hunger. The strength surprised him, for he had come to accept a life where he felt little at all beyond the constant pressures of his work. He gave a self-conscious glance around, worried that he might be attracting all sorts of attention, a grown man perched at the rim of the valley, seated upon a stump and clasping his hands in his lap. But no one paid him any mind at all. They were too busy with their own singing and hand waving and praying and chattering. A pair of young mothers wafted by, humming and dancing with little babies for partners, their laughter the clearest assurance he could have asked for that all was well and that he was welcome.

Ben bowed his head and gave a stumbling sort of plea. *I know I've been absent for a while, Lord. And I don't blame You if You've decided to turn Your back on me. But here I am. And I'm lost, plain and simple. I don't have any idea what to do. So I need Your help. Amen.*

He lifted his gaze and found himself staring at the golden shield of a near full moon that was almost free of the highest treetops. He felt nothing but a sense of relief at having made the confession. Perhaps that was all that he could ask for, coming to realize he had no idea what to do. None at all.

He stood and continued along the ridgeline until he arrived at the next downward-sloping aisle. For no other reason than a new longing to get closer to the heart of the valley and the night and the Gathering, Ben started down. Three dozen steps along, he passed an open space to his right. He was two steps farther along before he changed his mind and turned around. It might be nice to sit and join in, for a while at least.

It was only when he slid into the seat and turned to nod a greeting to the next person that he realized he had chosen a seat next to Dottie.

SEVENTEEN

Dottie Betham would not have been any more surprised than if he had reached out and spun her in a jig. "How did you find me?"

"I didn't . . ." Ben looked as shocked as she felt. "I wasn't . . ."

"You mean to tell me you just *happened* to come sit beside me?" She waved a hand out over a Gathering so large she still could not take it in. "Here, in the middle of *this*?"

"I don't have any idea how it happened," Ben replied straightforwardly. "But it's the plain and simple truth."

She dropped her hand, surprised at how shaken this left her. "If you weren't the most honest man I've ever met, I'd never believe that."

"I wouldn't either." He hesitated, then asked, "Would you like me to leave?"

"No, no, it's fine." But it wasn't. Nothing about this night was fine. "Of course you can stay."

Ben gave his patented smile, the one that barely touched his lips yet pushed dimples into his cheeks and put a special glint to that rifle-barrel gaze. "Thank you, Dottie. To be honest, it's nice to find a familiar face."

"Yes." She turned back to the valley and the stage, pretending to concentrate upon the next song. But the truth was, she could not have identified the words or the tune, even though she was staring straight at the screen.

The entire evening was turning into a shattering experience. Yet she could not tell *why*. Dottie had gone to the soup kitchen as planned and had helped feed a never-ending line of new arrivals. Then the music had signaled the beginning of the Gathering, and she had left with the others and walked to the amphitheater. She had moved over to one side, wanting to separate herself a bit. Night had strengthened. The moon had risen. The Georgia pastor had greeted them with a few administrative notes. More singing. As straightforward and normal as any other evening service she had ever attended, only larger.

Then why did she feel so pulverized?

The only way she could describe the feeling was, it felt as though her soul was being shaken to pieces. All the mistakes she had made seemed to be placed upon display. Not for the Gathering. For herself. Even before she had arrived here, perhaps even before the night itself had begun. Maybe it had started upon her arrival at the community. That was how it seemed to her now. As though all the discomfort and all the unease she had been feeling was merely a forethought, a first taste of what had been waiting for her all along.

But what was it?

The choir and the band swung from one number to the next, and the music filtered through her fogged brain. The song was "When the Roll Is Called Up Yonder." She heard Ben begin to sing from beside her, hesitant at first, but growing in strength and assuredness. He had a solid baritone, one that matched his stature and his bearing. Dottie opened her mouth, but no sound came. She remained mute, captured by the sense of unfolding disaster.

Nothing in her life seemed clear. Nothing seemed *right*. She stood and looked back at an existence built upon self-serving mistakes. She had always refused to join the regular staff of any publication, though many had invited her, and now she could see it as just another sign of how she had always tried to keep life at arm's-length. Ditto for any man in her life. Sooner or later the good ones always realized she kept too much of herself hidden away. Which meant that only the bad ones stayed around. This had always suited her fine, if truth be known, because the reasons to kick them out had always been easy to find. She had chosen a life of solitary confinement, safe and insulated from anything that might touch her too deeply.

Only now, as she stood trapped by the Gathering and the night like a fly in amber, she felt blasted by the loneliness, the *futility* of her existence. She would finish and she would be gone, and no one would ever miss her. No one would stand upon her grave and grieve. An hour after her passage, she would be forgotten. A candle blown out by a careless breath of wind, a wick left to smolder in the isolation of endless night.

Dottie found herself saturated by an anguish so deep it felt as though she was mourning her own passage.

With a start, she realized the singing had stopped and everyone around her was seated. She would have run away, fled the place and the horrid realizations, if only she could find the strength. But all she managed was to lower herself into the seat.

Ben chose that moment to reach over and take her hand. The simple gesture acted like a salve poured upon her aching soul, bringing her back from the wrenching despair. She would have looked over, but if she had met sympathy in Ben's gaze she would have burst into tears. So she gave her face a hasty wipe with her sleeve and kept frantic hold of Ben's hand.

It was good that Dottie was there beside him. But more than that. It was a miracle. If Ben had not had her hand to hold on to just then, he did not know what he would have done. Melted and flowed away, most probably. Devastated by the conviction that suddenly surrounded him.

He had never experienced anything like this. The sensation was so novel he could not even name it. As close as he could come was to suppose this was how a criminal felt, when he had been captured and was being confronted with his crimes.

It seemed as though the walk along the rim, the acceptance of his own inability to find answers, and then the prayer, all had been leading him to this point. Opening him so that he could now be confronted with a truth he had never before realized. Never wanted to see. Not even now.

The realizations were upon him with the force of an earthquake. He could no longer rest upon his own strength. He felt as though he had no strength at all. The gentle night, the stars, the moon, the singing, the crowds on every side—everything was impacted with a force so great he could neither flee nor turn away.

All his adult life, he had allowed his wife to worship God for him. She had always been the one of faith. He had gone to church because he wanted to be there with her. It was not so much that he had allowed his faith to wither with her passage, as it was that he had never had a personal faith at all. God had been someone left to his wife's domain. He had never sought a vision of the divine, never wanted to draw near. While his wife was alive, it had remained enough to let her pray for them both, study the Word, be involved in the church family, worry about neighbors and friends and family. After her death, he had refused to take up the responsibility of a Christian life of his own. He had simply continued the withdrawal, from earthly and heavenly worlds alike. He had become a drifter in all but name. The world might have seen him as a strong lawman. But now, as he sat surrounded by the mirror of this strange night, the vision he was confronted with was very different indeed. He saw himself as a holy loser. A man who had lost one opportunity after another, because he had never tried to *see*.

When Dottie lowered herself into the seat, Ben felt his hand move almost of its own volition, scrambling across the sanded planks, searching for something that would keep him anchored and safe. He breathed a sigh of relief when he found Dottie's hand. He could not turn and look at her. He did not dare. But he desperately needed the touch of a friend, someone who would help keep him from being utterly lost within the shattering power of this moment.

Ben sat and held himself together by gripping Dottie's hand. He watched as Charles Griffin rose from his seat. He felt as much as heard murmurs of anticipation. From somewhere far away, he heard a man's voice shout, *"Praise God!"* But Ben could not agree with the sentiment. He did not feel like praising. He felt terrified by the force of all that surrounded him.

The cry was caught up by a thousand other voices. The choir settled into their chairs, the band set aside their instruments, all eyes upon the stage were fastened upon the slender figure moving toward the microphone.

Charles Griffin appeared too unassuming for all the attention focused his way. Ben watched Chuck greet the Gathering and then bow his head and pray for guidance. Ben struggled to hold on to the words, but it was hard. Very hard. It felt as though the thundering revelations within himself kept pushing the words out of focus. But he struggled, leaned forward, and did his best to hear.

Chuck Griffin turned to the row of people at the back of the stage and said into the microphone, "What were those words you spoke at the beginning, Paul? No, you come up and say them again, will you?" He moved aside, and the portly reverend took his place. Once more the older minister raised his hands in benediction and said, "Come, oh come, blessed Spirit of our sovereign King. Breathe upon us and this Gathering. Fill us with Your mighty presence. Anoint us and this gathering. In Jesus' name. Amen."

"Amen, amen." Chuck patted the old man on the back. "Thank you, Paul. Isn't that the most beautiful prayer you've ever heard?"

All around Ben, people applauded and whistled and cheered and called loud acclaim. Ben could not fathom why. As far as he was concerned, the *last* thing he wanted was to feel something *more*.

PART
TWO

THE ELEVENTH HOUR

EIGHTEEN

When Mavis Drew called her to the phone Saturday morning, Dottie knew leaving *Newsday* a contact number had been a big mistake. The editor's voice grated unwelcome and brusque in this quiet home. "Ed Starling here, Dottie. How're things?"

"Busy." The contact number was a practice so ingrained she had phoned it in without thinking. Now she felt as though this harsher aspect of her life had invaded the Drews' house. "Can this wait until Monday?"

"Not a chance. What's going on down there in Kingdom Come?"

"I assume you already know or you wouldn't be calling." Mavis Drew cast her a peculiar look as she passed, clearly not pleased with Dottie's sharp tone. Which only irritated her further. "My mobile phone is on the blink. I think I forgot to plug in my recharger. I left this number for emergencies only."

"Which this is." Ed Starling had been born in Lima, Ohio, but he claimed it was an error of fate that he had corrected as soon as he could walk. He lived and breathed the New York editor's role now. It defined everything about him. "Wait, wait, I get it. You're hot because I haven't gotten the contract to your agent. Well, it's his fault, ducks. Not mine. The guy is a bloodsucker. He wants every drop. You've got to get on the line and tell him to lighten up."

Dottie did not dignify that with a response. The discussion had no place in this quiet country home, nor with this couple who had been so kind as to offer her and now Ben Atkins the use of their two free rooms. She stood in the front hall, the plank floor shining beneath countless coats of hand-applied beeswax. Dottie turned so as to look out the front door. The road into Hamlin, closed to motor traffic for the weekend, was filled with people and sunlight and chatter.

"Okay, okay. I get the message." Ed Starling gave a theatrical sigh. "You've got me over the barrel. Tell the bloodsucker he'll get his pound of flesh."

Dottie felt as though the conversation was sullying her and the day both. "I've got to go, Ed. Call me on Monday."

"Monday, nothing. I told you, I'll courier the contract over this afternoon. Look, there's something going on down there, isn't that right? Something big."

"How did you hear that?"

"Never mind. They say it's massive, what is it they're calling it?"

"A Gathering."

"A hundred and fifty thousand people swooping down for the weekend, is that right?"

"Nobody has any accurate figures." She thought of the revelations she had experienced the night before and shivered. "But I'd say you were pretty close."

"I tell you, Dottie, this is big. And word is getting out. The leader's denomination is holding its annual congress in Richmond as we speak. Word is, they're excommunicating this guy."

"Chuck Griffin?" Dottie felt as though she had been slapped. "They can't do that!"

"If what I've heard is true, they already have."

"This is absurd. It's crazy! Chuck is . . ." She struggled for proper words. "Chuck is a saint."

"Don't tell me you're getting hooked by these people."

"It's not that." She had never felt more confused or more fragile. "Look, I really have to—"

"I want you to fly out on Monday and talk to the guy responsible for kicking your high honcho into the street. Wait, I can't find my note. Okay, here it is. Reverend Thurgood Innes. He runs some megachurch down in Orlando. He's the guy who organized the process against Griffin. I want you to use the magazine's clout and arrange a meeting. My money's on this guy having the down and dirty on this cult."

* * *

Ben Atkins slept later than he had in years. He awoke to the smell of bacon and the sound of someone talking. Dottie. He recognized the hard edge to her voice, and guessed it was someone on the phone. He reached for his watch on the bedside table, then swung his feet to the floor and squinted, certain his sleep-addled mind had misread. But the hands stayed in the same place, showing eleven-fifteen. Ben rose and padded across the hook rug to the window. Through the screen he heard birdsong and people and the sounds of a world that had beaten him to the punch by hours. Fleetingly he wondered if the previous night had been a dream, but he knew it was real and half-wished it was otherwise.

Swiftly Ben washed and dressed and went downstairs. Dottie stood in the front hallway, her back to the stairs. She said into the telephone receiver, "And I am telling you this is *not a cult.*" Her voice was tense, one inch off genuine anger. "Listen to what I'm telling you. It isn't misreading a situation to tell the truth about it. Or are we going for tabloid journalism now, and reshaping the facts to fit the sensational headline?" She listened for a long moment, then finished with, "Yes, all right. I'll keep searching. Yes. I told you I would, Ed. First flight Monday morning. Yes. Bye."

She hung up the phone, turned around, and said in a voice that still grated hard, "Editors!"

"Good morning, Dottie."

Only then did she focus on him. "Oh. Sorry. That was . . ." She waved a vague hand toward the phone.

"Work," Ben supplied. "I understand."

She released the tension with a single explosive sigh. "Why am I doing this?"

"I would imagine because you're very good at it."

His words drew her further still from the telephone argument. "How are you feeling?"

"I'm not sure. I slept so hard, I feel numb." He examined her. "What about you?"

All she said was, "Exhausted."

A voice from the front porch called out, "Revivals will do that. The strong ones, anyway." The rocker creaked, and Hal Drew stepped over to where he could look through the front screen door. "Don't know a thing more tiring than a good hoot and holler for the Lord."

"I don't recall doing either," Ben replied.

"Not out loud, maybe." Hal Drew sounded impossibly certain. "But what was your heart doing? That's the question."

"No it's not," Mavis Drew said from behind him. Ben turned to stare down at the diminutive woman. She demanded, "All I need to know right now is, what are you having for breakfast?"

✠ ✠

The Saturday revival was scheduled to begin again at two. Hal Drew left right after lunch to mosey about the community, check on his volunteer wardens, and make sure all was as calm as it appeared. When Ben left the house soon after, the road was packed with people moving toward the amphitheater. Dottie's face looked pinched in the strong sunlight. She turned and squinted, as though looking straight into the afternoon sun and not at Ben. "Do you mind sitting with me again?"

"I couldn't think of anything I'd like more."

"Good. That's very good."

Ben fell into step alongside her. "You didn't help at the kitchen today?"

"I couldn't. Last night . . ."

When she seemed unable to continue, Ben confessed, "There was one point, just before the sermons started, when I thought I might just fold up my tent and be done with it."

"It was beautiful," Dottie said quietly to the pavement below her feet. "And it was awful."

"That pretty much sums it up," Ben agreed. "Wonderful and dreadful both."

She seemed oblivious to the throngs moving along on either side of them. "Do you really want to come today?"

"I've been asking myself the same thing ever since I got up," Ben replied. "And the truth is, I don't see as how I have much choice."

The previous night had not seemed to intensify further, so much as deepen its sense of *naturalness*. It was *natural* that Ben sat surrounded by a vast assemblage, yet felt as isolated as he had ever been in his entire life. It was *natural* that Ben heard sermon after sermon, yet never grew weary, or even counted the passing time. It was *natural* that he heard the teachings and sang the songs, and yet spent most of his time and energy locked in his own private conversation. It was *natural* that the one thing he clearly remembered about the night was his internal revelations.

"I've got to attend today," Ben said simply. "I don't know how to say it better than that."

"I feel exactly the same," Dottie said softly. Her mouth worked a few times, then she said softer still, "Thank you for holding my hand last night. It helped knowing you were there. A lot."

Ben started to protest that it was not for her that he had done so. But the words seemed dry in his mouth, as though neither intended nor necessary. So he said, "Do you want to tell me what happened?"

"I can't." No fervor to the protest, no anger over his asking. Her response was as quiet as the wind that softened the afternoon heat. "I don't think I could even explain it to myself."

"I understand."

"I really believe you do." She glanced over, swift as passing wings. "You are one remarkable man, Ben Atkins."

He could think of nothing to say to that. So they crested the rise and started along the ridgeline and descended to seats midway along the valley, all in silence. Ben exchanged greetings with those about him but did not join in the singing. For the moment he wanted to sit and savor the compliment. It had been a long time since someone had called him remarkable. If asked, he would have described himself as a fairly ordinary man, maybe with an overly developed sense of right and wrong, maybe a little too honest for his own good. At least, that's what he might have said until the previous evening. Now, as he sat and felt the music in his chest as well as heard it, he had no idea what he would say about himself. None.

For the moment, it felt as though reality had been suspended. He knew he would have to face the problems and the threats from Washington. But at this point, as he stood and bowed his head for the opening invocation, Ben felt as though what really had happened in his private prayer of the previous night was that he had separated himself from the outside world. Right now, the only thing that mattered was what was happening here. The rest would just have to wait.

The next song was "Blessed Assurance," another old favorite, a gift to help him ease the world into focus. He began singing along, remembering other times. His wife had enjoyed traveling with him to Wyoming country churches, white clapboard affairs that seemed as planted in the earth as the trees and the scrub and the hills. People stood around outside, the old-timers in their string ties and silver-and-turquoise belt buckles, their hands as hard and weathered as stone. Ben shut his eyes, not needing to see the words to sing along, carried suddenly by distant visions. Saturday evening songfests, country musicians on zithers and banjos and mandolins, reedy voices singing nostalgic hymns that left his wife's face wet with tears she did not even know she was shedding. Ben had always savored those moments, far more because of the effect they had on his wife than because of anything he felt himself. He opened his eyes then, and found the world swimming, filtered by how much he had loved that sweet, dear woman.

Paul Caldwell approached the podium and invited the congregation to sit. Ben was glad for the chance to duck his head and swipe at his eyes, hoping no one noticed. A woman took Paul's place by the front microphone, and for a moment it seemed as though his memories had come to life. She wore an ankle-length deerskin skirt, Western-print blouse, and high-heeled boots. Without accompaniment, she began singing "Amazing Grace," and Ben had to wipe his eyes again.

This time Dottie did notice, and silently she reached over and took his hand. It was only then that he realized the day was affecting him again. Yet strangely enough, this time he did not mind, for the memories did not come with pain. For so long, whenever he had recalled times with his wife, his heart had felt parboiled. But right now he sat and remembered earlier days with a clarity so laced with peace he could only say he was happy. Yes, happy—even though his eyes trickled the occasional tear and it hurt somewhat to breathe. Even so, it was a great and lovely day, and it seemed to him as though he was truly among friends.

The woman finished to cheers, and Ben was sorry to see her go. For with her went the memories. He drew an easier breath, and found the day suddenly so clear and crystal sharp that it seemed ringed by light. He watched as Chuck Griffin rose from his chair and approached the pulpit, as always to the sound of applause and the rippling undercurrent of excitement.

Chuck waited until the noise had lessened, then bowed his head and repeated the words from the previous night, "Come, oh come, blessed Spirit of our sovereign King. Breathe upon us, Father. Fill us with Your mighty presence. Anoint us and this Gathering. In Jesus' name. Amen."

Chuck raised his gaze and said to the crowd, "Today I want to speak with those who are not certain exactly why they are here. I suppose in some way that might include just about all of us. But I mean most especially those who cannot put a precise name to what it is they are feeling, other than perhaps curiosity or a sense of being unsettled or maybe just being hungry for more than what they have."

The words were spoken in a tone as mild as the man himself. At one level, Ben thought that if he had to describe Chuck Griffin, he would say the man would make a perfect Sears shoe salesman. But the thought was swiftly gone, for the other side to him, this newly awakening side, seemed to come alight. Something about what the pastor said, something in those first few words, left him unable to pay attention to his doubting, analytical side. Not here. Not now. To this awakening portion of his mind and heart, it almost seemed as though the quiet slender man was surrounded by angelic light.

The pastor continued, "Today I want to talk with you about one of the most remarkable points in the entire Scriptures. Turn with me, if you would, to the sixteenth chapter of the book of John."

Saturday afternoon, the westering sun burnished the wall opposite Wayne Oates's window and displayed a central office devoid of life. Wayne Oates sat behind his desk, mainly because he had nowhere else to go. Saturdays were the worst day of his week, had been ever since his wife had left him. Early in their married life she had complained that he had always kept a part of his inner being locked away, hidden from sight. By the end of their first year together, she knew what he had been hiding, and loathed him for it. The marriage had ended quietly three months later. She was a good girl, country born and bred, looking for a man who held to the earth and her values. She was glad to be rid of him. But it didn't make a week's final hours any easier, when everyone else was up and gone, and him there with time and regret on his hands.

He was trying to bury himself in paperwork when the outer door opened and the weekend duty officer, a young woman recently graduated from the academy, pointed a lean man across to where Wayne sat. The narrow-faced man crossed the central office, knocked, and poked his blond head into Wayne's doorway. "Agent Oates?"

"Yes sir." The man had Washington stamped all over him—the standard-issue gray suit, the jacket's crease where his gun dug in as he traveled, the bland expression. The features were evenly handsome, the eyes a strange washed green, like pebbles at the bottom of a swift-running stream. Warrior's eyes. Nothing revealed except a readiness to do whatever it took. "Can I help you?"

"Justin Ball. I'm in Theron Head's office."

Wayne was already up and moving around his desk. "I had no idea he'd be sending—"

"Officially I'm not here."

"Right. Sure." Wayne backed up. "Have a seat."

"No thanks. This is a quick in and out. Wanted you to have a chance to put a face to the name. I'll be your liaison."

Wayne could not hide his grin. "So it's really happening."

"One thing you'll learn, Mr. Oates—"

"Call me Wayne."

"You can take whatever Theron Head says to the bank."

Wayne nodded his understanding, recalling stories about the man. "Good and bad."

The gaze was as flat and bland as the voice. "You'd better hope it's only good. Theron Head doesn't offer second chances."

"Right. Of course."

"He assumes the people he signs on are all top-notch. Which

means there's no room for mistakes. Not ever." He reached into his pocket and handed over a handwritten card. "Contact numbers. Reach me day and night. Theron Head's people never go off duty. I'll need the same for you."

"Sure." He stared at the card. It felt alive in his hands.

"Now, Oates."

"Oh. Right." He returned to his desk, wrote out numbers for his home and mobile phone.

The man accepted it, then demanded, "Car phone, weekend getaway, anything like that?"

"No to both."

"Okay." Justin Ball pocketed the card. "Anything new about this Kingdom Come cult?"

"We're on it. There's some major event up there this weekend; traffic is snarled back ten miles and more. Agent Ben Atkins is on the ground—"

"Forget him."

"Excuse me?"

"From now on, Theron Head wants everything routed directly from you to me to him. I'll tell you what to feed Atkins." The pebble-hard eyes studied him. "You have a problem with that?"

Wayne swallowed. "No. No problem."

"Apparently Atkins thinks this cult deserves a soft-glove approach. That's just giving them more rope to hang us and them both. Come Monday, Theron Head intends to go in hard. Break some heads. Show these fanatics we're ready for anything they can throw our way." He handed over a second card. "We've received word that this cult is about to get the boot from their church's parent organization. This is the guy in charge of the ouster, as far as we can gather."

Wayne accepted the second paper and read the name, "Reverend Thurgood Innes."

"Runs a church in Orlando. We want you to fly down Monday

morning and check this guy out. See if there's any dirt serious enough we can use to bring charges against the cult leader."

"I'll be on the first flight down."

"Good." Ball reached into his jacket pocket and drew out a holstered revolver. "A little gift from your new boss."

Slowly Wayne unsnapped the guard strap and withdrew the gun. A nine-millimeter Glock with polished chrome barrel, mother-of-pearl stock and hammer, doeskin-edged grip. It was the finest weapon he had ever held. He said, almost without realizing he spoke at all, "A warrior's weapon."

The Washington liaison smiled thinly. "Mr. Head doesn't usually reach out to the smaller offices for his men. Some of us had our doubts. But I think you'll do." He offered Wayne his hand. "Welcome to the club."

Pastor Chuck Griffin's message that Saturday afternoon was drawn from the story of Jesus' walking on water. It was a story Ben had heard a hundred times before. But this day he heard it anew. And not because the preacher was a great orator. It was not that at all. Chuck addressed the Gathering as he would a circle of close friends, his tone conversational, his bearing almost meek. No. Ben could no longer ignore the fact that something else was at work here.

The previous evening's revelations, the painful reflections on his heart—Ben knew with utter conviction he was being introduced to something new. Had it always been there? Had he simply chosen to ignore what had actually been with him always? That was how it seemed to Ben as Chuck read from John's Gospel, the words cast upon the giant screen behind the choir. Jesus walked upon water. A story old as time, new as the freshening breeze. A story so powerful Ben felt as though he was in the boat with the apostles, tossed by a storm that had captured his life.

"Why would Jesus do such a miracle?" Chuck asked the crowd. "One that saved nobody and healed none? What could have been the purpose behind this act? And remember, we're not just talking about the Master coming out to the boat. Why did our King also allow Simon Peter to experience this with Him?"

Ben reflected that it felt as though he was listening to a personal friend of God's speaking here. A man who *understood*. A man whose words were accompanied by a power so vast it could work as gently as Chuck's voice. Ben sat and listened in utter certainty that an authority rested upon this Gathering, clear as the sunlight, strong as gravity.

Chuck continued, "Work through this passage with me now. Look to the previous verse. Jesus has just fed the masses. Commentators place the total number of men, women and children at somewhere around fifteen thousand people fed from those puny loaves and fishes. Imagine now, think how the disciples must have felt. They'd be filled to the brim with the power of this miracle. So what does Jesus do? He sends them out upon the Sea of Galilee in a little boat. And a storm comes up out of nowhere. A storm so vicious, it threatens to capsize their craft and send them tumbling into the raging waters.

"The contrast is so great, the paradox of the miracle against the storm, I feel in my very soul that there must be a message here. Something so great, so *vital*, the Master chose to address it with a miracle and not with words. Any idea what that might be?"

Chuck waited. He seemed to be in no hurry whatsoever. There might as well have been a dozen or so gathered in a semicircle about his chair, the way he stood there at the lectern and seemed to invite the crowd to respond. Ben took the opportunity to look about him. The crowd was so massive as to appear to be a human rainbow, stretched across the entire valley, encircling an open green expanse down at the base. Rows of wheelchairs ringing the empty field glinted in the afternoon light. Most of the people Ben could see clearly held Bibles open in their laps. They grasped pens and paper, poised there at the edges of their seats, willing to wait as long as Chuck held them there.

"Well, let's look at this passage together and see what it says to us in the here and now." Chuck lifted his Bible but kept his eyes upon the crowd. "Does it ever feel to you that the Spirit works the most incredible miracles at times when the entire world seems up in arms against you?"

A murmur rippled through the crowd. Ben found himself nodding a fraction.

"So the disciples were out there in the storm. Those of you who have experienced a storm on open water know it's not just the wind and the waves that are deadly. It's hard to *breathe*. The crests are blown off the waves, and they mix with the wind and the rain until the air becomes almost impossible to find. Every time you open your mouth, you risk drowning.

"And yet, here they were, the disciples out in this storm because the Master sent them. And in their terror they see Him coming across the water toward them. Here again is a mystery. I have spent a lot of time on this passage, asking God what the purpose might have been. And the answer I have come up with is this: Rough times are *not* symbols of divine punishment. Yes, all right, you are a sinner. And you might deserve something bad. But, brothers and sisters, the disciples were no better or worse than you. Do you hear me out there? Jesus did not send them out on the sea to be punished. Remember now, Christians are not promised a trouble-free life, but rather that God's peace will be with us always. He sends storms upon the righteous as well as the unrighteous. Tough times can be a conduit to great blessings. Storms can be a holy force, cleansing away the chaff of an unholy life. So right here, right now, God may well be positioning you not for a chastisement, but rather for a *choice*."

He waited a long moment, then continued softly. "My guess is, most of us here have recently experienced some form of divine miracle.

I would imagine that we've felt the Master's touch in one way or another, and that is part of what brought us here. We have, all of us, experienced our own miracle of the loaves and fishes.

"At the same time, either before we arrived or after we leave, we are also going to know the storm. It happens, brothers and sisters, it happens all too often. It is one of the tragic elements that defines the world we live in. And so a vital part of this message is, Wait. Be patient. Keep watch, for if you do, you will see the Lord come walking through your storm. Walking out to where you are tossed and frightened. Bringing the impossible gift of peace."

"Praise God!" The call was lofted upward from somewhere far along the row. It seemed to release the audience, for cheers and applause rippled from one end to the other. Ben clapped along with the others. He felt such a surge of energy in his chest, he had to do something. Applause was as good as anything else. He was pleased to find Dottie doing the same.

Chuck waited until silence was restored, then continued in his quiet way. "I said that God might be positioning us for a choice. Look again now at that passage. Has it ever occurred to you that Jesus did not *invite* Simon Peter to join Him? And have you noticed how none of the other disciples came with Peter? Think on this a moment, if you will. When the storm strikes, do you remain focused upon reaching safety and the ending of the storm? Or do you cast all aside and step out upon the water?"

Chuck had to wait through more tumult. "Let us be clear about one thing. A walking-on-water experience is an *opportunity*, not a requirement. It is our chance to move to higher ground in the experience of living a godly life. Obedience at the impossible moments of life puts us in the right place at the right time. It positions us to see miracles. It readies us for the grand impossibles of life.

"To be a water-walker means wanting to do what is impossible without God's direct intervention. It means searching the storm for

Jesus' coming, and when He arrives, moving out to meet Him. Leaving behind the safety of what you know, and attempting the impossible. Risking to do what you have never done before.

"*Risk*. That word is defined as the possibility of loss or injury. Living on faith's cutting edge. Going beyond the bounds of what you can do alone. What we are talking about here is doing what you have never done before. Acting with the absolute knowledge that success is only possible with God's hand upon you."

He raised his hands high, the Bible still gripped in one hand. "But it means something else, brothers and sisters. I stand here before you today to say that if you are blessed with the vision of your King coming toward you through the storms, if you have the strength to walk forward to meet Him, you will be more alive than ever before."

Chuck waited through the ferment, gave the crowd time to quiet, then invited them to pray. When all had settled back down, he bowed his head and continued. "Lord, show us where You walk. We will strive to walk there also. No matter that our worldly eyes might call this impossible. Show Yourself to us. Reveal Yourself, and then give us the strength to ... ."

Afterward Ben was unable to say whether the pastor ever finished his prayer. He did not know if the sermon was completed, he did not know if the sun still shone. He did not know anything, in fact, except for what happened within his own private universe. For in that moment, everything changed. Everything.

It seemed as though a wind swept down from outside and inside at the same time. He did not know whether he imagined the external noise, but he did not think so. For it appeared that it blew in from the east, a rising storm that felled the people in the valley like sudden summer hail. The instant before he was struck himself, he could see them over to his right, wailing and shrieking and flailing about and falling over. Or so it seemed in the quick instant before he himself was struck.

He did not want to release himself to the experience. Part of his reluctance was terror. But mostly it was his background. The years of training had worked their way deep into his psyche. Ben gripped the wooden seat so hard he broke four fingernails. He strove to maintain focus upon the stage and the world about him. But it was hard. Oh yes. So very hard indeed.

Back in college Ben had worked a variety of construction jobs. His senior year he had obtained a commercial license and started driving a cement truck. His days had consisted of driving some-where, then sitting and waiting while the contractor got ready for him to crank the levers and unload the wet cement. But the final hour of every shift had been the hardest work he had ever done. Harder even than the worst of his FBI basic training. Although the job had paid almost double anything else he was offered, he had lasted only three and a half months. For after unloading the cement and pulling back into the yard, Ben had been required to climb inside the round rear container. The hole though which the cement flowed was so tight Ben had been forced to slide in with one arm out in front and the other held tight to his middle. Once inside, a yard worker would pass in a pneumatic drill, a helmet, safety goggles, and the kind of heavily padded ear-protectors used by jet mechanics. The yard worker was always smirking when he did so. Ben then used the pneumatic drill to chip off all the cement that had dried and hard-ened around the inside of the revolving vessel. Otherwise the next shift's load would dry and clot faster. Every last bit of cement had to be turned to dust; otherwise the yard boss would fine him half a day's pay and force him to clean out another truck. Using the drill had been a dreadful experience. The cauldron fired back the noise and the vibration directly at Ben. It was not a noise he heard through his padded ears. The racket was so loud he felt it inside his entire body.

It turned every bit of muscle and bone into one giant tuning fork. It bounced him and bombarded him so hard he felt it and heard it for hours and hours after it was over.

That din was nothing compared to what he now felt.

Only this time, the sensation was positive. At least it was so long as Ben could hold on to his tight-fisted focus.

And still the wind roared about him.

⚒ ⚒

Gradually the force waned, until Ben managed to look around and find the world still intact.

"Are you all right?"

Ben turned to Dottie, and was not the least surprised to find her face streaked with tears. He touched his own face. His cheeks were dry. It meant nothing except that his own weeping had all been internal. "How long was I out?"

"I . . ." Dottie shrugged. "Fifteen minutes, maybe more. I don't really know."

Fifteen minutes was impossible. Ben was certain it had been hours. Or days.

He looked around. The rotund little pastor stood before the microphone. All the others who had been seated in the chairs ringing the stage were down in the central field. The grass was now almost completely covered, lost beneath the feet and knees of hundreds and hundreds of people. They gathered, knelt, raised arms in supplication, joined hands in prayer, or sprawled supine beneath the brilliant sunset. The choir and the band sang a gentle melody, one echoed by thousands of people around the valley, singing the refrain over and over: Humble thyself in the sight of the Lord, And He shall lift you up, Higher and higher.

The pastor said, "All right now, those in the field, we ask you to return to your seats. There are others who want to come down. Everyone in the field, please give us a hand here. And to those who have waited so patiently, let the others return up the aisles before you start down. Wait for my signal, please. Move along, that's it. Thank you."

The field gradually emptied itself, a multihued tide that simply flowed back up and into the bleachers. Ben knew it took time, but in the state he was in, time did not seem to count. As though the flow of power was far more important than any earthly measure. Eventually the pastor said into the microphone, "All right, those who have not come but would like to join in the field of prayer, you are now welcome to move down. There's no rush, folks. We're not going anywhere. We'll be here until everyone who wants to has joined us here. So take it easy and offer your neighbor a hand."

Dottie turned to him and said, "Will you help me, please?"

Ben wanted to say that he wasn't sure how much help he could give to anyone. But he also wanted to go, and it was good not to go alone. So he merely nodded and took her hand and slipped from the row and joined the downward flow.

All the while, the greater part of him remained trapped by an image that had formed in the midst of that hurricane force. The image had been of a blazing sun, yet not a sun at all. A light so great it filled the entire universe. One that melted him just to be near it. He did not need to look at the light, for wherever he turned his attention, the light was there. A single voice sang. A man's voice. It sang words of eternal praise. And though Ben knew he would ever remain unworthy to join in this song of praise, he could think of nothing he would like more. Just to stay there in the holy chamber, and sing praise to the Giver of life and of love.

He stepped off the final stair and started forward, Dottie still there beside him. He heard her begin to weep anew and felt a rightness to it. Such was the strength of the moment, as they gathered with others who were strangers and yet also his closest brethren, that Ben considered his own dry eyes as a weakness. It was not only right to cry, it was called for. The joy was that strong.

NINETEEN

Orlando was a city that had totally reinvented itself since Disney's arrival. Dottie Betham's plane flew over the endless green of central Florida, giving way to the mirror surfaces of hundreds and hundreds of lakes. The water was surrounded by carefully tended golf courses. Then came equally precise housing developments, parks, hotels, and finally the airport itself. Everywhere was the sight of green and water, even as she disembarked and took the electric train to the central concourse. Dottie knew she should be taking notes. Such initial impressions were vital to setting the emotional and physical scene to longer journal articles. But her hands remained still in her lap. Her mind refused to follow the natural course. This day she was not an experienced journalist following a story. She was lost. The sunlight and the carefully tended palms and lagoon outside the monorail only heightened her sense of being utterly disconnected.

She carried her purse in one hand and her overnight bag in the other, and walked to the car rental station and picked up her vehicle. She studied the map and laid out a course to the church. Her mobile phone remained inert in her purse, as she had forgotten yet again to plug in the recharger. Dottie decided not to call ahead. She would just go and see the church's layout and arrange an appointment with this Reverend Thurgood Innes in person. But all this was handled by a tiny part of her, the robot brain of normal actions. The vast majority of her remained locked in shock.

She found herself thinking of an article she had done three years earlier for *Life* magazine on the effects of trauma. She had interviewed almost two dozen survivors of car pileups, life-threatening illnesses, airplane accidents, sudden losses of loved ones. Interviewing these survivors of modern nightmares, then writing how they had struggled to pull themselves back together, had made it the hardest article she had ever done.

Though she had no personal tragedy to point at except the sense of a wasted life, this was how Dottie felt. As though she had been shattered by the experiences back there in the valley, and now nothing made sense any more. Her mind could not reform itself into the person she thought she was. And yet the experience itself, the revelations and the *power* she had known back in the amphitheater, was so different from anything she had known before, it did not seem real either. Even though she remained spiritually and emotionally blasted by the force, she could not bring herself to accept that it was genuine, or ever had been. She was left feeling like an empty shell, just going through the motions, clutching at sunlight and street names, driving through an alien city, feeling that she would never belong anywhere. Not ever again.

The Church of the Redeemer was not hard to find. It was the largest building in the area. It dominated the skyline, a modern structure with an earth-tone bell tower standing to one side. Dottie pulled into the parking lot and pretended to study the neighborhood. All the buildings she could see in every direction had the church's logo in the signs; she saw a crisis pregnancy office, a teen walk-in center, a school, a homeless kitchen, a bowling alley, and a glitzy shopping arcade with a neon sign over the entrance.

In truth, however, Dottie was thinking of what had happened that morning before her departure from Kingdom Come. She had come downstairs an hour before dawn to find Mavis Drew already up and brewing coffee. The older woman said she had noticed Dottie's state the previous evening and thought perhaps Dottie might need a friendly word before returning to the workaday world.

Dottie had stammered that she felt uprooted and could not explain why. Mavis Drew then pulled two cups and saucers from the cupboard and poured the coffee, all her motions very deliberate, very slow. She waited until Dottie was seated and sipping from her cup to say, "When Paul met Jesus for the first time on the Damascus Road, the experience blinded him. I happen to think it was not his eyes that were blinded, but his *mind*. The power was just too great for the man to handle."

"I understand," Dottie murmured.

"Paul's blindness gave him a time to sit and think things through. To come to the realization that accepting what he had experienced meant turning away from everything that had defined his life up to that point." Mavis took a careful sip. "Perhaps that's what you need to do now."

For some reason, the idea filled Dottie with panic. "I can't."

Mavis nodded, as though expecting nothing less. "I imagine you don't *want* to."

"I've already taken too much time off."

"Time off from what?" The old woman's eyes were a smoky blue in color, but the irises were ringed by a lighter shade, which turned her gaze into something that held and penetrated, no matter how gentle the face or the tone. "From something you're being called to give up anyway?"

Dottie repeated weakly, "I can't."

"Well, it's not the Lord's habit to force somebody into the fold. But I think you'd be better off keeping an open mind to His call. Will you do that?"

Dottie made a pretense of checking her watch. She took a card from her purse and wrote out her mobile phone number and the warning that it had not been working for two days. "Would you give that to Ben when he wakes, please?"

"Certainly." Mavis fitted the card into the pocket of her apron. "Fine man, there. Don't know what the pastor and the Lord have in store for him, but I'm certain he will do well by them both."

Dottie rose and said, "I have to be going."

Mavis walked around the table and embraced her. "I'll be praying for you, honey. And don't you try too hard to run away, now. The Lord might just let you get away."

⚊   ⚊

"Mrs. Betham?"

"It's Ms., actually." She rose to her feet and faced a handsome man in his early fifties. His full head of hair was brushed lightly with silver, his shirt starched, his silk tie darkly subtle. He wore the vest and pants to a striped gray suit, and his shoes were polished to a brilliant sheen. "Reverend Innes?"

"So nice to meet you." He gave her a warm smile and handshake. "You're a journalist from *Newsday,* did my receptionist get that right?"

"Yes. But I just stopped by to make an appointment, not—"

"It's no problem, Ms. Betham. I can spare you a few minutes." The reception area was separated from the back offices by a waist-high wall. Thurgood Innes pushed open the little swinging door. "Why don't we go to my office?"

"I'm really not prepared to speak with you yet."

"A professional. I like that." He pointed her down a long hall. "We can take a few minutes now to get acquainted and talk further when you're ready. How's that?"

"All right." She really had no choice.

As they passed through the pastor's outer office, a middle-aged secretary said, "Miller Kedrick is on the phone."

"I'll get back to him in ten minutes. We should be through by then, wouldn't you say, Ms. Betham?"

"Sooner." Snap interviews were a common and in many instances vital part of her work. People often gave better quotes when unaware of the line of questioning. But Dottie was not ready. She slipped into the chair in front of his desk and desperately wished for something that would bring her mind and her world into better focus.

"You'll have to excuse me, Ms. Betham. But I don't believe I've ever spoken to someone from a major newsmagazine before. How on earth did you get my name?"

She had no choice but to launch straight in. "I understand your denomination has censured Reverend Charles Griffin."

The pastor winced. "I see. It's about that."

"I could come back." Almost pleading now.

"No, no. I suppose I should have expected it." A long breath. "Were you there at Kingdom Come this weekend?"

"Yes."

"Was it . . ." He hesitated, then finished, "I hear it was a rather large affair."

"Huge."

Dottie watched as the pastor seemed to struggle with himself. Or perhaps she was simply seeing a reflection of what she felt inside herself. Certainly his charming smile was gone. Thurgood Innes said very carefully, "I cannot speak for the synod, Ms. Betham. I have only recently been elected. I can simply tell you what concerns me personally. All right?"

"Fine." She reached into her purse and extracted a pen and pad.

"Sadly, America's history is filled with examples of new sects that rise up swiftly and just as quickly disappear. They seem at first glance to be very spiritual. But in truth they are power and ego driven. They are the creations of self-serving leaders, and they rapidly fall apart."

His voice gathered strength and timbre as he continued. "My concern is that we are faced with another of these extremes. Emotionalism plays well in the beginning. It attracts a lot of people, most of them desperate for something that will help bring order to their worlds. But these sects don't last. And their answers, sadly, are not based on the eternal message."

He was indeed a handsome man, and his words were most convincing. His tone was experienced, his voice professional. His smile and his expression were as practiced as an actor's. Dottie made notes of what he said, and knew it was good copy. She also found herself personally shaken, as hearing this man talk made it even harder to believe that what she had experienced in the valley had been genuine. "Could you give me your personal opinion as to why the synod voted as they did?"

He formed a steeple of his fingers. "The Reformed Church of America is a denomination rich in heritage. We are more than two hundred years old. Our rules have stood the test of time. Our traditions have helped build this nation's faith. We care about our people. We birth them, we raise them in the Lord, we teach them and help deepen their faith and strengthen their walk, we help usher them Home, and then we stay around afterward to comfort those left behind. We are here for the long haul, Ms. Betham. Sects like what this Reverend Griffin is establishing merely play to the moment. They are flashes in the spiritual pan. They come, they go. And we are left to pick up the tragic pieces of their terrible mistakes."

Dottie walked back along the church offices' long hallway. As she passed through the reception area, she heard the receptionist say something. But she could not make out the words. Or perhaps she could, but her internal confusion blanked it out before the meaning could take form. She stepped into the sunlight and leaned against a pillar supporting the entrance portico.

"Are you all right, dear?"

Dottie squinted. But she could make nothing out, as the sunlight seemed to have congealed around the person standing in front of her. "Excuse me?"

"You look all done in." A hand reached forward. "Can I help you with something?"

"I . . . I was just inside. I had a meeting with Reverend Innes."

The figure stepped into the shadows and became a woman about her own age. Heavier than Dottie, wearing the expandable shift of late pregnancy, with a belly to match. "My name is Sally Crane. Why don't you come back inside and let's have a little chat."

Dottie allowed herself to be taken back through the reception area. She entered a large antechamber whose door held a handwritten sign stating simply PRAYER ROOM. Inside sat just one other woman, who rose to her feet as Dottie entered. The woman leading Dottie said brightly, "Oh, hello, Rebecca! This is perfect. Come join us. I'd like you to meet . . . I'm sorry, I don't know your name."

"Dottie. Dottie Betham."

"Rebecca is a missionary back here on leave from Saint Catherine. That's an island in the Caribbean where we run a school and a pottery factory and several other things. Rebecca is also one of the strongest prayer partners I've ever met." The woman continued to talk cheerfully as she led Dottie over and seated her on a sofa by the back wall. "Would you like a glass of iced tea?"

"Yes . . . no, thank you. That is . . ."

The woman seemed to understand perfectly. "You just sit right down here." She settled beside Dottie and reached for her hand as though it was the most natural thing in the entire world. "Would you like to talk about it?"

Holding the woman's hand seemed to bind her more closely to earth. She managed weakly, "I don't know if I could find the words. Which is crazy, since I'm a writer."

"A writer?" Rebecca stepped over, moving so hastily she twisted her long skirt around her ankles. Impatiently she flicked it straight and dragged over a chair. "What kind of things do you write?"

"Everything. I'm a freelance journalist." Dottie watched as the missionary moved in so close their knees almost touched, yet she felt no sense of intrusion. Which was odd, as Dottie had a lifetime's experience of keeping people and the world at a comfortable distance. Here in this little windowless room, however, Dottie sat with one stranger holding her hand and another crouched on the edge of a plastic chair, their faces scarcely a foot apart. And all she felt was a gradual focusing, an ability to return to the here and now. "Name any national magazine you can think of, and I've probably done a piece for them."

"Are you working on an article now?" Rebecca had scrubbed and lightly freckled features, and the clearest eyes Dottie had ever seen. Up close she could make out the tight, weary lines running from her eyes and mouth. "Is that why you came to see Reverend Innes?"

"You don't have to tell us anything if you don't want, dear," Sally added. There was no criticism to her words, just a quiet little reminder. "We don't want to pry, just help."

"No, no, it's fine." To Rebecca, Dottie explained, "I came down for some background on an article I'm doing for *Newsday*. But what I found . . ." Dottie struggled to give voice to her confusion. "It leaves me wondering if I'm asking the right questions."

Her words pressed Rebecca back into her seat. The blue eyes blinked once, twice. But the woman said nothing more. Just watched her carefully. Sally asked, "Would you like us to pray with you?"

Dottie confessed, "I don't even know what to pray for."

Sally gave the calm smile of one who had heard it all before. "Then perhaps illumination might be a nice request to make, wouldn't you think? To have the light that penetrates the deepest darkness fill your mind and your life with clarity."

TWENTY

The prayers went on a long time. Or at least that was the way it seemed to Dottie. Sally prayed, then Rebecca. Then they stopped and waited for Dottie to offer a prayer of her own. Dottie did not wish to speak, but the silence was so powerful in that windowless room that she had no choice. It was either speak or be swallowed whole. Afterward she had no real idea what she said, only that it did not take long. Her voice sounded shaky and thin to her own ears.

Dottie emerged from the prayer room feeling that the air in the reception room was too compressed, almost impossible to draw into her lungs. Thankfully, the receptionist was elsewhere, and the room empty. Rebecca moved up beside her in scuffed shoes. "Are you all right?"

"I'm not sure." Dottie glanced at the tall woman and found herself wondering how it was possible to hold to such calm. The world was a billion shades of gray, and life was made up of one hopeless choice after another. Yet this woman seemed totally at home, both with life and herself. "Thank you for your prayers."

Rebecca offered a thin smile and said, "Do you have a card?"

Dottie hesitated, but could not think of a reason not to hand one over. "I'm not available at that address right now."

"Of course, you're up at the Kingdom Come community. You said that." Rebecca scrutinized the card. "Is the mobile number here correct?"

"Yes, but my phone's on the blink. I think maybe I forgot to plug in the charger. Things have been kind of crazy lately."

The missionary hesitated, then said, "Could I ask you something about your writing? I know it's not the proper—"

A voice from down the back hall said, "Mr. Kedrick, I'm sorry, you can't just come in here and—"

"Stow it." The second voice was more of a bark. "Thurgood's in there, I know he is. And I'm going to see him."

"Sir, he is in—"

"*Now!*"

Dottie noticed Rebecca backing away from her and the room, moving toward the outer doors. The missionary kept her head down, hiding her face behind her hair. Dottie was tempted to follow her, but the argument called to her journalistic spirit. Especially when she heard a door open and a voice she recognized as belonging to the pastor said, "Really, Miller. There are few things in life that can't wait a half-hour."

"Stow it, I said." The man sounded like a human bulldog, all snarl and yap. "Are you still meeting with the feds today?"

"I told you I was. They called, and I agreed."

"And *I* told you it was a big mistake."

"I have nothing to hide, Miller. And neither does this church."

"That's not the point! You let them in the door, they'll start snooping around here, looking for something to pin on you. Believe me, that's the *last* thing you want."

"That's not the way it is at all. They want to talk about Chuck Griffin's cult, just like the reporter."

A hushed pause. Then, "*What* reporter?"

"She was just here. A woman from *Newsday*."

The voice growled, "She was asking questions about the Carolina dingbat? Why did she come to you, Thurgood?"

"I was the synod's spokesman on the topic. There's nothing sinister about—"

"Never mind. It's gone too far. The only thing to do now is to give them what they want, and hope they'll leave us alone. Make them see us as too valuable to make trouble for."

"You're not making sense, Miller."

"Don't you worry about it. I'll take care of this mess, too. Just like all the others."

"Miller, wait—"

But the bulldog was already on the move. Dottie knew because at that moment the ungainly man charged through the reception room's rear entrance. He glared at her as though seeking an outlet for his rage. When Dottie remained silent, he harrumphed angrily and stalked across the room. He pushed the outer doors so hard the metal frame hammered the church wall.

Dottie hesitated a long moment, then followed him outside. Either the sunlight was too strong or her vision too weak for the day. She blinked and shaded her eyes, searching the empty lot. The missionary was nowhere to be found.

For reasons she could not explain, Dottie followed the path the stocky man had taken. She crossed the lot and entered an open-ended hallway. Overhead was a sign that simply said THE WAY. The building reminded her of the garish arcades of her youth, running like a square mouth through a squat white three-story structure. Above the arcade's entrance hung illuminated signs embossed with spangles and Day-Glo letters. The effect was jarring and tawdry.

Dottie entered the arcade corridor. Gospel music blared from tinny overhead speakers, the song turned to almost painful clamor by the tiled floor and stucco walls. Shops with glass windows fronted both sides of the hall. She passed a bookstore and a boutique carrying a vast array of clothes bearing a religious logo of one sort or another. Then came a large music shop with music blaring even louder than in the arcade hallway. After that came a thrift store and a café and a store selling secondhand baby clothes and toys. Dottie walked slowly, wondering what it was among these businesses that would have interested a man like Miller Kedrick.

"Can I help you?"

The door to the last shop on the right was open, and just inside stood a smiling young man. "You look lost."

"That's exactly how I feel," Dottie replied.

The smile grew brighter. "An honest answer. What a nice way to dress up a beautiful day. Come inside."

"I'm not really interested in buying."

"That's okay. I haven't sold a thing today; why break a perfect record?" He stepped into the corridor, offering his hand. "Neil Hadley."

"Dottie Betham."

"Come on inside, Dottie. Please. I'm bored out of my skin here." He walked her back inside and shut the door. Instantly the noise was comfortably muted. "Coffee?"

"No thank you."

"I usually love this job. I'm studying at Rollins College, and I can come over here and get paid by the hour to sit and do my homework. But I'm all done and the book I brought to read is so totally tedious I'd rather watch paint peel. I've even caught myself singing along with that noise outside."

The store was by far the largest of those along the corridor. Dottie stared back through three large rooms packed to overflowing with hand-wrought knickknacks. "I was actually trying to follow somebody."

"This place is beyond empty. Things don't pick up around here until the kids arrive after school. I heard one of the ladies in the café say children these days should have their noise glands removed. But they come, and that's the most important thing." The guy sprawled back onto a sofa of rough-hewn wood armrests and overbright cushions. A placard on the wall said it too was for sale. "The only person who's come through here lately is my boss. And nobody in their right mind follows Miller Kedrick around."

"You work for that man?"

"Have a seat." The young man shifted his load of books and papers from the sofa to the coffee table in front of him. "He owns this place."

Dottie lowered herself down. "Funny, he doesn't strike me as the kind of man who'd sell African curios."

"First of all, they're not African, they're Caribbean. And second, he doesn't own the shop. He owns the whole building. Leases it to the church for a dollar a year."

"You're kidding."

"I know, I know. He doesn't strike me as the do-gooder type, either." The guy settled one sockless loafer on the coffee table. "But hey, the pastor trusts him, he leaves me pretty much alone, and my paychecks arrive on time. Not to mention the fact that this work helps finance mission projects."

"There's a lot of people I couldn't say that much about," Dottie agreed.

"Yeah, I could add some names to that list." The young guy grinned. "But it doesn't excuse the fact that Miller Kedrick acts like a bear with a migraine."

"Where is he now?"

Neil cocked a thumb at the side window. Across the street rose a mammoth structure of steel and dark reflective glass. "That's his new headquarters, as of last year. Kedrick Construction. Kedrick Components. Lots of other stuff, all starting with Kedrick."

The building revealed nothing. Dottie turned away and glanced around the shop. It was packed to overflowing with clay pots and woven reed baskets and kitchen implements and garish artwork and rough-hewn furniture. "So you sell a lot of these things?"

"Not here. But Mr. Kedrick is always bringing people through, showing the stuff off, then selling it in mass quantities to other places."

"So this is a wholesale and distribution center." Dottie shook her head. "Sorry, the whole idea of a senior corporate type taking an interest in Caribbean cookware is, well . . ."

"Straight out of Looney Tunes," Neil cheerfully agreed. "It gets worse. I didn't believe it either when I first got started. So I asked around. Everybody at the church has a Miller Kedrick story, most of them about how the guy has singed their hair. According to the scoop, though, he went through a bad spell several years ago. Almost lost the whole circus. Then his wife left him. That was when he started getting interested in the church and took charge of their mission outreach down in Saint Catherine. That's one of the leeward islands."

"I know where Saint Catherine is."

"Sure you do. So Kedrick finds God and throws himself into this work, stepping on about a gazillion toes in the process. But he turns the mission project around. Suddenly this stuff is selling like hotcakes. Now the money funds four missionaries, a clinic, and a school."

"I met one of the missionaries."

"Yeah, I'd heard Rebecca was back on leave. You won't find her in here, though."

"Why not?"

"They can't stand each other." Neil laced his hands behind his head. "Get those two in a room together and the sparks fly."

Dottie decided this was leading her nowhere. She rose to her feet. "Thanks for your time."

The guy gave an easy shrug. "You kidding? This is the high spot of my day."

TWENTY-ONE

M r. Wayne Oates?" A blond woman with overquick gestures moved toward the airport arrival gate with hand outstretched. "Sheila Walters. Federal district attorney's office."

She was immensely attractive and a small, tight bundle of energy. Wayne had the hunch she was braced now for a come-on, so he kept his face utterly bland and his voice touched with country twang. "You a lawyer or a gopher?"

She smirked and relaxed a trifle. "Both. The low girl on the totem pole, newest addition to the Orlando office, the first to become plant food. You've risen through federal ranks, you know what that means."

"I know."

"Do you have any luggage?"

Wayne hefted his carry-on. "Who sent you out to meet me?"

"Justin," she said carefully. "The name mean anything to you?"

"A lot," he agreed. Justin Ball, the hatchet-faced assistant to Theron Head. Hearing the name was enough to accelerate the day.

She waited until they were out in the humid Florida warmth to ask, "Is what they say about the gun true?"

Wayne followed her across the road to the multistory parking lot. She halted by a square, gray, federal-issue car and opened the doors. He tossed his bag in the back and climbed into the passenger seat.

When they pulled up to the pay booth, he slid the gun from its holster and held it with both hands.

Her eyes were round as she studied the Glock shining in the sunlight. "It's beautiful."

"Shoots better than it looks," Wayne said, sliding it back into the holster. "I spent two hours at the firing range last night. Got a blister on my finger. Tore the center of ten targets to shreds at a hundred yards."

"I hear most federal agents never get a chance to use their weapons," she ventured.

Wayne remained silent as they drove toward the church, not the least bit bothered by that prospect. Something told him Theron Head did not expect these weapons to remain firing-range ornaments.

Sheila seemed satisfied with his relaxed silence. "I was told you wanted to see Reverend Thurgood Innes. I've gone ahead and set up an appointment with his office."

"What can you tell me about him?"

"Big church. Huge. Recent appointee to the church's central body. No dirt on him, far as we know."

"I'm not here to find dirt on Innes." He glanced over. "Am I in the daily log?" All federal prosecutors were required to keep time sheets listing all their official meetings.

"Absolutely," she replied, not taking her eyes from the road. "Every visitor from Washington who wants an excuse to bring the kids to Mouseland has to be listed."

"I'm not from D.C., and I don't have any kids."

"Even so," she said, casting him a cool look, "that's how we're playing it. Okay?"

"Fine. No problem at all," Wayne said as they approached the church parking lot and pulled into a visitor's space.

The church was big and new, the office area muted and professional looking. Wayne made no protest when Sheila followed him and the receptionist down the hall and into the pastor's outer office. When the secretary went inside, however, she offered him a chance to push her away by asking, "How do you want to play this?"

"I told you," Wayne replied. As far as he was concerned, if Justin Ball asked her to meet him, that was all the recommendation he needed. "Thurgood Innes is not under investigation."

The meeting proved utterly futile. The reverend had no intention of giving them anything with teeth. Wayne had met people like Innes before, trial lawyers and big-time deal-makers and successful people of every ilk who had worn the public face so long they had trouble realizing they were still spouting from the soapbox. Wayne sat the man out, giving him nothing but the professional investigator's mask in response.

The first time Sheila Walters spoke was to thank the man upon their departure. They walked back down the hall and reentered the sunlight. As they returned to the car, she said, "What a waste."

Before he could agree, however, a voice called from behind them, "Wait a second!"

They turned to confront a red-faced, bullish man with the muscled jaw of a dedicated teeth grinder. "Tell me you're the agents."

Wayne demanded, "Can I help you?"

"If you're who I think you are, pal, it's the other way around. Definitely the other way." The man wore a wrinkled shirt, the bottom half of a pin-striped suit, and a tie at half-mast. He looked to Wayne like somebody who put the clothes on because other people expected them, not because he cared. "Are you the FBI agents down investigating the Carolina caper?"

Sheila answered for him. "Who are we addressing?"

"Head of church finances." He was sweating far too hard for the day. "I've got some stuff for you. But first I want to see some IDs. Need to make sure you're not some ringer down from a newsmagazine."

Wayne opened his leather wallet and demanded, "A reporter was posing as a federal agent?"

"Not exactly. She was down asking questions, same as you."

Wayne exchanged a glance with Sheila. The news was doubly disturbing, first that someone knew they were coming and used that information to her advantage. And second that the newsmagazines were taking an interest. "She was asking about the cult in North Carolina?"

Miller Kedrick's grin was not a pretty sight. His teeth were so flat they looked filed. "Man, you don't know how nice it sounds to have somebody else call it that besides me."

Sheila's voice pushed hard. "We need to know about this woman, sir."

"She met with the pastor, maybe Innes can tell you something. I didn't hear about it until it was over."

Wayne had no interest in returning to the pastor's office. "Do you have information about this cult that we need to know, sir?"

"I'll say. Come on over here." He led them to where a Cadillac Esplanade sat with the motor running. Wayne climbed inside and was instantly engulfed in stale cigar fumes. The SUV's temperature was barely above refrigerator level. Even so, the burly man continued to sweat as he balanced his briefcase on his knees, twirled the locks, and pulled out a bulky file. "Here you go. That should burn them good."

Wayne scanned the first sheet, then the second. From her position on the backseat, Sheila leaned forward to read over his shoulder. He heard the quick catch to her breathing as she realized what he was holding.

"Tell me I'm right." Kedrick's grin was fierce. "This is enough to bury Kingdom Come deep."

━ ✠ ━

"There is definitely evidence of a serious diversion of funds," Wayne Oates declared. He sat in the assistant federal prosecutor's office in downtown Orlando, speaking on a secure line. Sheila Walters sat across from him, listening on the extension. Staring at her somber expression helped keep his voice steady. "No question about it."

Theron Head responded with the same fixed tone as always. "But this information did not come from the pastor himself, do I understand you correctly?"

"That's correct, sir. Thurgood Innes had nothing of any substance to offer."

"Pity. It would have helped to have an official complaint lodged against this Charles Griffin by his own governing body."

"Reverend Griffin has been expelled from the denomination," Wayne pointed out. "But we can't use that as a basis for our own investigation."

"Wouldn't you consider such an expulsion as an indication of wrongdoing?"

"Certainly, sir. But there is nothing to the synod charge that we can apply. Innes made it out to be strictly a doctrinal issue."

"Oh. I see. Very well, Mr. Oates. Proceed."

"Yes sir." Wayne paused long enough to press the sweat from the hair over his temples. Sheila cast him a sympathetic glance, then returned her own gaze to the papers strewn over the desk. Once again it helped him focus. "We met with the church's financial officer. He has prepared a detailed survey of confidential information from over a dozen churches. They've had funds siphoned off by the cult."

"*All* of them?"

"Seventeen in all. Every single one has lost funds, sir. Many of them have even detailed the specific families who have stopped meeting pledges and, when questioned, have said they are transferring their donations to the Kingdom Come cult."

"Oh, this is good. Very good indeed."

Wayne exchanged an easier glance with Sheila before saying, "There's more, sir. In over a dozen cases there is also evidence that money officially on the churches' books has been transferred to the cult."

"You don't say."

"Yes sir. Apparently this was done at the written request of the donors."

"But if the donations were listed on the books of a federally tax-exempt body, this could be construed as an illegal diversion of funds." The tone sharpened slightly, like a soft velvet lash. "It appears we finally have what we have been seeking."

Wayne knew he had no choice but to pour water on the moment. "Sir, I have to tell you, the source struck me as a man with a shadow."

"You're sure about this?"

"No sir. But my gut tells me the man was hiding something."

"We can't be seen as accepting tainted evidence. We will need to keep this source under wraps, and if we go to trial we will dig deeper and offer the man immunity from whatever he wants to keep hidden."

"That's why I thought I'd best mention it up front."

"You did so correctly, Mr. Oates. All right. This is what we will do. I am hereby authorizing you to set up a money-laundering investigation. Make it a two-pronged attack, diversion of federal funds for private housing, and diversion of funds from tax-exempt sources."

"I'm on it, Mr. Head."

"I will bring the relevant bodies together this afternoon and contact you upon your return to Charlotte. Is there anything else?"

Again he hesitated, then Wayne said, "Yes sir. Maybe it's nothing, but . . ."

"Get a move on, Oates." The impatient lash once more.

"The source mentioned there was a reporter sniffing around. She met with Innes. The pastor's secretary told us her name was Dorothy Betham. From *Newsday*."

"All right. Fine." No apparent concern at all. In fact, there was perhaps a hint of satisfaction. "It had to happen. Fax those documents to me now."

The phone went dead. No farewell at all. Wayne settled the phone back on its cradle and struggled to find an easy breath.

Sheila Walters said, "I feel that way every time I talk with that group. Like I'm walking a tightrope to victory."

"Are you planning a switch to the FBI?"

She gave him a full-watted stare. "You didn't hear this from me, all right?"

"No problem."

"It's the other way around. Theron Head is pushing to become the assistant secretary for criminal investigations at the Department of Justice."

Wayne nodded slowly. It made sense. The FBI was one arm of the Justice Department, the federal prosecutors' offices around the nation were another. Their connection came in taking cases to trial. But there was one other conjunction. At the highest possible level. The Department of Justice had an assistant secretary who was responsible for every major case, handling all the public relations and coordinating the resources brought in from all the different divisions. "I didn't know the slot was open."

"It isn't. Not yet. But it will be soon. And Theron Head needs a major headliner to get him into the public's eye."

"Anybody who helps him find that notoriety," Wayne thought out loud, "might make the climb with him, wouldn't you say?"

"A NASA space launch comes to mind." She offered a tight smile. "We're talking serious nosebleed altitude. You have any trouble with that?"

Wayne Oates smiled in reply, glad to meet someone whose ambition matched his own. "None at all."

TWENTY-TWO

Her mind a jumble, Dottie spent another fruitless half-hour drifting about the church. The missionary had vanished. No one knew where she was, and in truth Dottie had no idea why she even wanted to speak with Rebecca again. Finally she admitted defeat and drove her rental car back to the Orlando airport.

She dropped off her car and took the shuttle bus to the main terminal. Once there, however, she felt the day's confusion wash over her. Dottie was pushed to a halt by a sweeping sense of lonely isolation.

Loneliness was a way of life with her; why would it strike her now? Even so, it was all she could do to carry her briefcase and overnight bag as far as the next group of chairs. She collapsed into the seat beside a pay phone. Then she recalled the card Ben had given her at their first meeting. She scrounged about her purse until she came up with the crumpled card. Suddenly she was filled with an urgency that left her hands fumbling both with the pay phone and the numbers. She punched in the first number and had difficulty keeping from panicking when there was no answer. On and on it rang—ten, eleven times. Finally she accepted defeat and dialed the second number. It clicked instantly, apologizing that the mobile phone was neither switched on nor accepting messages. She replaced the receiver, feeling bitterly let down. It did not matter that the sentiment was utterly illogical. She needed Ben and he wasn't there. Finish.

She started to hang up the phone, when it occurred to her that at least one man did want to hear from her. She dialed the magazine's number from memory, and when her editor came on, she declared, "Talk about a wild-goose chase."

"Dottie?" Ed Starling's voice carried the delight of an editor after a scoop. "Is this the woman with my lead? I've been trying to call you all day."

"My mobile's on the blink."

"Where are you?"

"I'm sitting in the Orlando airport," she replied. And suddenly she found herself listening to her own voice, as though it was coming from a stranger seated nearby. A voice pounded flat and emptied of every shred of emotion by big-city bitterness. Utterly without hope in mankind or herself. "I'm surrounded by a million kids wearing mouse ears. It looks like a rodent epidemic."

"Skip the travel fluff. Did you get the story?"

"Wait, wait. Now I'm looking at a little girl in a Snow White hat, you know the kind? It looks like a dunce cap with sparkles. There's a purple nylon ribbon trailing off behind. She's carrying a Goofy doll." Dottie sighed, suddenly feeling that she would give anything to trade places with that weary mother holding the little girl's hand. Anything and everything. For just one day of having someone whose joy and skipping excitement and childhood dreams were more important than her own sleep. "What am I doing here, can you tell me that?"

"Chasing a lead," Ed reminded her. "Tell me you talked with the pastor."

"I got the interview."

"Great." His voice rose like a motor revving to redline. "I'm looking at tomorrow's deadline with a hole in the magazine big as Africa. Give me fifteen hundred words."

"Ed, I don't have anything but a billion questions."

"Fine. Then ask them on paper." When she didn't respond, he

whined frantically, "I know you, Dottie. I could send you to cover a cupcake bake-off, and you'd give me headline drama. But my nose tells me we're looking a major story in the face. Write it for me. Do it now. I'm dying up here."

She inspected the emptiness of a life without lasting purpose and sighed, "Why not?"

"Great. Just great. Twelve hundred words will cover the hole, fifteen hundred would be perfect, two thousand max. Can you work all night and have this to me by dawn?"

Again there was only one answer. "Why not?"

"You're great, Dottie. The best. Check into the finest hotel you can find. Do lots of room service."

She set down the phone, picked up her bags, and followed the signs toward the airport Hyatt. A family passed her, the kids still amped from seeing Mickey in real life, the parents sunburned and weary but very pleased. She carried her acrid emptiness into the hotel lobby, signed for the room, took the elevator up to the eleventh floor. Her room was spacious and well-appointed and as empty as her life. She set up her computer on the desk and started to write.

Dottie worked until four in the morning. Several times she registered outside sensations. The windows rattled as planes took off or landed. Her empty stomach growled. People passed in the outside hallway, laughing and talking loudly enough to disturb her ornate cocoon. Her neck and shoulders ached. Her eyes became gritty with fatigue and stress. She noticed it all, then pushed it away. She gave herself over totally to the work and the unloading. It was not so much an article as a catharsis.

She wrote not one piece, but three. Fifteen hundred words each. The first covered her departure from New York, and the life she had known, following the invitation from Charles Griffin. She described every early sensation she could remember, and every doubt she knew. She unloaded everything, holding nothing back. How the place and the friendly people and the quiet fervor of their faith did nothing but dig holes in her psyche. How she had found not rest, but further sleeplessness and troubled dreams.

The next segment dealt with the arrival of the FBI, the arrest of Pastor Chuck Griffin, and the events leading up to the revival. This second article felt as though it was going to tear her apart to write, for she wrote with two voices: One spoke with a journalist's detachment, asking all the right questions, giving none of the answers. The other voice simply wept. All the tears she had not yet shed Dottie poured onto the page. She cried over the revival's power. She lamented her own inability to respond. She went through each day, describing the people and the intensity and her desire to pretend that it had not been there at all.

The third article began with the conflicting emotions she had felt upon departing for Florida, relief on the one hand, agony on the other. And how this confusion had followed her down to Orlando. She gave a detailed description of Reverend Thurgood Innes and his analysis of the Carolina experience. She laid it out, including the baffling quandary she found herself facing. She concluded with an honesty that raked her soul.

Now as she sat in this faceless hotel room and struggled with just one more deadline, she observed her own internal conflict with the honesty of utter exhaustion. The logical journalist wanted to discount everything she had experienced, everything she had *felt*. Her mind wanted to remain with what she knew, what she found comfortable. And yet . . . Her heart cried out for what she had undergone in that sweet-scented Carolina valley, surrounded by people who were gathered from the four corners of their vast nation. People who had nothing in common with one another, and yet there on that star-flecked night had shared in something so strong they had left united in heart and in faith. She wanted that. Her wounded and divided life cried out a yearning so vast not even her frightened mind could silence the wail. She could no longer say if the experience were real. But if it were not, perhaps it should have been.

Dottie sent the three articles off by e-mail. Then she lay down on the bed without taking off her clothes. She did not sleep. She was too spent even to close her eyes. She lay and watched as dawn streaked the ceiling with light.

The first time the phone rang, she was unable to move. The second time, however, she managed to reach over and grab the receiver. "Yes."

"You know what you've sent me?" It was her editor. "A headache, that's what."

She used her free hand to rub her face. "Will you run it?"

"Some of it. Sure." Ed Starling's voice sounded strained. Uncomfortable. "But other parts . . . Dottie, you realize I don't have room for all this."

"I know."

"I ask you for a story, and you give me a personal epic." Even the jaded Ed Starling seemed shaken. "Are you all right?"

"No."

"You don't sound all right. What you've given me . . ." Nervously he cleared his throat. "I could send down somebody else to take your place."

She was tempted. But where would she go? She had no place, no one. "I'll stay on it."

"Are you sure? All I've done is read this, and I feel wasted." When she did not respond, he hurried on. "Well, keep a close watch on this thing. We're not done here. This is going to be a major break, a headline maker for weeks to come. And Dottie—"

"What?"

"Remember the first rule of journalism: Never get too close to your story."

She mouthed a good-bye, then let the receiver flop onto the bed beside her. A recording came on, telling her to hang up. Then the beeping started. She did not move. She felt nothing at all, and yet sensed a rightness here. The beeping grated inside her skull, another crass sound from a mechanized and uncaring world. She blinked, and one tear escaped to scald a line down her cheek. She did not wipe it away. For there in the distance she sensed something, soft as a violin played in the wind. A single note, whispering to her battered and confused soul. That here in this space she had finally arrived at a point where she could truly turn *from* one thing and *toward* another. That the act of honestly confessing to the page in her articles had brought her to where she could face a new tomorrow.

Dottie finally managed to roll over and hang up the phone. She lay back and felt the aching void begin to ease slightly. Not filling with anything permanent, no. Yet at least there was a comforting sense of some reason to it all. Something beyond the confusion and the confession and the empty dawn.

She found herself recalling a distant time. Her grandmother had died when she was seven, but until then she had loved to travel to the Pennsylvania Dutch country to visit the ramshackle house where her father had been raised. He had taught physics at Penn, and had always seemed vaguely embarrassed by his mother and her simple ways. But that final summer, when even the young Dottie could see that the woman was in pain, the old woman had spoken words that had left Dottie very confused and her father very shaken. There is a light in my darkness, her grandmother had said. Soon enough it will rain in the desert. Soon enough the door will open wide. Dottie had not thought of the woman in years. Now, though she did not understand the words, she found herself comforted by the memory. Enough so that she could finally shut her eyes and drift away, carried by the sweet scent of water falling upon a parched and empty land.

TWENTY-THREE

Deputy Assistant Director Evan Hawkins returned from lunch to have his secretary meet him halfway down the hall. She was too old and too heavyset to run comfortably, but she managed to kick up quite a pace as she rushed toward him. "You've got to hurry." She jammed the folder into his hands. "They started without you."

Evan did not need to ask who or what, only, "Theron's private conference room?"

"Yes. Hurry."

He turned and ran, cursing Theron Head with every step.

The Federal Bureau of Investigation's headquarters had two distinct faces. The tour guides did a fine job of showing off the library of active, pending, and solved cases. The labs were given time, always a great source of interest. As were the training division and the Hoover museum. The high point for many visitors, especially the kids, was a trip to the firing range, where they were given a bullet-ridden target as a souvenir.

But the FBI was a bureaucracy, and most of the headquarters was a warren of standard-issue federal offices. As deputy assistant director of the Criminal Investigative Division, Evan Hawkins occupied the largest office on the CID's third-floor corridor. This same corridor also contained all the next tier down, the section chiefs, as well as their own assistants and many CID agents assigned a tour of duty in Washington.

Because of this, some of the ambitious preppies doing time as aides to the higher echelon—the director's office, the deputy director, and the assistant directors like Theron Head—liked to call the third floor Munchkin Row.

Every floor had a central number-one hall leading straight off the elevators. But only the seventh floor had a Hall One. This was the corridor containing the office of the FBI director, always appointed by the president and confirmed by the Senate Judiciary Committee. Also here were the deputy director, the director of congressional affairs, the chief of staff, and several of the more powerful assistant directors. The assistant director with the greatest clout and the largest staff was unquestionably the chief of the Criminal Investigative Division, the position currently held by Theron Head.

Theron Head's suite of offices was three doors down from the director's, which was as close as Head would ever come to the directorship. He was utterly lacking in the charm and charisma required to push for the top slot. But Evan had heard the latest scuttlebutt, that Head was planning an end run, putting himself up for the position of assistant secretary of criminal investigations within the Department of Justice. The thought left him cold. Theron Head was everything Evan despised about Washington bureaucratic life—utterly ruthless, brilliantly ambitious, and sneaky as a Teflon snake.

He did not even bother to pause by the one aide's desk that was manned, just stalked to the conference room opposite Head's private office. He knocked once, then entered. To his utter dismay, the people inside were up and moving for the door. The meeting was over. Enraged, Evan walked straight to the chair opposite Theron and slapped down his folder. Hard.

"Evan, how nice of you to join us." Theron gave his flat little smile. "We were just discussing—"

"A case that requires my input! This meeting should never have been called without me, Theron."

"We tried to reach you, of course." If anything, Theron seemed pleased by Evan's outburst. "Didn't we, Justin?"

"Absolutely, sir. I called his office just as soon—"

"Oh, come off it! You knew I was at lunch. What could possibly have been so vital that you couldn't wait for me to return?"

Theron turned to the little group clustered by the door. "Thank you, ladies and gentlemen. Tomorrow at nine. Please be prepared." When his aide did not move, Theron added, "Give us a few minutes, will you, Justin?"

"Yes sir. You have a meeting with the director in ten minutes."

"I doubt seriously we will need that long." Theron waited until the door was shut before turning back to Evan and announcing, "I've just heard there is an opening for a special agent in charge of the office in Omaha."

"Don't threaten me, Theron!"

"On the contrary," he said, everything about him soothing and insipid. "You're the one who entered here in attack mode."

Evan Hawkins jammed a finger across the table. "You try to shut me out and I'll bring you up on formal complaint. How do you think that would look, with you gunning for higher office? Your own number two, the one with the *real* field experience and *real* arrests under his belt, accusing you of foul tactics?"

Though his tone remained as bland as ever, Theron's gaze turned hard and hot as brimstone. "Careful who you go after, Evan. I'll hand you your head on a platter."

"You're the one who's started with the skirmishes!"

"Only because you haven't shown the stomach for this investigation."

"I've done nothing but say we need conclusive evidence before we proceed," Evan shot back.

"Which we now have." Theron Head tapped the folder before him. "Direct evidence of diversion of tax-exempt funds."

The news slammed Evan back into his seat. "Ben reported this?"

"Ben Atkins is finished." Theron's features did not seem able to move in proper balance. His dark hair fell down like a schoolchild's, almost masking the frown creasing his forehead. His face was then split by mud-brown eyes, which held little emotion save a sullen rage. His mouth was the most mobile part of him, pulling and stretching those thin bloodless lips like a puppet. "And if you don't cut yourself loose from him, you'll go down with him."

"The resident agent in Charlotte," Evan guessed. "Wayne Oates."

"A fine man. Does good work." The folder was tapped a second time. "We now have the ammunition to move this Kingdom Come investigation from preliminary to criminal."

Evan felt the ire drain away. Not only did it mean that his friend Ben Atkins was wrong, it meant his career was finished. "May I see the documents?"

"You already have them." Theron pointed at the file in front of Evan. "If you'd bothered to look at what we sent you before bursting in here, you'd know it too."

He opened the folder, as much to give himself a chance to recover as to survey the data.

Theron took Evan's silence as an admission of defeat. "Clearly Atkins has inflated the quality of his personal scrutiny. The man is over the hill. He's due for a SAMMS review; I've had Justin check his file." The Special Agent Mid-Management Selection group confirmed or declined the placement of all senior officers. "I'll make sure they downcheck him."

"That's a crying shame." Evan knew his protest would do no good, but he felt the urge to speak nonetheless. "Ben Atkins is one of the finest agents I've ever met."

"*Was* a fine agent," Theron corrected. He leaned across the table. "We'll find him some appropriate final assignment. Processing applicants, perhaps. Let him wallow in paperwork until he gets the message and takes early retirement."

Evan realized Theron was no longer speaking of Ben at all, but rather about Evan's own career. He felt the ashes of his former anger almost choke the words, "So what now?"

The cauldron within Theron's gaze heated further. "We attack this cult. Hard. The only question I have for you is, Are you with us or against us?"

Evan knew he had no choice. "With you. Of course."

"Good." Theron leaned back, the mouth pulling up into a satisfied smile. "I never doubted you, Evan. Not for an instant."

TWENTY-FOUR

Ben Atkins walked the street leading from his apartment into the town of Douglas, a troubled man. The day was charged with gray power, the wind low and sullen and laden with a coming storm. Thunder echoed in time to his footsteps, as though the clouds walked with him. He was tired. He had not been sleeping well. He had spent two full days tracking across every trail he could find, making as careful a survey of the enclave and the parkland as he could. He had a lot of experience in this, for his days in Wyoming had taught him how to read a trail that his eye said ran true but actually would lead him in a gradual circle and back upon himself. Exactly as his life was doing now.

Ben had purchased a surveyor's map and sectioned Kingdom Come into quadrants. Then with a compass and great patience he had driven every single road and lane and track on the map, marking them off one by one. He had pushed his way along fire trails running the high ridges, doing the paintwork on his rental car no good whatsoever. Those trails too small to drive, he had walked. And found nothing. No sign of anything dangerous, no secret gathering point, no arms cache, no training ground.

But the truth was, he had not really gone looking for any such thing. He had known before he started what he would find. So why had he done it? That was the question that plagued him. For if Ben did not know better, he was showing every sign of a lawman getting to know a new patch of turf. A place he was aiming to claim as his own.

The vast reaches within the encircling fence were taking on a feel of their own. He saw Kingdom Come now as an enclave, one with a distinct personality. There was no danger here. No threat. The Gathering was not an isolated event. It *defined* this place. On the surface his search had found a strange mixture of urgent construction and calm countryside, of high-tech projects and timeless farms. Of people in a modern-day hurry, and calm anticipation of what lay utterly beyond their control.

Ben pushed through the door to the diner on Main, and was greeted by quiet chatter and the smell of bacon frying. The fierce argument he had witnessed on his first morning seemed years ago. Ben slid into a booth, his back to the wall. There was no warmth to the waitress's greeting, but no hostility either. He waved away the menu and said, "Scrambled eggs and wheat toast, please, Madge."

"You got it."

Ben sipped his coffee and watched the world move slowly past the window. He found himself recalling his confused reaction to the argument he had witnessed his first visit here. Then he had been searching for the criminal. Now . . . What was he feeling? Ben smiled his thanks as the waitress deposited his plate, and realized that quiet understanding was gradually developing. He did not feel the same sense of being commanded to come that these others perhaps had. And yet there was a new yearning within him. Ben ate his eggs and toast and pondered this. Was this how it had begun for them? Or had they been more ready than he to listen when God called? He shook his head over that thought.

Madge stopped by his table. "Something wrong?"

"What?"

"You were shaking your head at the plate. Did Harv burn the eggs again?"

"No, they're fine." When she didn't move, he said, "Really, Madge. The eggs are great."

When he was alone again, he returned to his surprise over that realization. In the past few days, God had become a far stronger force in his life. One that might be drawing him into making a move that even a week earlier would have seemed totally ludicrous.

Ben swiveled in his booth so that he could look back into the diner. He no longer saw an odd assortment of cult followers. Not at all. Ben studied the faces, then studied himself. He knew he was looking at people who were simply trying to follow their God the best they could. Humans all, prone to err and fall and fail. But giving it all they could.

A voice above him asked, "Mind a little company?"

He looked up to find Pastor Griffin standing by his table. "Not at all. Have a seat." But it was the person next to the pastor who caused him to smile. "Hello, Dottie. When did you get back?"

"A couple of hours ago. I should be asleep, but I'm too tired to go to bed." Dottie slid in beside the pastor and tried to return Ben's smile, but in her exhausted state it came out as a tight grimace. "I guess that doesn't make any sense."

"Been there myself many times. You do look all done in."

Dottie nodded her thanks as Madge set down a mug of coffee. "Four years ago, I took the flu vaccine and had this terrible reaction. For a week afterward I walked around feeling as though I was only partly there. That's how I feel right now."

"Disconnected," Ben said, understanding perfectly. "Like you're spinning one way and the world is going the other."

The pastor observed, "You look tied up in knots yourself, Ben."

Ben wondered if he should try to give voice to his reflections, but decided it was too early. So he mentioned his other concern. "I'm mighty worried over what Washington might have planned."

"It seems like only yesterday you were counting yourself among those folks in the capital," the pastor observed.

He nodded slowly, convicted by the statement's simple truth. "Ever since the revival I haven't been able to raise my boss. He's there, but he's not available. Which leaves me pretty certain they're coming out against the community here. Yet the evidence is too flimsy. There's nothing solid. Even so, I'm concerned the FBI might be starting a criminal investigation."

Chuck Griffin neither criticized the government nor condemned Ben for being a part of it. Instead, he sipped from his mug and said, "It's a pastor's prerogative to poke his nose into other people's business. Would you allow me to make a personal observation?"

Ben pondered this. He did not feel worried over what was coming, but rather sharply aware. If he had learned anything during his stay here, it was that Chuck Griffin did not attack, nor did he seek to destroy. It shamed him to think he had ever suspected the man of either. "All right."

"Your problem, Ben, is that you're still trying to heed two voices. You haven't *declared* yourself. You've been invited, but you have not *entered*. And the struggle is tearing at you inside."

"It's hard," Ben quietly agreed.

"You cannot be both of this world and of the next. You can't serve two masters," Chuck told him. "I know this lesson all too well, I'm sorry to say. It's the same problem with a great deal of our church today, my own denomination included. We condemn the world while accepting much as part and parcel of our daily walk. This is why I felt such a sense of rightness in accepting the call and putting this community together. The time and place of the Second Coming is in God's hands. Here and now, I want to show how a Christian community can live in this world yet not be a part of it. And serve as a beacon to those in darkness."

Ben opened his mouth, then shut it. He knew the words he wanted to ask. But they were hard. Chuck sat and waited with the patient stillness of a man who had learned not to rush events of the spirit. Ben took a long breath and glanced at Dottie. Her gaze emerged from plum-ringed hollows. She looked so tired. Yet her eyes were alert and seemed to reflect his own indecision. Staring at her and not the pastor, Ben confessed, "I wish I knew what to do."

"Let me share with you something that happened last week," Chuck told him. "I received a call from Thurgood Innes, a pastor I've known for years. He was telephoning on behalf of my denomination's ruling synod. They were giving me an ultimatum. Either I disband the cult and issue a general disclaimer, or face expulsion."

There was a gasp from somewhere inside the diner, and a quiet murmur, quickly extinguished. Ben realized others were listening to their discussion, but did not turn to look. The moment was too strong to permit outside interference. Chuck continued, "I did my best to convince him that this was not a cult. Thurgood Innes replied that the time for such discussions was over. Either I acted now, or I would be lost to my church family. Keep in mind, Ben, I've been a member of the Reformed Church of America all my life. I was born into it, and my family has been members for generations. I went to their seminary. I've served in six of their churches. I was married in the church, and I had always expected to serve out my earthly days within its fold. This was devastating news. Do you understand what I'm telling you?"

Ben felt an odd intensity to the moment, a hint of the same force he had experienced that evening in the valley. As though he was trapped in an amber of light. He understood all too well.

"There was nothing I could do but set down the phone and fall to my knees. I prayed, hard as I've ever prayed in my life. For the second time in my life, I lived the words, praying until the blood sprang from my brow. The first time was on my wife's deathbed."

Ben wet his lips but could not find words to speak. He recalled a time like that of his own. The moment's hold tightened further, drawing him so close he felt as though he could hear the pastor's words before they were spoken. Chuck went on. "Over the next two hours,

I received a succession of telephone calls. But they were not from other churches within the denomination, as I might have expected. Not one came from friends and colleagues, phoning to tell me how I needed to mend my ways. No. All nine of those calls were from different spin-off communities with problems they needed my advice on. I found my answer there, Ben. I found God's voice speaking to me through these other people. I was called to help these communities do what they feel is God's call to service.

"So now I prayed again, and this time I asked God to reveal to me what I was not seeing. I asked Him to show me where I was not obeying as I should. I begged Him to make me a better servant. To live His will for me and for my community more fully."

Outside the window, thunder rumbled softly. The diner was so quiet Ben could hear grease hissing on the griddle, the ticking of the wall clock, the flick of a toaster popping up. The only other face he could see belonged to Dottie, and she looked as stricken as he felt. As convicted.

Chuck asked softly, "Would you like to pray such a prayer with me, Ben?"

He nodded. But it was not enough. Hard as it was to speak, he wanted his voice to be heard. Such a rightness, such a power demanded a public response. "Yes, I do."

Chuck turned then, acknowledging the other listeners for the first time. "Gather round, everybody. Come on, draw in close. Lay your hands on our friend here. Let him know your welcome as well as God's." Only when the day and the shadow of coming storms were blocked by a human wall of compassion did Chuck say, "All right, let us pray."

Ben retreated to his apartment, a private man embarrassed by this public display. But the atmosphere was too confining. He made a cup of coffee he neither wanted nor drank. Then with an exasperated bark at the blank walls, he grabbed his keys and headed for the door.

He drove aimlessly for a half-hour or so, along streets that were becoming increasingly familiar. Finally he wound his way back to the center of Douglas, not really certain where he was headed until he pulled up in front of the police station. His unconscious destination left him smiling as he locked the car door and walked the shaded path. Where else should a lawman go but here?

The same youth who had greeted him that first morning with Wayne Oates was behind the counter. Ben searched his memory, feeling as though he was reaching through the cobwebs of years instead of days. Jeff Cummins, that was his name. The young man waved an easy greeting, the phone stuck to his ear. "You don't say. Well, if that don't beat all." He waved Ben around the front barrier. "Well, now, Mrs. Blake, we're a little shorthanded just now. Hal is all the way over in Hamlin, looking at . . . "

Ben hesitated a long moment, then pushed through the swinging door and entered the official domain. He shook his head when Jeff pointed toward the coffeepot on the corner table. Jeff continued speaking to the telephone. "I'm sorry, Mrs. Blake, I can't. I've explained that to you before. I'm not allowed to leave this office. Yes ma'am, I understand. Urgent. Yes ma'am. Soon as he gets back. No ma'am, I won't dally. All right, ma'am."

Jeff hung up the phone, shook his head, said, "That was Mrs. Blake."

"I think I've heard that name before."

"Reckon you have. She calls here every day, seems like."

Ben snapped his fingers, recalling a conversation overheard that first day. "Invaders."

"Dropping out of the sky," Jeff agreed. "Right into her very own backyard. Climbing over the fence, stomping through her tomatoes."

"Every precinct has at least one eccentric," Ben said.

Jeff cocked his head to one side. "Been some changes since the last time you came by." He grinned. "Hear there was a little prayer circle over at the diner."

"News travels fast."

"You can say that again. Had three people stop by already, wanting to make sure I heard the news." Jeff stopped as the radio crackled, but when nothing but static came through, he went on, "Thunder does that."

"Big storm coming in," Ben agreed. "Sky's dark as twilight." It seemed the most natural thing in the world to rise up then, and offer, "I could go see to Mrs. Blake if you like."

"Are you kidding?" Jeff's feet hit the floor with a solid thunk. "Hal would call you a friend for life."

"Write out her address for me."

"No problem." The young man did so from memory. He started to hand over the paper, then reached into the drawer and drew out a familiar item. "Might as well take this too."

Ben accepted the paper and the silver star. "You have the power to deputize me?"

"We're pretty casual about rank and responsibilities around here. Not to mention the fact that Hal's been wishing you'd help out ever since he took you and that Washington fellow for a ride." Jeff reached into another drawer, pulled out a radio handset, and handed that over as well. "Channel 4 is open, heard by everybody from the fire chief to Pastor Chuck's secretary. Channel 3 is reserved for me and Hal and now you." He dropped back into his seat with a comfortable sigh. "You be sure and tell Mrs. Blake I said howdy."

━ ⟟ ━ ⟟ ━

Dealing with Mrs. Blake and her noisy fears took Ben Atkins right back to his earliest days on the force, when junior station officers were used as gophers to track down the least likely leads. Ben did not mind in the slightest. As he drove back to the station, he found himself wishing for a world where the only fiends were those seen by lonely old women. Where schools were places for growth and protection, where kids played up and down the middle of streets, where even police cars had to stop for a rolling ball. Where a town council held open meetings that were full to overflowing, where people asked what they could do to help. A place where metal detectors were unknown.

The radio crackled on the seat beside him. "Ben? Ben Atkins, you there?"

"Right here."

"This is Hal. Go to channel two."

Ben steered the car to the side of the road, then turned the radio dial around in time to hear Hal say, "You there?"

"Go ahead."

"We got us a situation over at the temporary housing."

"The apartments where I'm staying?"

"Nah, the new ones going up behind you. Weirdest thing you ever did see."

Ben's mind sorted through a category of possibilities, all of them bad. "Can you give me something more?"

"Some newcomers showed up wanting accommodations." A long pause, then, "Let's just say they aren't what we were expecting."

"They making trouble?"

"Not so you'd notice. Not yet, anyway. I called on account of wanting some backup when I tell 'em we don't have room."

A faint alarm bell went off. "Don't do that, Hal!"

"Ben, you don't understand. These aren't our kind of folks. They might as well have just landed from one of Neptune's moons."

Ben jammed his car into gear and floored it, ignoring an oncoming vehicle's squeal of brakes and an angry horn. He drove with one hand, shouting now. "Don't tell them a thing! Run back and tell the housing authorities to let them in!"

"Ben—"

"I'm on my way!" He tossed the radio to the floor and used both hands to keep control of the car as he did a four-wheel spin around the corner. Blaring the horn in place of a siren, he barreled through the heart of Douglas and hit seventy before he passed the town limits. He lifted the car up on two wheels making the entrance to the apartment complex, wishing for suspension made for high-speed chases.

He skidded to a halt in front of the sheriff's car, opened his door, and called over, "Did you tell them?"

"Got there just in time." Hal Drew gave him a sideways glance. "What's got you so worked up?"

"Maybe nothing. I hope not, anyway. But I smell trouble."

"In that case, you just hang on a second." Hal walked over, reached through the open window of Ben's car, and picked up the badge. He pinned it over Ben's breast pocket, then asked, "You got a problem with that?"

"There's no law against deputizing a federal agent."

"That's not what I mean, and you know it." He cocked a thumb toward the middle apartment building. "Let's go."

As soon as they climbed the stairs to the second floor, Ben knew he had guessed correctly. Four extremely odd characters stood poised for argument. A slender, middle-aged man stroked a tiny white dog with one beringed hand. He wore a single dangling earring, peroxided hair, and an open sneer. "My goodness gracious, what on earth do we have here? Two big strong sheriff types just to open our little door?"

The second man was Indian or east Asian, overweight and surly. "Is there a problem here?"

"No problem," Ben said. He had already retreated behind his official mask. "How are you gentlemen today?"

"Tired," the dark man snapped. "We want to get inside and get settled."

"Of course you do." Ben turned to the wide-eyed young lady sent over from the housing office. "May I see that, please?"

She surrendered her clipboard without a word. "Thank you. Let's see, Mr. Abel and Mrs. Lawrence, do we have that correctly?"

"Obviously not," the smaller man said. "It's *Mr.* Lawrence, as you can well see."

"Sure. But everything else is correct? You're in the process of relocating from Philadelphia and you have requested subsidized housing? Is that right?"

The first hint of uncertainty entered in. "Precisely."

"Then it looks like everything is in order here." Ben turned to the second couple, silent and watchful. "And here we have Mr. Ibn Rashid and Ms. Goldstein. Formerly of San Francisco. Also applicants under the subsidized housing rule. Correct?"

"Yes."

"Fine. Both of these are just fine." He handed back the clipboard and asked the young lady, "Did you bring keys?"

"Yes, but—"

Ben silenced her with as hard a warning glance as he could possibly muster. She fumbled in her purse, dropped the keys, and let Ben retrieve them. He checked the apartment numbers and handed them over. "I hope you all have a very nice stay with us here. Just let us know if you need anything."

He then turned and ushered the sheriff and the young lady back to the stairwell. As he started down the stairs, Ben turned as though struck by a sudden thought. "Just one thing more," he said in his mildest voice. "North Carolina has some of the strictest decency laws in the United States."

The heavyset man bristled. "Are you threatening us?"

"Not at all, sir. Just doing my duty and informing you that we uphold the law here." He nodded politely. "Welcome to Douglas."

Only when they were halfway across the parking lot did Hal demand, "What was that all about?"

"They're here on orders of the FBI," Ben replied grimly, angry now that it was over. He cast a glance behind him, caught four surprised and disappointed faces staring at them over the balcony railing. He gave a little wave and turned back. "Civil Rights Division."

"Come again?"

"They're seeking to provoke a federal offense," he explained. He asked the young lady, "Have you used federal funds in building these temporary accommodations?"

"I'm sorry, I don't know, I just started—"

"Absolutely," Hal replied. "Federal and state both. I know that for certain."

"Which means that anyone requesting subsidized assistance must be granted accommodation, regardless of race or creed or marital status. They sent these people in *hoping* we would turn them down. Then every official within the local government here, every person involved in the housing organization, everyone remotely connected to the event, could be charged with violating their civil rights."

Hal Drew jammed an angry arm out behind him. "You mean to tell me we got to put up with this mess?"

"I mean to tell you," Ben replied harshly, "this is only the beginning."

TWENTY-FIVE

The storm broke just as the last person entered the police station. Lightning flashed so close the blasts of light and thunder caused those gathered to flinch. The world outside became lost behind a torrent so strong the window looked submerged. Overhead, rain drummed hard upon the roof. Ben Atkins had to raise his voice to be heard. "I've asked you here because we need to prepare for attack."

The lawyer, Phil Trilling, responded from where he leaned against the far wall. "I've been saying that for weeks."

There were fourteen people stuffed inside the station's front office. Ben did not know half of them. Chuck had made some calls, as had Dottie and Hal. Phil Trilling was not the only person who watched Ben with wary hostility. This had to be addressed. "A number of you have every reason not to trust me. If you prefer, I'll lay out what I know and what I suspect. And then I'll leave so you can plan in privacy."

Chuck seemed to have been expecting this or something similar. For he spoke up as soon as Ben stopped, saying, "I'll vouch for Ben."

"So do I," Hal said. "The man saved our bacon today, and that's the truth."

"Me too." This from Jeff Cummins.

"For what it's worth," Dottie added, "I do too."

The rotund little pastor who often acted as Chuck's number two, Paul Caldwell by name, said in his soft southern drawl, "Shoot, I'd be happy to have four folks this fine speak up for me at the Pearly Gates."

The lawyer's stiff stance eased slightly. "I suppose that's all right, then," he said grudgingly.

Ben decided this was the best he could expect at the moment. "Today federal inserts arrived seeking temporary housing. They were intentionally outrageous. The scheme was to provoke a negative reaction. They wanted you to deny them housing, which would result in a federal lawsuit being brought against the community and its leaders."

He had their full attention now. Ben went on, "My guess is, this was only the opening salvo."

"What's that supposed to mean?"

"Something has happened," Ben replied. "Something that elevated the case against Kingdom Come from a preliminary investigation to a criminal case."

"They don't have a thing against us," Trilling scoffed.

"They think they do," Ben countered. "And what they think is important here. I've been trying to contact my superiors back at headquarters. They won't take my calls. This is the clearest possible sign that things are heating up."

Ben's tone and expression had as much effect as his words. He could see the grim cast settle upon most of the faces watching him. Someone asked, "What comes next?"

"More inserts," Ben predicted. "Investigators from different segments of the federal government. They won't seem coordinated from the ground. But believe me, they won't be what they seem."

When no one spoke, Ben pressed, "Has there been anything out of the ordinary over the past few days? Any unexpected meetings? Any unannounced visitors from Washington?"

A middle-aged woman in a burnt-orange suit and shiny pumps raised her hand. "Glenda Wasmuth. I run the bank in Hamlin. We've had the auditors in for our quarterly review. They're about a month early, is the only reason I mention it."

"Have they ever been early before?"

"Now that you mention it, no."

"Then they're not just auditors." Ben found himself tensing further. "What is the worst these guys could do?"

The woman paled. "Revoke our banking license. But—"

"That's what they're after. Believe me. Whatever dirt you have, they'll find."

A square-jawed man spoke up from his place by the door. "I had the IRS show up this morning."

"Your name?"

"Chad Prebble. Prebble Mills. I run the textile company."

Hal was next. "I've spent all day going through the park with two guys from the Department of the Interior. Something about a review of the plan to hand over control of the land."

"It's not going to happen," Ben predicted. "They're after something that they can point to as serious wrongdoing on your part. They want to shut Kingdom Come down."

Chuck broke in with, "What should we do?"

"It's time to circle the wagons," Ben said tightly. "We need to show these guys a single face. Let them know at the outset that we're onto their little games, that we're not going to stand by and let them attack us. Show them we're going to fight back, and fight hard." He waited, giving them a chance to speak up and take over. When they remained silent, he said, "One person should go around and give them a brief, in-your-face warning. Then we put monitors in place. We dog their every step. We look for anything we can use as a basis for a case against *them*. And we'll need to get a legal team organized to begin court actions."

"Leave that to me," Trilling barked. The lawyer was already in fighting mode. "I'll hand those guys their hides."

"That's the idea," Ben agreed.

"I'm not so sure about that," the rotund Georgia pastor countered. "We are a Christian community. We are told to turn the other cheek."

"I can't answer for that," Ben responded. "I can only tell you what I would do under these circumstances. And that is, take the attack to them. Fight hard. Strike the first blow. Don't give them a single solitary inch."

One by one, all the faces in the room turned toward Chuck. He was ready for them. "In this imperfect world, sometimes we must be ready to defend what has been placed in our care. We have to stand up for what's right."

The words seemed to bind them together; even the older pastor seemed willing to nod his acceptance. Chuck turned to Ben and said, "Do what you feel is best."

Ben felt the mantle of responsibility settle upon him. "You're sure about this?"

"I told you from the beginning that I felt you were brought here for a purpose," Chuck replied calmly. "Get to your work."

<hr />

The rain had halted by the time Ben drove over to the textile company's main office. Every surface glistened in shimmering welcome to the returning sun. Clouds loomed on the horizon as Ben walked across the puddle-strewn lot. The sound of more approaching storms only strengthened his resolve.

The man from the IRS could have been cut from a mold. Overweight, black hair matted to his forehead, wrinkled white shirt with shirttail protruding where his belly pushed over his belt, tie at half-mast, dark-framed glasses, flat eyes. He had taken over the company owner's desk. He looked up as Ben entered, noticed the star shining on Ben's lapel, and said, "Don't tell me I double-parked."

"Mr. Seymour, do I have that right?" Ben had stopped by his

apartment and outfitted himself for the occasion. He wore a square-cut dark suit, Stetson, and polished boots. As close to a stern uniform as he could get on such short notice. "Do you have some identification?"

"What is this, a shakedown?" The man had a smarmy whine to his voice, the sign of a permanent chip on his shoulder. "Am I getting rousted here?"

"Looks to me like you're the one doing the rousting." Ben held out his hand. "Identification."

"Is this any attitude to take?" The guy played for innocent. "Is this the way you treat—"

Ben leaned over the desk. "I asked you for an ID."

"Hey, look, you just better take it easy." Even so, he reached into the jacket draped over the chair back and retrieved a billfold. He slid out a plasticized card and handed it over. "You know what I mean?"

"No. What exactly do you mean, Mr. Seymour?" Ben made careful note of all the details. "Is this address correct?"

"None of your business!" The guy jammed his glasses square. "I'm here on assignment from guys big enough to fry your hide, so you better back off!"

"I'll tell you how it is," Ben said, flipping the plastic card back across the desk. "In about three minutes an attorney is going to be marching in here. He is going to make certain that you get all the information you need and that you fill out all your forms exactly right. Am I getting through here?"

"I don't believe this," the guy huffed, nervous now. "You're looking to charbroil what's left of your career, is that it? Spend the rest of your life patrolling the back streets of San Juan?"

"The very first sign we have of you juggling figures or contriving to deny legitimate deductions," Ben went on, "we're going to enter court actions against you. The law now states that IRS agents can be held personally liable for any abuse of power. We'll hit you seven ways from Sunday. We'll tie you up in knots so tight you'll wish you never even heard of this place."

"Must be you're hiding something big," the man blustered, "taking this attitude before I even get started."

"You're the one with the attitude and the hidden agenda," Ben lashed back. "I'm just spelling it out for you in the plainest language I know. Up front and honest. You go looking for trouble, that's exactly what you're going to find."

━━ ✠ ━ ✠ ━━

When Ben Atkins pulled up in front of the Hamlin bank, four cars were there to meet him. The bank's manager remained nervously by the front doors, awaiting Ben's signal. Phil Trilling walked over with a younger man in tow. "This is Bill Witchell, he works in my office."

"I-I'm just a paralegal," the young man faltered. "I don't know a thing about banking law or how to—"

"It doesn't matter, son." To Phil, Ben added, "This is just fine."

Hal stepped over from his patrol car. Jeff Cummins was with him. Hal asked, "You sure you know what you're doing?"

"No, but it's all I could come up with at short notice." Ben nodded to Jeff. "Who's watching the store?"

"Two ladies from the town offices." Jeff gave his contagious grin. "I couldn't just sit there and miss out on all the fun."

Dottie walked up, and Ben asked, "You know how to play this?"

"You kidding? I cut my baby teeth doing hostile interviews." Even so, her features looked tight and wary. She motioned to the pastor accompanying her. "Paul asked if he could come along."

"Decided there ought to be an official representative of our council," the pastor said.

"Okay. Game faces, everybody. Here we go."

Ben marched in at the head of the group, following the manager's silent directions through the main foyer and past all the astonished glances. They pushed past the waist-high swinging gate, a remnant of a more tranquil bygone era. Ben strode up to where the two dark-suited men sat pouring over the bank's confidential records.

Before the men could recover from their initial astonishment, Ben leaned over the desk and got up tight in their faces. The expression he showed beneath his hat brim was enough to push them both back in their seats.

"Here's how it's going to play out," Ben snarled quietly. "We're going to go at this straight by the books. We've got the law here and we've got appointed representatives of the town council. There will be no suggestion made that the bank has failed in its duty to the community. There will be no reference to illegal usury, or bad loans being carried in secret, or money laundering."

"Ah, excuse me." One of the men cleared his throat. "But just exactly who might you be?"

"I'm the guy who's going to turn you both into meat loaf if you step one inch out of line."

"Any charges against the bank will be for us to decide," the other declared sternly.

"You'd better be ready to back them up in court," Ben shot back. "Because that's exactly where we're headed. We're drawing up the papers today."

"But we just got started here!"

"We're doing this in anticipation of your trumped-up regulatory maneuvers," Ben hammered on. "We are *expecting* you to find short-comings that don't exist. We are preparing a counterattack. We are going to have a petition signed by the majority of this entire county, stating in the clearest possible terms that this bank is responsible and upright. That this bank acts as a friend to this community. Which is more than anybody will ever say about either of you."

Ben straightened. "So I suggest you men do your job and do it properly."

———※——※———

By the time Ben arrived home that night, he was as tired as he had been in years. But there was no regret to his decision or his actions. Even the fatigue contained a well-earned edge. It was good to go back to the basics of law enforcement, protecting a community that he was coming to call his own.

Ben halted by the refrigerator, where he found a note taped to the door. He read and he smiled as he stripped off his tie. Mavis Drew wrote that she had learned of his work from Pastor Paul, and seeing as how he probably would be too busy to cook for himself, she and a few friends had stopped by with some provisions. He opened the door and gave a low whistle. The shelves were stuffed to overflowing. Each foil-wrapped plate or plastic tray contained a description and heating instructions. Ben got midway through inspecting the first shelf before hunger took over. He decided on Texas-style chili and homemade sourdough bread.

The IRS had also shown up at the warehousing operation and one of the construction companies. Ben had repeated his little welcoming visit, but obviously word had been passed before he got there, for he was met with stone-faced resistance. To his astonishment, when he had returned to the police station he had discovered a crowd of three or four dozen people milling about in front. Thunder rumbled in the distance, and the wind carried the sweet fragrance of yet more rain. But all attention had been focused on the pastor standing on the police station's front stairs.

Paul Caldwell met Ben with a defiant glare and the words, "There is no reason why we can't add God's good spice to the day." He swept an arm out over the gathering. "These here are some of the finest prayer warriors it's ever been my pleasure to serve with. We're going to spread out and spread the good Word. We're going to pray right around the clock, letting these visitors see just exactly who it is we serve. Inviting them to join not us, but Him."

The reverend set his jaw then, ready for a quarrel. Ben had rubbed his chin hard and worked to hide his smile. When he was certain he could keep his voice level, he said, "I can't think of a single thing that would work better right now."

Now he stood by his kitchen window and watched the clouds do heavenly battle with the setting sun, displaying all the lights of Armageddon across the sky. When the phone rang, he was reluctant to turn from the simple pleasure of his meal and the display. But he thought of Dottie, and decided he could not risk missing her.

Instead it was Evan Hawkins, his boss in Washington. The bureau chief demanded, "What in the world are you doing?"

"Watching the sunset and eating some of the finest chili I've had in years," Ben replied, spooning in another mouthful. "I do believe they used real Angus steak."

"I mean, what are you doing *there?*"

"My job," Ben replied, snagging a chair and pulling it over.

"That's where you're wrong!" The man sounded shriller than Ben could ever recall hearing. "You're committing professional suicide!"

"Well, now," Ben replied, settling himself down. "That's where you and I disagree."

"Listen to me, Ben. Theron Head has real ammo against Kingdom Come."

"I figured he *thought* he did. Otherwise he wouldn't have risked moving this to the criminal level."

"This is the real thing. I've got the file here in front of me. There is direct evidence of the cult illegally diverting funds from tax-exempt sources."

"I've already told you, Evan. This isn't a cult."

"*Listen to me!*" Evan's breath rasped down the line. "Churches within Reverend Griffin's former denomination have supplied us with documentary evidence of funds being diverted to the cult's own coffers."

"Wait, let me see if I might read this a different way." Reluctantly Ben pushed the remains of the chili aside. The meal was too fine to flavor with this discussion. "Believers from the churches in question have withdrawn their support and given it instead to the community here. Which of course has the established churches pretty hot under the collar." When Evan did not respond, Ben finished, "Go tell Head he's going to have to do better than that. Any charges he trumps up based on this nonsense will wind up sending him down in flames."

"Ben, listen to me. Theron Head is going to come hunting for you. The big guns are out and armed."

"I reckon we're ready for them," Ben replied grimly. "You tell Theron Head he'd best go looking for the guilty and stop harassing innocent citizens."

There was a moment's amazed silence, then, "They've got you hooked, haven't they? You've been turned."

"Something like that."

"You of all people. I'd never have believed it." A rough sigh. "Ben, I'm through with you. You're beyond help."

"I wish I could show you," Ben replied, "just how wrong you are."

TWENTY-SIX

When the call came that Thursday morning, Wayne Oates noticed nothing out of the ordinary. Later he would look back from the position of perfect hindsight and see how, yes, this was indeed a major turning. But when Theron Head made what had become his daily call, Wayne Oates sensed little beyond a definite lack of progress. It had been several days since they stepped up their activity against Kingdom Come. The morning phone calls had become a normal part of Wayne's routine. Theron liked to call just after eight. That morning Justin placed the call as usual, no greeting or small talk, just "Hold for the chief." A click, then the familiar banal voice demanded, "Anything new?"

"Good morning, sir. No, nothing significant."

"I didn't ask for you to judge what was and was not crucial, Oates. I asked for change."

"Right. Sorry, sir." Wayne slid to the edge of his seat, positioned now at academy-style rigid attention. "On Saturday we brought in the highway patrol as you instructed. Explained we were working to stamp out a dangerous cult, requested their assistance."

"Any trouble there?"

"A few officers complained that this amounted to unnecessary harassment, particularly those who have contacts inside. We made note of them. I have a meeting scheduled with the regional chief today and will request they get assigned elsewhere."

"Good. Go on."

"We've stepped up the halts of cars coming in and out of the compound. We're ticketing them for everything from exceeding the speed limit by one mile to faulty taillights to erratic steering. But the results so far are so meager I'm not sure I should even waste your—"

"Skip the analysis and the apology and give me the data!"

Wayne caught himself up short. It was the first time Theron Head had spoken in anything but his dull little monotone, the first time his insipid mask had cracked. Clearly the man was feeling the strain as well. "That's about all from this end, sir. Is there anything new about Ben Atkins?"

"He has taken a leave of absence. Apparently he has not had a vacation in three years. He put the request through official channels and it was accepted before I could . . . Never mind." The moment's silence spoke volumes. Agent Atkins was proving a serious nuisance, coordinating activities within the community, anticipating many of their actions. Definitely counted now among the enemy. "Forget Atkins. He'll be staked out and skinned with the others. What about our inserts, anything new there?"

Wayne had dreaded the question. "No progress, sir. The locals continue to dog their every step. And their numbers are growing."

"Any threats? Pressure tactics? Abuse?"

"Nothing but prayer, sir. Apparently they work like tag teams, always a dozen nearby the inserts, following them wherever they go inside the compound, meeting them as soon as they return, standing around wherever they're working."

Theron Head faltered. "They are praying?"

"All the time. Hundreds of them." Led by a pastor shaped like a bald butterball with glasses and a Georgia drawl, according to the IRS agent auditing the construction company. But Wayne Oates decided there was no need to mention that. "It's got some of our people rattled, I can tell you."

"All right, that's enough. The gloves are coming off. We're moving to full-on tactics here. We have got to force these people's hand. Something needs to be found that can be turned against them, and it needs to happen now." The voice tightened slightly. "Officials from the Department of the Interior should arrive this morning. They will determine that parkland has been encroached on in some way. The Bureau of Alcohol, Firearms and Tobacco is also going to begin its own inspection. We'll harass Kingdom Come to the point of no return, if necessary, until they show their true, deadly colors."

Wayne felt his hand begin to tingle, as though the phone it held had become a tuning fork for Theron Head's compressed rage. "What do you want from this end?"

"Coordinate their inspections, for starters. But what I *want* is to hear you have found something we can use to bring in the big guns."

"But sir—"

"I have a meeting with two reporters at four, and at five I am being interviewed for national television. Do you hear what I'm saying, Oates?"

"You need concrete evidence. But—"

"More than that, Oates. Far more. I need a *case*. I need it *now*." When Wayne did not respond, Theron gave the screws a further turning. "Our careers are riding on making this case, Oates. Yours and mine. Tomorrow the American people are going to hear about this with their morning coffee. The day after that, I and my little team will move into the national spotlight. After that we have the leverage to catapult into the highest federal realms. Do I make myself clear?"

"Perfectly," Wayne replied, suddenly breathless.

"Evidence of criminal wrongdoing at Kingdom Come, Oates. Bring it to me. Now."

The phone went dead.

Dottie was just locking her front door when her mobile phone rang. She fumbled in her purse, pulled out the recharged phone, and, assuming it was her editor, answered with, "I'm not ready for another go. Not yet."

But a woman's voice said, "Is this Mrs. Betham?"

"It's Ms. actually. Who is this?"

"My name is Rebecca Painton. I don't know if you remember, but we met—"

"At the Orlando church. Of course." Dottie slung her purse and started for the stairs, wondering what possible reason the missionary had for calling. "How are you?"

"Are you still looking for a story?"

The blunt question halted her midway down the stairwell. "Actually, I wasn't down investigating Reverend Innes. My assignment is about—"

"But you'd be interested in a story about the church, wouldn't you? Something big?" The missionary held to her same subdued tone, but now it was the quiet of hypertense control.

"I'm not sure. Possibly."

"We've uncovered, that is, I'm afraid there's something horrible—" She sounded as though she was choked off.

"Ms. Painton? Rebecca?"

"I'm at a pay phone outside the church. I can't talk."

"Can you get to a more secure line?"

"No, no. There's no time. This is *urgent*."

"Does it have anything to do with the Kingdom Come affair?"

"The community up in North Carolina? I don't see . . . oh, I don't know, I wish I knew what to do. All I know for certain is this is *serious*. It's worse than that. It's *tragic*."

Dottie stepped over to where the open stairwell permitted the sunlight in. She fished in her purse and drew out a pad and pen. "What is it exactly you're facing, Ms. Painton?" When the woman didn't respond, Dottie pressed. "Can you give me something specific?"

"I can do better than that. I can show you. But you have to come."

"Where, to Orlando?"

"I'll meet you at the airport. There's a Delta flight leaving from Charlotte in two and a half hours. I've checked. I'll be waiting at the gate."

"All right." Dottie sighed, already regretting her decision. "I'll come."

TWENTY-SEVEN

Thurgood Innes liked to take part of Thursday afternoon to do the initial outlining of his Sunday sermon. Two hours every week were set aside from an overpacked schedule, hours that his secretary had long since learned could never be interrupted. The entire church staff trod softly during this period. Which made the tumult echoing from his outer office even more surprising.

Thurgood tried to ignore it, but in truth he was not getting any work done. That morning he had received a call from Lloyd Bowick, the synod's elder statesman, who had personally visited the cult enclave. Bowick had called to report that without question they were facing another bona fide transformation within their church. Why Charles Griffin had elected to establish this isolated community, Bowick could not say. But the revival was definitely happening. Innes had not spoken a word during the entire conversation. Lloyd had concluded by saying that similar communities were sprouting up everywhere, smaller Kingdom Come enclaves in eighteen states now, and he was going to go join one. Thurgood had hung up the phone a thoroughly shaken man.

Outside his office the voices rose another notch, loud enough for Thurgood to recognize that one of them belonged to Miller Kedrick. Thurgood rose from his desk and walked over and opened the door. "What on earth is going on out here?"

"I told him, sir. Over and over." The secretary's face was beet red. "But he just won't listen!"

"You've got to fire this woman!" Kedrick's voice was louder, his face almost purple. "And get yourself somebody who knows how to follow orders!"

"That is exactly what she is doing." Innes wanted to scream as well, furious over the man and his exasperating habits, angry as well over the confusion he felt about this cult business. Logic told him he was right in condemning the Carolina commune. His mind shouted that all was going exactly as it should. Yet there was something about this whole affair that just would not leave him alone. "I left explicit orders not to be bothered. After all the time you've spent here, you should know this for yourself!"

"Never mind that!" Miller waved the papers he bunched in one fist out in front of him. "This won't wait."

"It most certainly will." Thurgood glanced at his watch. "I have another fifty minutes to put together—"

"The FBI office closes in a half-hour! You've got to call your contact up there in Charlotte and tell them what I've found!"

"I won't—" Innes ground to a halt. "What did you say?"

"I've found it!" The papers were crumpled and tattered from Kedrick's tight-fisted grip. "What we've been looking for all along. This is going to nail Kingdom Come's hide to the wall!"

"Aren't you the person who didn't want us to get involved with the FBI?"

"It's too late for that now! This just came in from a church in South Carolina. I've had feelers out, and we've finally hit pay dirt. Their senior elder joined the cult, and he left a *serious* personal mess behind when he left. We're talking major A-bomb type ammunition here!"

"Then would you mind telling me," Innes said, "why you don't just pick up the phone and call the FBI yourself?"

Anger turned to bluster. "I can't do that. I'm not the head guy. My name doesn't carry any weight. Besides, you're the one the FBI contacted, not me."

"Let's try another question, then." Innes crossed his arms. "What's your problem with Kingdom Come?"

"I . . . What are you talking about? You're the one who took the case before the synod!"

"I know I am. And it was with your backing. As a matter of fact, ever since their name first came up at the church meeting, you've been attacking them."

The arm dropped to Kedrick's side, the eyes narrowed. "And you haven't?"

"We're talking about you," Innes said, holding to his quiet tone with difficulty. "I want to know why you have despised them so."

"Despise is right." Kedrick ground his teeth. "I can't believe we're having this conversation. The clock is ticking!"

Innes remained firmly planted. "I'm waiting for an answer, Miller."

"You want the FBI back down here again, sniffing around?" Miller shot back. "You never know what they might turn up."

"You're saying there is a problem with our books?"

"Of course not! I check them personally!" A faint sheen of perspiration dotted the bullish man's brow. "Federal attention can't do us anything but harm. They might threaten our tax-exempt status. They could fall on us like a horde of locusts. You haven't seen what it's like when you get stuck under their microscope. I have. Believe me, you want to keep the guard dogs on the other side of the fence."

Innes hesitated. His gut instinct was that something else was at work here. The FBI had only recently been called in, yet Miller had been opposed to Kingdom Come since the beginning. "They're dealing with the Carolina cult, not us."

Miller rattled the pages once more. "Which is why you need to call them right now!"

But Innes was not ready to let this one go. His secretary remained seated at her desk, following the conversation, her head moving back and forth, her mouth hanging open. Innes could well understand her surprise. He never confronted Miller. It just wasn't his way. "Even so, I fail to understand why—"

"You still don't get it, do you?"

Innes stopped. He had heard those words before. It took a moment, then he remembered. At the synod, Miller had said the exact same thing. "Get what, Miller?"

"You can't have two top dogs." Miller's voice had descended to a rough growl. His lips were pulled back tight enough to reveal teeth flat as tombstones. "Not to a business, not to a synod, not to anything."

"Chuck Griffin is hardly a senior official of—"

"Not now. But you don't hear things like I do. I'm on the phone all the time to the other finance guys. I know things. Like how the churches are getting bled by this cult business. It's growing like wildfire. It's sucking in people, and it's sucking out our money." A finger punched the air between them, the pages bundled in the fist rattling for emphasis. "There's only one way to handle a threat from the competition, buster. And that's to grind them into the dust. Bury them. And do it fast."

If the elder's phone call had disturbed him, it was nothing compared to what Innes sensed now. He felt his skin crawl. "What if they're right?"

Miller's eyes widened with surprise. "Right about what?"

"What if it's not a cult at all?" The confession of his own fears wrenched him. "What if it really is a revival?"

"So what?" The sneer tightened. "You know how it is. These things come and they go. History is full of losers, Thurgood. The world only remembers the winners."

Thurgood had heard enough. "If you have something for the authorities, call them yourself."

"But—"

Innes stepped back inside his office and shut the door. He stood there, leaning against the door, his stomach churning. He walked to his desk and sat down. This would definitely be a week to pull a sermon from the files.

TWENTY-EIGHT

Evan Hawkins walked down the back second-floor hallway to FBI headquarters, doing his best not to appear furtive. He knocked on the open door. "Mrs. Tottler? May I have a minute?"

The woman had been holding her forehead with one hand. When she looked up, her eyes strained to focus against the overhead light. "I know you, don't I?"

"Evan Hawkins. I'm deputy assistant director of the Criminal Investigation Division."

"Oh, right." She made an effort to draw herself together. "Sure. Have a seat."

"Thank you." Evan checked the hallway before shutting the door. The woman had been assigned an office on the second floor, in the administration and personnel division. He walked over and sat down. "I just wanted to have a word about the Carolina investigation."

Her face pulled into a thousand strained furrows. "Mr. Head said I was all done with that."

"You are, you are." Evan smiled tightly. He had not been invited to the woman's debriefing, had not even known she was back from her unannounced vacation. That morning Evan's secretary had heard from a friend in personnel of Tottler's sudden appearance. Fran Tottler's assignment to the administrative division apparently carried

Theron Head's personal signature. "It's all fine, Ms. Tottler. I just wanted to ask a couple of questions, if that's all right."

"I suppose so." Her face said it was anything but all right.

He should not be here. It was going outside channels and directly against orders. He knew Fran Tattler was out of bounds. But Evan needed to know. He *had* to find out more. "Could you please tell me what's happening down in North Carolina?"

"It was a nightmare."

"Why do you say that?"

"A thousand things. You wouldn't understand. No one does." Fran Tottler was a woman on the edge. Her hair had the ragged appearance of someone who had done her personal grooming with garden shears. Her eyes were sunken. Her face sagged with a great burden of weariness. "You'd have to have been there yourself."

"Could you give me anything specific that I could—"

"They prayed over me."

"—use in justifying charges against—" Evan stopped. "I beg your pardon?"

"All the time. In stages. They were always there. Ringing my doorbell and asking me to come here and there. They knew I was inserted as part of an ongoing investigation. But they were always after me. They took me to church."

Evan leaned back in his seat. "To church."

"It was . . . intense." She dug in her purse, pulled out a pack of cigarettes. "Sorry, I need to go outside. Now."

"Just one minute more." Seated here with this distraught woman, he could not get the last conversation with Ben Atkins out of his mind. How calm the man had seemed. How divorced from the bureaucratic fray. "Did you see anything illegal going on?"

"They showed me what they wanted me to see." She rose to her feet with a jerk. "They tied me up in knots."

"But did you see anything that might point to—"

"Look, I know I blew the investigation and my career." She bounced off the desk as she tried to round it. "I'd give anything to change things around and never set foot in that place. But I can't."

Evan reached over and touched her arm. Reluctantly the woman stopped. The cigarette pack was crumpled and knotted by her tense grip. "Please, Ms. Tottler. Did you see anything that could justify us opening a criminal investigation against Kingdom Come?"

She scarcely seemed to see him at all. "I tell you what it was like. You know the training films they show us about the brainwashing of prisoners? How kidnappers can turn their victims to their side? That's how it felt." She wrenched her arm free. But when she reached the door she halted once more. Without turning back, she added, "I dream about the place. It's the worse nightmare I've ever had. I wake up feeling like I'll never be the same again. Never."

⚊⚊

Wayne Oates sat surrounded by all the fears he had hoped to have left behind forever. Beyond the inner window spread the activity of another normal day. The Charlotte office was following sixteen cases at present—not too heavy a load, but enough to keep the phones ringing and the agents moving. Wayne was the only officer not active. He could not find the energy to do anything but sit there and watch the biggest chance of his entire career go straight down the drain.

The truth of the matter was, he had not turned up anything that would justify lodging criminal charges against the Kingdom Come cult. He knew the threat was there, he *knew* it. Yet he had failed to come up with anything substantial. In order for them to move, they needed something major. Then they could classify this as a dangerous cult that had to be surrounded and shut down immediately. The problem they faced was, as Ben Atkins had irritatingly stated, there was no evidence of lawbreaking, no reason to penetrate and take them out.

Wayne swiveled to the sun-splashed outer window and said to the empty room, "Theron Head is going to cook me over a slow fire."

Strange that those words would come to mind. It had been a favorite expression of his father. Only for his father the threat had always come from the banks. Every autumn, once the tobacco harvest was in and the auctions made and the money counted, that was what his father would say. The banks were gonna roast him alive. His daddy had spent a lifetime hanging on to their farm by the skin of his teeth and eighteen-hour days. Year in, year out, until the strain of never making it to safety finally got to be too much. Ten years ago this coming autumn, the old man had been out walking the fields and chanting his worries, when he stopped, keeled over, and was gone. Now it was Wayne's older brother who moaned about the bank and the debt and the prices and the anti-tobacco people. When Wayne went back to the old homestead, which was not often, he always left feeling like his daddy had bequeathed the chant to Wayne's brother as a legacy.

Wayne had always hated the farm. Loathed it with the bitter taste of a child's sweat. Wayne's most vivid memory of his childhood was as a six-year-old, lugging a burlap sack down the rows of plants and pulling the tobacco worms off the lower leaves. The bottom leaves always ripened first, and the worms would devour a two-foot leaf in a matter of hours. The worms were grayish green and wet and thick as his thumb, with little suckers that had to be ripped free of the leaf. The July and August heat became trapped inside those long rows, baking the earth and the boy dragging that squirming burlap bag. The smell of ripening tobacco would leave him dizzy and oftentimes give him a headache that pounded worse than the heat. By the time he finished the field, he'd have close to fifteen pounds of worms. His brother and his father used them for fishing bait. Those nights Wayne dined on hush puppies and cole slaw. The childhood Wayne would have rather starved than eat fish that had consumed one of those worms. Still to this day, Wayne despised seafood.

He stared out at the sunlit day and could feel the same sense of being held down and trapped that he had known all through his growing-up years. He would do anything to keep from going back there again. Anything at all.

At the knock on his door, Wayne turned slowly around. The other staff all knew he was working under Theron Head's direct supervision. They all treated him with a newfound respect. He had come to love it. "Yes?"

"Are you in for a call?"

"Who is it?" Not Theron. Nor Justin, his Aryan assistant with the stone-killer eyes. He did not want to tell either of them that the inserts had turned up nothing at all.

"He wouldn't give his name. But he knew yours. And he said it was something to do with your investigation, and that it was urgent."

Wayne reached for the phone. "Oates."

A hard-edged voice demanded, "You still looking for dirt on that cult thing?"

He sat up straighter. "What cult are we talking about?"

"Come on, give me a break. We both know what I mean."

"Who is this, please?"

"Nobody, that's who. And I'm not calling. We never spoke. You got that?"

Wayne recalled a bullish man in a Cadillac Esplanade outside an Orlando church. Wayne waved frantically for attention. "All right. I'm listening."

"You still haven't answered me. Are you looking for dirt?"

The staffer returned to his doorway. Wayne cupped the phone and mouthed, "Trace this. Fast." Then he continued to the phone, "Any evidence you have that would help us with an ongoing investigation would be appreciated."

"That's what I wanted to hear." The man's voice rasped hard, as though he was fighting a battle just to make the call. "Go to your fax machine."

The line went dead. Wayne rose from his chair. The staffer met him as he exited the office with, "No chance. The connection was too brief."

"Try the fax line." He heard the fax machine begin to purr and walked faster. When a secretary reached for the emerging page, he snapped, "I'll take that."

As he read, he felt the world lift from his shoulders. It was almost too good to be true. He checked the address. A church less than thirty miles beyond the South Carolina border. Easy enough to follow up. He read the next page, which was better. Court records were hard to doctor.

"Excuse me, Wayne?"

Reluctantly he turned from his reading. "Did you trace it?"

"No, too short a signal." The staffer showed wide-eyed apology. "And Theron Head's assistant is on line four."

He had to laugh. The timing was that perfect. "I'll take it in my office."

When the call was forwarded to his boss, Wayne was still smiling. "Mr. Head, how nice to hear from you again."

"I'm still waiting for you to deliver. And I hate waiting."

"I have located something that might interest you." Wayne read out the details.

"This is excellent," Head said. "Outstanding."

"I haven't had a chance to double-check anything yet."

"Do it."

"I'll get back to you within the hour."

"Make it faster."

Wayne waited for the phone to click, then softly settled the receiver back down. And took the first comfortable breath of the day. He scanned the sheets one more time. Things were definitely about to take a turn for the better.

TWENTY-NINE

Dottie Betham came out of the tunnel connecting the plane to the Orlando airport terminal, and instantly spotted the missionary. Rebecca Painton wore yet another wraparound skirt and sun-bleached blouse. But her expression was utterly hostile and wary. She watched Dottie approach with no sign of welcome whatsoever.

When Dottie set down her overnight bag and her briefcase, Rebecca announced, "There's been a terrible mistake. You shouldn't have come."

"What are you talking about?" Dottie asked. "*You* were the one who called me, remember?"

"That was the worst mistake of all." The voice was flat, the gaze pinched. "I can't imagine why I ever thought I was being divinely urged to trust you with . . . Never mind. I'm sorry to have disturbed you."

"Why on earth did you wait until I got here to change your mind?"

"It wasn't until I arrived at the airport that I saw how wrong I was to ask you. I thought you were an answer to a prayer. And then I got out here and realized what a dreadful blunder I was making."

"Something here at the airport made you change your mind about . . ." Her gaze followed Rebecca's as it glanced over to the terminal's corner. There in front of the newsstand entrance was a floor-display containing the latest issue of *Newsday*. "Oh no."

"I'm sorry I can't offer to repay you for your journey. I don't have—"

"Oh, don't tell me." Dottie held out her hand. "Give me your copy."

"I threw it away. I couldn't bear to keep it."

"Oh no, no, no, *no*." Dottie moved off, then turned back and ordered, "You wait right here."

She bought a copy and started back, flipping through the pages. Then she stopped, horrified. She scanned the article, scarcely believing what she saw. She forced herself to return to where Rebecca stood, though the shock and shame left her sick to her stomach. She said weakly, "This isn't what I wrote."

"How can you say that?" Rebecca cried. "Your name is there on the page!"

"They've changed it. They've changed *everything!*" Dottie dropped the magazine, then grabbed Rebecca with one hand and her briefcase and bag with the other. She started toward the nearest seats. Ignoring the glances cast by passing travelers, she shrilled, "They've completely shredded my work!"

"I don't have time for this." Rebecca tried to drag her heels. "I've got—"

"You have got to sit down and *read*." Dottie unzipped her case, drew out her laptop, and pulled up the file containing Monday night's work. She deposited the computer into Rebecca's lap. "This was my article!"

As Rebecca read, Dottie strode back and picked up the magazine. She started to reread the piece but could not finish it. Furiously she ripped out the pages, then tore them into ever-smaller bits. A mother gripped her child's shoulder and steered a wide course around Dottie.

When Rebecca raised an astonished face toward Dottie, Dottie walked back over and collapsed into the next seat. Rebecca whispered, "What they did is just *horrible.*"

"I put my heart and soul into that piece." Dottie looked back to where the pages lay in tatters and saw not the article but her career. "It was the best thing I ever wrote. The very best."

"But why did they *do* it?"

"The magazine had decided to take a certain slant." She had seen it enough to know. In fact, she had done it often enough herself. "They went after what would make for headlines and satisfy their readers. People like to consider the very religious to be extremists. So that's how they decided to cover Kingdom Come, as a group of extremists with the power to sway the normal, to distort perception, and to draw in the unwary." She stared down at the paper fragments, her mind reforming the pictures Ed Starling had inserted around her twisted words. The photographs the magazine had selected were all of cultish disasters—the burning buildings from Waco, the Jonestown suicide horror. She looked away, took a breath, swallowed against the rising rage. "This is what sells."

"But it's not the truth!"

"No," Dottie agreed quietly, dirtied by the part she had played. Not merely this time, but in the past. It was, she bitterly decided, a fitting punishment. "But the magazine can justify its actions by saying, this *could* be the truth."

Rebecca stood, walked over, and picked up Dottie's bag. "Come on, then."

Dottie had trouble finding the strength to follow. "Where are we going?"

"We have a plane waiting over in the private hangar." Rebecca was already walking toward the monorail to the main terminal. "It's a little hard to explain, hard even for me to believe. But recently a man who flies products from Saint Catherine has come to the Lord. And what he's told me, if it's true, has to be told to the world."

THIRTY

When the phone rang, Ben Atkins was so busy with troubles already unfolding that he hesitated over whether he could handle any more just then. Hal was driving flat out, the siren whooping away overhead, the noise so alien that people were halting and turning and pointing as they passed. When Ben did not respond to the ringing, Hal offered, "Either that's a phone in your pocket or you got yourself a mighty strange case of indigestion."

Ben pulled out the phone and said, "Atkins."

"Oh, good. I didn't want to leave a message."

"Dottie?"

"Yes. Listen, I'm in Orlando. At the airport. I'm chasing down a story."

He gripped the dashboard as Hal took the corner at a tire-screeching speed. "I tried to call you."

"Is that the siren I hear?"

Ben decided there was nothing to be gained by sharing his woes. "It can wait."

"All right." She sounded very tense herself. "I'm flying down to Saint Catherine."

"The island in the Caribbean?"

"That's right. Apparently transport via a private airplane has been arranged by a missionary I met. I don't actually know what's behind

237

all this. They say it's easier to show me than to try to explain. I just wanted someone to know where I was, and I called you."

Ben tried to put a little more emphasis than needed behind the words. "I'm glad you did."

"Listen, there's something very important I need you to do for me. Have you seen the latest issue of *Newsday*?"

"No."

"There's an article in there about Kingdom Come. It's just horrible, Ben." Her voice broke momentarily. Another big breath, then, "It has my name on it, but it's not what I wrote. It's important you tell everyone. Please. This is vital."

"I'll tell them." Hal turned down the Hamlin main street, and Ben finished with, "Things are heating up, if the press is coming out against us."

"You sound worried."

"I'd like to tell you, but now's not the time." Ben was already unstrapping himself before Hal pulled to a halt and cut the motor and siren. "How long will you be gone?"

"I'm not sure. A couple of days, probably. I'll call you later."

"Good. I have to go now." But even under these circumstances, the words were not complete. As he rose from the car he used the moment's isolation to say, "Dottie, I've been thinking about you a lot."

Her tone lightened immensely. "It's so good to speak with you, Ben. You just don't know."

When Ben cut the connection, Hal walked around the car and offered, "Dottie's about as fine as they come."

"Yes." Then he put it aside. He had to. The crisis brewing inside did not permit any room for what warmed his heart just then.

The rotund Georgia pastor stepped through the law office's doorway and said, "This time they've gone too far."

Ben allowed himself to be ushered inside. The entire group of elders, everyone who had been seated upon the stage that first town meeting, was crammed inside Phil Trilling's office. "Why aren't you at the town offices?"

"We didn't want this to get out until we had a chance to prepare a response." Phil waved him and Hal to spaces by the window. "Sorry, there aren't any seats left."

A gray-headed woman exclaimed, "I want to know what we're going to *do* about this!"

"Just a moment, Sandra." To Ben, Phil Trilling asked, "How much do you know?"

"Only that one of the people has been arrested."

"Three of them, actually. A family. Have you met Lando Buhler?"

"Not that I recall."

"A fine man," someone offered. "Solid as they come."

"Lando is a dentist here in Hamlin. He's originally from some-place, Austria maybe—"

"Hungary," the woman supplied. "Budapest."

"Anyway, he's a naturalized citizen." A big breath. "He's divorced. His wife left him three years—"

"Four," Sandra corrected. "Almost five."

Phil gave the woman an exasperated glance. "Today the police arrived and arrested him for parental kidnapping and child abuse."

The woman moaned softly, shook her head.

Ben demanded, "Does anybody know this family? I don't mean on an occasional basis. I mean, is someone close enough to be certain these charges are unfounded?"

"I lived next door to them for six months, until our house was ready." This came from Sandra. "Those children were a delight. And Lando was one of the finest fathers I have ever met."

"He lives for his children," another agreed. "He was always making time for them and their activities."

"You see things," another offered. "Like how he would show up at a soccer match, and his children would shout and jump and wave to him. These are not abused kids. No way."

Resignation hollowed Ben's voice. "Then the FBI is behind this."

"How can you be so sure? The state police made the arrest."

"They must have been acting on a federal warrant." He turned to Phil. "Let me guess. Since Lando has been taken into custody, further charges have been leveled against him. Maybe unlawful flight to avoid prosecution."

"And the harboring of noncustodial children," Phil agreed.

"These are common tactics," Ben explained to the room. The knowledge he was correct left his chest aching. These were his people, being attacked by the organization he had given his life to serving. His loyalties were set now. But it made this no easier. "The strategy is called *gathering companion cases*. The FBI wants to level as many different state and federal offenses as they can against the defendant. Then the agency can go public and wave this great sheaf of papers in front of the cameras. 'Look at everything that's happening down there in North Carolina,' they'll say. 'We don't have any choice but to bring in the troops and disband the community.'"

Sandra protested weakly, "How can you be so sure?"

"I've seen it happen a dozen times before with big cases that warrant national attention. You might as well know, I just got a call from Dottie. She says we've made the big time. *Newsday* is carrying an article about Kingdom Come this week, and it is highly critical. She wanted us to know that even though it carries her name, she did not write it. Having one of the national magazines draw attention our way means the feds will be under pressure to act fast."

Phil asked, "What do we do?"

"There's no choice," Ben said, pushing himself off the wall. "We have to intensify our counterattack."

Ben drove Hal's official car toward Charlotte. Chuck Griffin sat in the front seat beside him. As they were preparing to depart, the pastor had announced that he needed to come along, and that Paul Caldwell and Hal were to remain behind and pass the news along to the community. Phil Trilling and one of his associates sat in the backseat. In the rearview mirror Ben caught occasional glimpses of Phil's suspicious face. Clearly the attorney was having difficulty seeing Ben as one of the good guys. Ben understood completely. After all, it was his own organization who was on the offensive.

Other than insisting that he needed to come along, Chuck had not spoken at all. It was only as they sped through the community's perimeter that Chuck murmured, "I've always loathed that fence."

"What?" Ben cast the pastor a swift glance. "Why?"

When the pastor did not speak, Phil said from the backseat, "But you were the one who said—"

"I know I was. And I still don't understand why the thing is there." Chuck sank down low in his seat and said tiredly, "Every time I go through, I wonder. I can't help it. Why were we called to build it? Are we preparing an island against the tide of Armageddon? Are these truly the end times? Or is there another reason?"

Phil's young associate asked, "What does God say?"

"Nothing." Chuck shook his head. "God chooses when and where to speak. About the fence He has not spoken, other than that it needed to be built."

Phil offered, "I was amazed at how easy it was to get all the property owners to agree."

"I kept hoping someone would object," Chuck confessed. "A refusal would be the perfect excuse not to go ahead." As they crested the rise, he turned and said, "Look at that thing, will you? It shines in the sun like a beacon. Like a magnet for all the trouble we're facing." He swung back around and muttered, "Poor Lando. Those poor kids."

Phil objected, "You can't think all this is because of the fence."

Chuck did not respond. Ben gave a single jerk of a nod. He agreed with the pastor's unspoken response. The fence was definitely something the outside world could point to and use to justify their indignation.

The car remained silent until Ben pulled onto the state highway. Then Chuck said, "Sometimes it isn't necessary to know God's will about a particular action He has simply called us to *do*. I still don't know the ultimate purpose behind our settlement. Is it to establish a new form of Christian community, a point from which revival will rise and sweep through the country? Or are we to remove ourselves from a society that is becoming increasingly depraved? Or is this a mark of the Second Coming? I have no idea." He turned toward Ben and added, "I still don't know what purpose God has in store for you here in the community. I can only accept that He is calling you."

A stiff wind had started up, tossing about the surrounding trees and causing the sunlight to shiver across the windshield. Ben started to object that his work seemed pretty clear, but he found himself answering the question before he spoke; the pastor was not talking about the here and now.

It took a while for him to digest this, the idea that his work in the community might not be just for the moment. It was only when they turned off the four-lane highway that he asked, "How does God speak to you?"

Chuck responded so swiftly he had clearly either been expecting the question or had answered it many times before, at least in his own mind. "You see how the sunlight hits this car? You see how natural it is? So normal we can easily forget the majesty and the power behind it."

They entered downtown Charlotte and pulled into the parking lot attached to the city tower. They walked through the connecting tunnel and entered the foyer. They passed through the metal detectors, showed the guards their IDs, and took the elevators to the secure floor containing the entrance and visiting rooms for the county lockup.

Ben could not help but reflect on his last visit there, when he had watched Chuck Griffin being interrogated. From the tight-eyed glance cast his way by Phil Trilling, the attorney was clearly wondering what his motives were this time around.

The guards had obviously been expecting an attorney to show up for Lando, but not one accompanied by a federal agent. The policeman at the entrance control-booth examined his badge and said to Ben, "You're with them?"

"That's right."

"But I thought you guys said to hold things up."

Ben cast the pastor a glance. "There's been a change in plans."

"Right. Okay. Sure." He pressed the button, and the door buzzed. "Interrogation room six. I'll have the suspect brought right down."

"Thank you."

When they were alone in the windowless chamber, Chuck asked him, "What is this going to do to your career?"

"I doubt seriously," Ben replied, "that I'll have much of a career left by the time this is over."

Phil's gaze eased somewhat. A trace of uncertainty, a lingering inspection, then he turned away as the outer door clanged and the shackled prisoner was led inside. The man spotted Chuck and sobbed with relief. "Reverend, I didn't do this. You've got to—"

"Easy, brother." Chuck gave him a solid embrace, then moved aside for the attorney to do the same. "Do you know Ben Atkins?"

"I've seen you around." His own gaze reflected Phil's alarm. "But it's you guys who arrested me."

Ben waited for the guard to lock Lando's wrist to the metal table and depart. Only then did he say, "I had no part of what's going on here. My only job right now is to get this cleared up. And fast."

Lando was fine-boned, perhaps five-ten with dark hair, black eyes, and a slightly liquid accent. "Pastor Chuck, they took my children."

"We'll work on that as well."

"They're going to give them back to their mother." The thought choked off both air and sound. He swallowed so loudly Ben could hear it from his place by the door. "That would be a terrible thing. You can't let it happen."

"Why not?" This from Ben.

"Because she's manic-depressive." Lando's gaze remained fixed upon the pastor. "She's been in and out of mental institutions. Twice while we were married, and twice since then."

"This is good," Ben said to Phil. "Very good."

"No it's not!" Lando's features were wrenched with agony. "It's a nightmare! The children are terrified of her! One minute she's fine, the next she's a totally different person, screaming nonsense at them. It's the only reason I agreed to the divorce, to get them away from her."

Phil was taking swift notes. "Where was she institutionalized?"

"The Harley Spring Center, down in Columbia."

"She checked herself in?"

"Once. I did it the second time, that's why she divorced me when she got out. And then the social workers put her back the last two times. I heard about this from one of our neighbors. When she gets off her medicine, she's a menace."

Ben had heard enough. "All right, this is how it's going to play out." He pointed to Phil's young associate. "You get started on Lando's release. Pastor, you go talk to the social workers; their head honcho will probably be somewhere in this same building. If not, they can tell you where to go. Find out where they've stashed the children." Ben ignored Lando's moan. He said to Phil, "You come with me."

Reluctantly the attorney rose to his feet. "I ought to stay and make sure the release—"

"Your associate can handle that. You need to be there when I speak to the care manager at the clinic in Columbia. How long a drive is it?"

"An hour and a half."

"All right. There's a coffee shop off the foyer; we passed it on our way in. We'll meet up there in six hours. Then all together we're going over to the newspaper."

Phil was still struggling to catch up. "Why involve them?"

"Because we don't have any choice." Ben hammered on the door to attract the guard's attention. "You know what a fire wall is? When a brushfire threatens to get out of control, the firefighters will light a strip of downwind terrain, a controlled burn broad enough to halt the wildfire's progress. That's what we've got to do." He noticed that Chuck was smiling slightly at him and demanded, "Something the matter?"

"Not a thing. Not at all." He raised his hand, a benediction as gentle as his voice. "Blessings on your trip and on your quest."

THIRTY-ONE

But things did not start out well at all. Ben walked the long prison corridor, passing by the bars with prisoners' hands protruding, their voices ringing loud, their curses crashing like blows. It was like that in every prison where he had ever been—except the empty lockup at Kingdom Come. Here the jailers walked their slow endless passage, the keys and the sticks rattling from their belts, and the prisoners stood with their forearms resting on the horizontal bars. To walk down a prison corridor was to pass a long line of slack hands, tattooed and dirty and limp. When he was in a hurry, like now, he could make it down the entire line and see not a single face, just hear the curses strike him and observe the long line of empty hands.

Then he turned the corner and almost ran into Wayne Oates.

There was nothing mild mannered about the special agent today. Oates backed off a pace and gave a feral snarl. "I never would have believed it if I didn't see it with my own eyes. A federal agent turned traitor."

"There's only one traitor in these parts," Ben shot back. "And he's not standing inside my boots, that's for certain."

Wayne cast a furious glance at the lawyer halted alongside Ben. "Don't tell me. You've gone against direct orders and released my prisoner."

"Nobody's ordered me to do a thing. But I sure would have disobeyed this one. In a heartbeat." Ben shook his head. "As for orders, bub, there's a code we're supposed to follow. In case you've forgotten."

"Don't you try to tell me my business!"

"At the top of the list is our order never to subvert justice in order to advance a case." Ben plowed on. "Which is exactly what you're trying to do."

Wayne took a menacing step forward. "That Buhler man is the worst sort of criminal! Do you know what he's done to those kids?"

"I do indeed. Everything in his power to give them a decent home."

"You're demented!" Wayne stepped in close enough for Ben to see the spittle on his lower lip. "This case has been granted top priority, and you're insisting on standing there like a blind fool with his finger in the dike!"

"I'd say that sums things up pretty well," Ben agreed. He eased by the other agent. "Come on, Phil."

Wayne shouted after him, "You're shredding your own career! Theron Head is personally going to see you fry for this!"

Ben nodded to the cluster of prison officers gawking at them from behind the control station's bulletproof window. It wasn't often they had the chance to watch two federal officers go head to head. When the outer door buzzed, he pulled the door open and held it for Phil, and said back to Wayne, "Of that I have no doubt."

Phil was silent as they took the elevator down and walked through the connecting tunnel to the parking lot. Now that it was over, Ben was shaking from the strain. "Do you mind driving for a while?"

"Not at all." Phil accepted the keys, slid in behind the wheel, and said, "I think I owe you an apology."

"No you don't."

"I had no idea this was the situation."

"It's okay, Phil." When his words did not erase the other man's stricken expression, Ben forced himself to say, "When I started out investigating Kingdom Come, I was exactly what you thought. Looking for a crime and ready to convict."

Phil nodded slowly as he pulled up to the pay station. "What changed your mind?"

Ben could think of no other answer than, "God."

That one word relaxed all the attorney's remaining reserve. "What are we looking for now?"

Ben slid down in his seat and let his mind roam. "We're after supporting documents and testimony to exonerate Buhler. But eventually we're going to have to go after the source."

"Looks to me like you just had your run-in with the man who's trying to set us up."

"Wayne Oates is getting his string pulled by somebody in Washington. And that somebody, Theron Head is his name, is obtaining documentary evidence from someplace else. We need to find that source and attack it."

"Can you do that?"

"We have no choice. I've been involved in this work for a lifetime. Long enough to know that an attack on the principal source of damaging information is the only thing that will bring a public investigation down like a house of cards." His gut tightened at all that was riding on his strategy. "It's our only hope."

———※——※———

Phil Trilling was exultant upon their return to Charlotte. They gathered the pastor and the attorney and Lando Buhler and walked the three blocks from the city tower to the offices of the *Charlotte Observer*. Ben had called ahead, and they were ushered through the newsroom to the managing editor's office. The editor was a redheaded woman with a face like an unsheathed blade, hard and brilliant. She wore a tight green dress and a grim expression as Phil Trilling laid out the evidence on her desk. She was flanked by two reporters assigned to the story, a young woman wearing very thick glasses and an older, heavyset man with a quietly watchful gaze.

"In summary," Phil concluded, hard-pressed not to trumpet the findings, "Dr. Buhler's former wife has been determined to be in no condition whatsoever to take care of juvenile children. She has a history of failing to take her medication. The resulting disasters are carefully documented both by the courts and the police records you see here. Going even further, the South Carolina doctor was so horrified over the idea that the children might be returned to this woman that he authorized the release of the affidavit you see here, stating unequivocally that she is, in his own words, only marginally capable of taking care of herself."

He set down the final pages with a flourish. "And this is a copy of the court records from the final hearing over the care of the children, dated eleven months ago, just prior to Dr. Buhler's move to North Carolina. As you can see, everyone from the clinic doctor to the court-appointed social worker to their neighbors and the local pastor all praised Dr. Buhler as a model father. That expression was used over two dozen times; I have highlighted them in yellow."

The managing editor leaned back in her chair, folding her arms tightly across her chest. "Interesting."

"It's more than that," Phil Trilling declared. "It's conclusive."

"About this particular issue, maybe. But we have been presented with evidence of a number of other very serious felony charges related to Kingdom Come."

"Let me guess." Ben spoke for the first time from his position at the back of the office. "Diversion of federal and tax-exempt funds, harboring of illegal arms, subverting local government."

The brilliant green gaze turned his way. "Sorry, I didn't catch your name."

"Ben Atkins. Special agent with the FBI."

The trio behind the desk showed genuine surprise. The managing editor demanded, "Can I see your ID?"

He passed over his badge, waited as each inspected this in turn.

"You realize, of course, that your own agency is responsible for raising the majority of these charges against the community and its leaders."

"I'm here because they're wrong to do so," Ben stated flatly. "These people are absolutely innocent."

"You don't say."

"I've been living inside the community. I've gone over every inch of the terrain. Traveled every road. There are no arms. There is no militia."

"What about the fence?" the editor shot back.

"The fence," Chuck moaned softly. "The blasted fence."

All eyes turned toward the pastor. He shook his head back and forth. "I can't tell you why it's there. Except many of my community felt there might come a time when we would want protection against the outside world."

The managing editor demanded, "Does this protection extend to automatic weapons?"

"No. Absolutely not. You've heard Ben Atkins. Many families have guns, but it is a personal matter. We take no position on this at all."

"Are you armed?"

"No," Chuck stated flatly. "I used to hunt, but I haven't touched a weapon since before I was married."

She turned to Ben. "And you?"

"I am required to carry my weapon at all times. You know that. But the sheriff keeps his gun locked in the drawer of his office."

The editor shot a questioning glance to the older reporter, who said, "This flies directly in the face of everything we were told by the feds."

"All right. Here's what I'm going to do." She leaned back across her desk. "I'm going to pull the story we were planning to run tomorrow."

The young lady whined, "But I've spent *days* on it."

The managing editor ignored her. "I want you to let us send a reporter up to nose around Kingdom Come. Unhindered."

"I'll arrange for the person to have an apartment for as long as he or she cares to stay," Chuck offered.

"What about a pass to move around freely?"

All of them smiled at that. Chuck replied, "We don't use anything like passes. Your reporter is welcome to go wherever he or she wishes."

This news seemed to shake the trio more than anything. The editor said, "This is not exactly what we'd expect for a cult large enough to run a commune of this size."

"It's not a cult," Ben replied. "Come and see for yourself."

She studied him intently. "Maybe I will. What keeps you around if there's no crime being committed?"

"Somebody has to protect them against my overzealous colleagues." The words left a bitter taste. "Some Washington officials have gotten it into their heads that the community poses a danger."

"I'll say." She cocked her head. "This can't be doing your career any good."

"There are some things more important than my career," Ben replied. "Like my oath."

The overweight man murmured, "Could be a story here."

Phil Trilling could contain himself no longer. "I don't get you people! All you've said so far is you won't run a story we've just proven to be blatantly false! What about writing something to counter all these claims? Why don't you write something *good* for a change?"

The managing editor did not respond; she merely sat and eyed Ben. He understood perfectly. "They can't."

Phil turned reluctantly from glaring down at the editor. "What?"

"This is just one local paper. The national news media has already come out against us. There's only one way for us to stop this from steamrolling into a national sensation where we are tried and convicted by the press."

Phil glanced at the editor, who merely nodded. He turned back to Ben and said, "What you told me on the way down today."

"That's right. We've got to find the FBI's key source of information and discredit it." Ben turned to the managing editor. "Can you help us with that?"

She gave her head a decisive shake. "You know that would be the last thing the feds would share with us."

Chuck Griffin rose to his feet and lifted the others with him. "Thank you very much for listening."

She accepted his hand. "I'm not promising I won't run this damaging story sometime soon. But I will send a reporter up to corroborate what I've heard here, and I'll make up my own mind." When it came time to shake Ben's hand, she added, "You referred to the community as 'us.'"

"That's right. I did."

"Anything further you'd like to say about that? For the record."

Ben did not need to hesitate. "These people aren't saints. They're just decent American citizens trying to live a good and holy life."

"Behind a fortified fence," she shot back.

"That's their privilege," Ben responded. "The fence is on their land. They've broken no law."

"But you have to admit it seems highly eccentric."

"Maybe. But that doesn't mean we should persecute them." When she did not say anything else, Ben added, "I started off with the same suspicions you have."

"And now?"

He tried to put together thoughts so new many had scarcely been formed in his own mind. "The pastor has spoken about how the word *holy* really just means 'set apart.' They aren't closing themselves off from the world. Everyone who wants is welcome to enter. But they are trying to make a new sort of community. One that focuses first upon God."

She pressed, "What about the fence?"

"To be honest, I find the thing doesn't bother me any more. Maybe it's because I don't see it as a barrier now. More like a marker. Inside this line, we seek to live a God-centered existence. Maybe we fail more than we succeed, but we try. Outside, well, outside is the world."

Ben found himself so disconcerted by his own words that he turned and walked out the door. The others did not catch up with him until they stood by the elevators. It was there that Chuck told him, "I don't know about the woman back there, but I found a lot of comfort in what you had to say."

But Phil's elation was fully deflated. He sighed and spoke with bitter frustration. "What happens now?"

That much was simple. Ben turned to the lawyer and said, "We need a miracle. And fast."

THIRTY-TWO

This time it was Wayne Oates who placed the call. This time he was so enraged he felt not the slightest bit intimidated by speaking to Theron Head. In fact, he did not speak at all. He shouted, "Ben Atkins is *insane!* He's a menace!"

"Calm down."

Wayne stalked the confines of his office. "Do you know what he's done now? First he sprang our prisoner, the child molester! Then he traipsed into the *Observer's* office and convinced them to pull the story!"

"Don't worry, he'll be stopped."

Wayne swung a fist at the invisible Ben, striking only air. "I don't want him stopped, I want him ground into dust!"

"That too." Theron Head did not seem the least bit disturbed by Wayne's fury. "Lower your voice. Others are listening."

With great difficulty he reined in his rage. "Why don't you crush him?"

"It's not that easy. Ben Atkins is a highly decorated agent with twenty-one years of service under his belt. He has allies."

"He's the enemy," Wayne smoldered. "I want him demolished."

"I'll bring him down, don't worry. But it'll take time."

"We don't have time. That dimwit is standing in our way!"

"Then we'll just have to go around him."

The calm directness gave Wayne a fraction more clarity. "You've got a plan?"

"That's my job. To make plans. Yours is to bring me results. Are you ready to overcome our enemy, Mr. Oates?"

"Absolutely."

"No holds barred. Not any more. The stakes are too high."

"Just tell me what to do."

"In order for us to move, we need something so big the nation will sit up and recognize this cult to be the threat it is."

"And give us the lever to bring them down," Wayne agreed.

"Precisely. The arrest of that dentist has at least alarmed them. What we need now is something that will push them over the edge. A more secretive assault that, when discovered, will leave them ready to roll those Kingdom Come gates shut and declare themselves to be the peril we know they are."

Wayne walked around to the desk and swept aside his papers. "All right. I'm listening."

THIRTY-THREE

Ben waited until late that night, then called Evan on his home phone. When his longtime friend and colleague came on the phone, Ben asked, "Is this line secure?"

"I'd hate to think we'd gotten to the point where we were spying on our own men." But Evan's tone said he would not be surprised. "I won't ask how you are because I don't want to know."

"I'm fine. Really."

"You can't be. Not unless you're utterly oblivious to the storm you're raising."

"Evan, listen to me."

"No, Ben. No. I'm done with you. This is not going to be a multiple career suicide."

But Ben would not be halted. "You learned the academy lessons the same as me. The sole purpose of an investigation is the obtaining of evidence for prosecuting under federal statutes."

"Don't lecture me," Evan snapped.

At least the man did not hang up. "I know you've sold yourself into this. But Evan, please hear me. *There is no case.* This is no longer just a question of overemphasizing questionable evidence against Kingdom Come. They are *manufacturing* evidence."

"You don't know that!"

"Theron Head and his minions are resorting to tactics that fly in the face of justice! They have declared these people to be un-American, when in truth the community is being subjected to a federally sanctioned invasion!"

"Oh come on, Ben. This isn't—"

"Head's cadre has sent in the IRS, they've harassed motorists leaving and entering the community, they have arrested the main pastor and held him without charges, they have brought in investigators from a half-dozen other agencies, they are trying to choke off the local banks, they have fed slanderous information to the media. What else could you call it?" Again he waited, and took comfort from the fact that Evan did not break the connection. "Just think about it, will you?"

"It's about all I do." The words were almost a moan. "You realize this stance is going to cost you your career."

"I know." Ben wished the admission did not hurt so much, but he knew there was no turning back. "Listen, there is something I need."

"Ben, I can't—"

"Just hear me out, okay? I need to know who is the principal source. Somebody is digging up, then feeding Theron and his cadre, this damaging data." Again the silence, if not heartening, at least was better than outright refusal. "The financial data. The charges against Buhler—"

"It all came from the same person."

Ben's heart leapt. "Who?" When Evan did not respond, Ben pressed hard. "A name, Evan. Don't freeze me out here. Please. Give me a chance to see if we can clear this up."

"I don't know the name." Evan sounded more than resigned. He sounded old. And eternally exhausted. "But it originates from a church in Orlando."

"A church?" Ben searched his mind, tried to recall the name of the church Dottie had spoken with down in Florida. "You're sure?"

"Part of the denomination that your community leader used to belong to, back before they kicked him out." Speaking the words opened the gates, revealing Evan's internal agony. "Ben, they're breaking this as a national case. You're going to get crushed like a bug."

"What was it the Revolutionary War general said? 'My conscience and my God give me no alternative.' Something like that."

"Your God? Did I really hear you say that?" Evan tried for scorn but failed. "They've really gotten to you, Ben."

"Come back down here," he quietly urged his old friend. "Stay a while. See this place for itself. Not like they want you to see it, not like the media's painting it. See it for what it is."

The moment stretched long and silent, broken only by Evan's rasping breath. Then he silently put down the receiver, breaking the connection.

Ben sat there holding the mobile phone for a long time. He realized there was only one thing he could do, only one response to the surrounding night. He set down his phone, then slid off the sofa and onto his knees.

⚊⚊

Evan Hawkins arrived at FBI headquarters as tired as he had ever been in his life. He wore the same clothes he had on the previous day. His ankles and feet were sore from the hours of pacing. His mouth felt coated in fur from the coffee he had made and drunk all night long.

He took the elevator to the seventh floor and walked down Hall One. He entered the office with the embossed seal on the door. He gave his name to the secretary and settled onto the sofa. People came and went. He saw nothing but his own internal agony.

All Evan had ever wanted was to rise within the agency. He was a good leader, he knew that. For over a dozen years he had been aimed toward the assistant director's slot. He realized he did not have the charisma or the political connections for the top slot. Yet he hoped he would be recognized for the job he did, and appointed number two. He wanted it so much it woke him sometimes at night, his hunger a great aching void in his gut.

In the previous night's darkest hour, however, he had accepted that he could not live with himself if he did not speak. It had come down to a choice between his lifelong dream and his life.

Evan sat now in the director's outer office, so torn apart it seemed that his clothes were all that kept him from splitting in two. He could not remain silent. It was just not possible.

"Mr. Hawkins?" The secretary gave him a worried look, the smile extinguished before it was formed. "The director will see you now."

He mouthed a thanks, but his lungs could not gather enough force to form the words. He stumbled as he crossed the carpet and followed her down the hall. They passed the conference room, then the assistant director's office. Evan stopped and stared at the empty desk and the flag and the trophy wall. It would never be his. He knew that now.

He tasted nothing but ashes as he was ushered into the inner sanctum. The director rose and gave his polished smile. "Evan, how are you?"

"Fine, sir."

"You don't look fine. You look like death. Would you like something? A coffee?"

"Nothing, thanks."

He glanced at his watch. "I'm afraid we're tight today. I'm scheduled to be at the White House in a quarter of an hour. You know what Washington traffic is like."

"Five minutes of your time is enough, sir." As the secretary began to back out, he added, "Perhaps it would be good to have her remain, sir. As a witness."

A new gravity settled upon the room. "Take a seat there."

Evan remained standing. He took the hardest breath of his entire life, then said, "Sir, I wish to lodge an official complaint against Theron Head and his investigation of the Carolina community."

"You mean this cult?"

The second breath came no easier. "Sir, I have every reason to believe that it is not a cult at all."

THIRTY-FOUR

Rebecca Painton led Dottie from the main passenger terminal to the smaller hall for private planes. This compact structure was clearly built for people with money enough to afford private transport. There were a couple of expensive boutiques, a café, two bored customs officials, and very few people. Rebecca seemed to know her way around, leading Dottie straight through the terminal and out into the bright sunlight on the other side. Dottie squinted through the glare reflected off the concrete runway, and faltered.

When Rebecca realized Dottie was no longer keeping up, she turned and demanded, "What's the matter?"

Dottie waved toward the plane. "This isn't exactly what I was expecting."

"It's not mine. Hurry, now."

Dottie had thought they would be taking a one-prop puddle jumper, something barely able to make the distance to the islands. Instead, Rebecca stood at the base of a brand-new double-engine jet. The sleek silver-white vessel positively shrieked of money.

Dottie had always abhorred stepping into circumstances where she was giving up control. It was one of her defining characteristics. Even so, she felt compelled to trust this woman she had only spoken with twice before in her life.

A dark-skinned man in a brilliant white uniform stood at the top of the plane's stairs. He glared so fiercely at Dottie, her blood ran cold. Then he spoke with a heavy island patois. "You can trust this one?"

Rebecca said simply, "I feel God's hand upon our journey."

The words were enough to turn the pilot away. They also released the final chains tying Dottie to the known and the expected. She handed up her briefcase and overnight bag, and climbed inside.

The plane's interior was beyond ornate. The seats were white doeskin, the cabinets and tables walnut burl lined with what appeared to be sterling silver. There was a four-screen television and stereo complex built into the main cabin's front wall. Dottie did a slow turn, took in the fully-fitted kitchenette, the wine rack, the crystal goblets and decanters, the fold-down double bed with silk sheets behind a sliding shoji screen, and could only say, "Good grief."

The starboard engine whined through the start-up procedure. The pilot called from up front, "Close up the stairs, now."

"Give me a hand," Rebecca said. Together they pulled the stairs into place and locked the door. "Take this first seat. Don't touch anything."

The seat was soft as butter. "Whose plane is this?"

"Just wait. Please." Rebecca strapped herself in. "You'll find out everything soon enough. We both will, I hope and pray."

The jet was already taxiing as both engines whined up to full revs. "You don't know?"

"I know what Matthew has told me."

"Matthew is the pilot?"

"That's right. And a new brother in Christ. We decided it was too risky for him to go in and show me, then come back with someone else. I returned to Orlando hoping to find someone who could tell this story for us. Someone with more authority than just another washed-out missionary." There was no bitterness to her voice, only a quiet determination. "When I came upon you in the church, I thought perhaps you were an answer to a prayer. Especially when you said you'd become involved with the Kingdom Come community."

Rebecca waited through the noisy takeoff, then demanded, "Do you mind if I ask what it's like up there in Kingdom Come?"

"Like I said in my original articles," Dottie replied quietly. "Awesome. Frightening at times. Painful also. But wonderful."

Rebecca seemed comforted by the words. "What Matthew has told me is too big to be talked about in some secondhand fashion. So I'd like to ask that you wait and let us see this together."

Dottie repeated, "You say it's big?"

The question drew such a tragic expression from the missionary that Dottie thought she was going to start bawling. Instead Rebecca said, "All I ask is one thing in return. If the story proves to be true, I want you to tell Reverend Innes first. Before you write anything. Tell him what you've found."

"Why?"

"Will you do it?"

Dottie could not miss Rebecca's intense concern. "Yes. All right. If there is a story here, I will reveal my findings to the pastor in Orlando before disclosing it publicly."

Rebecca settled back. She said to the side window, "I don't think he's involved. I hope and pray . . . I want him to have a chance, that's all."

"A chance to what?"

But Rebecca did not respond.

<hr />

Rebecca did not speak again until they began circling into their descent. She motioned for Dottie to join her by the port window, and said, "We're flying over the Anegada Passage, which separates the British Virgin Islands from the American. The big island to the southwest there is Saint Croix. Up at the top there you can see Tortola and Virgin Gorda. Saint John and Saint Thomas are off to your left."

The sea was a sparkling universe of bottle green. Clouds floated in picture-postcard precision, looking as planted in the sky as the islands were below. Each verdant island was surrounded by a slender strip of white beach. Most rose into conical mountains at their center. "Where is Saint Catherine?"

"Almost directly below us." Rebecca leaned back. "The islands with tourism or banking are doing well. Those that have not been developed are mired in poverty. Saint Catherine is a very small island and has a shortage of freshwater wells. Most of the aquifer system is controlled by two big banana companies. They don't want development. They want a docile population that will work for pennies and be easily controlled."

The plane went into a swift descent. They leveled off so close to the water Dottie could see faces in the sailboats below them. The sun splashed the plane's interior with a brilliant glow. The place was too beautiful to be a threat to anyone.

They touched down and slowed with the incredible swiftness of a small private jet. They taxied over to the collection of private planes by a freshly painted hangar. Many of the other jets dwarfed their own. Beyond the hangar Dottie spotted the central terminal. She read the name on the roofline and exclaimed, "We've landed on Saint Thomas!"

"That's right."

"But—"

The pilot's door slapped open. "You move quick now."

Rebecca unstrapped and started for the door. "Shouldn't we wait until after they unload?"

If anything, the pilot was more tense than upon Dottie's arrival. His features were creased so tightly his eyes were mere slits in an ebony face. "I don't call them yet. Better you go first."

"All right." Rebecca waited for him to unlock the door and fold out the stairway. "We'll see you tomorrow, yes?"

"The hour before dawn." The pilot cast Dottie a single tight glance, then returned to his station. "You be ready."

"We will. Come along, Dottie."

As soon as she passed through the doorway, Dottie was greeted by the most incredible mixture of fragrances. The warm air was permeated with the pungent odor of jet fuel. Even so, she caught an exhilarating waft of sea and spices.

"Hurry," Rebecca urged. Dottie stumbled down the stairway, briefcase in her hand and overnight bag slung over her shoulder. Rebecca carried nothing save a battered leather shoulder-bag. Dottie caught up with the scurrying missionary and asked, "What was that all about?"

"Matthew stayed in Orlando during the plane's maintenance inspection. He's carrying back supplies for his people." Rebecca walked past a half-dozen security guards slouched beneath the terminal's overhang, then pushed through the doors. Only then did she slow somewhat. "We needed to get off and away without them seeing us."

Dottie followed the missionary through throngs of sunburned tourists in garish island prints. "Who are his people?"

Rebecca did not answer. Instead she pushed through the terminal's front doors and stepped toward the first taxi. An old man emerged from behind the wheel and almost sang the words, "You are welcome, ladies. Oh yes, most very welcome indeed. You like a sunset tour of beautiful Saint Thomas, yes?"

Rebecca climbed in, slid over for Dottie to join her, and said, "Take us to the port, please."

"The port, sure, sure, but first we climb the mountain and see the jewels of the Caribbean, yes? Oh, so very beautiful."

"Not today. Just directly to the port."

Once they were underway, Dottie started to speak, but Rebecca halted her with a brief shake of the head. The drive took them along a winding road sheltered by giant coconut palms. Traffic was an island hodgepodge of carts and dilapidated jalopies and brand-new Mercedes limousines. The road began to parallel the water, and they passed one luxurious resort after another. They entered a dusty township in the process of being reinvented with tourist dollars. Crumbling structures with wrought-iron balustrades and old-fashioned wooden shutters stood alongside modern glass-and-stucco buildings sporting familiar commercial logos.

They halted by a harbor filled with brightly colored native boats and massive, foreign-owned yachts. The smell of fish and seaweed was very strong.

Rebecca used her shoulder to push open the taxi door, paid the fare, and said, "Wait here."

Before Dottie could respond, the missionary was already scurrying across the road. She halted by three fishermen laughing and smoking on the harbor wall. Dottie murmured to herself, "What on earth is she doing now?"

"Your lady friend, she hires boat. She knows the islands, yes?"

"Yes."

"Sure, she knows. She talks alone to make price low. They see you, they think *Tourist!* and double prices." The ancient driver chuckled. "She one smart lady, sure."

Dottie was ready when Rebecca turned and waved her over. The fisherman at the center grimaced when she appeared, while his two fellows laughed out loud. He started to complain, but Rebecca cut him off sharp.

The three of them descended seaweed-slick stairs to a ramshackle wooden boat that reeked of its latest catch. The dour fisherman started the engine, which belched black diesel fumes, then began to chug steadily. He cast off the vessel and used the oversize tiller to steer them away from the harbor. Rebecca pointed Dottie into the bow seat beside her. The sun was almost touching the horizon as they cleared the harbor wall. Had it not been for the boatman's angry muttering in the stern and Rebecca's own worried expression, Dottie would have called this one of the most beautiful settings she had ever known.

"There are dozens of islands like Saint Catherine," Rebecca told her, pitching her voice low enough to be masked by the chugging engine. "Small and poor and undeveloped. The young people are trapped in a poverty that offers them no hope of a job or education or any real reason not to despair. Perfect hunting grounds for the foul and the despicable."

Night gathered with astonishing swiftness. The sun melted and poured itself into the sea, the stars came out, and the heat was replaced by a gentle evening wind. Rebecca reached into her voluminous purse and pulled out a shawl. She draped it around her shoulders and continued, "I've been working down here for fifteen years. I love this place."

"I can see why."

"Don't be blinded by the beauty," she warned. "There are aspects of this world that will horrify you."

An island grew from the sea to form a dark shadow silhouetted against a starlit sky. They entered a harbor much smaller and more dilapidated than the one on Saint Thomas. Several large sailboats and yachts were anchored out toward the harbor mouth, but far fewer than on the larger island. The boatman pulled up alongside a grimy rock wall, waited for them to disembark, accepted Rebecca's payment with a grunt, then pushed off and departed. He had not spoken a word since Dottie's arrival.

"We won't find a taxi," Rebecca said softly. "Can you walk a half-mile or so?"

"Sure."

"Let me have one of your bags."

Again there was the fumbling in the voluminous purse, and this time Rebecca came up with a compact yet powerful flashlight. The beam revealed a tired seafront town, with no signs of modernization that Dottie could see. It was good they had the flashlight, for there were no streetlights and the road's surface was pitted and scarred. Dottie avoided the potholes by taking a meandering course as close to the side of the road as she could. She heard soft voices and scraping steps, and saw gleams off the clothes and eyes of passersby.

They skirted an open store, where a group of men gathered around a boom box blasting gangsta rap. The men all held bottles, and their voices were slurred roars. Dottie picked up her pace. Farther on they passed a restaurant stretched out beneath a giant pepper tree, whose limbs were festooned with colored lights. A brazier cast off the scent of wood-coal and roasting meat. Dottie's stomach grumbled with hunger.

As though reading her thoughts, Rebecca said softly, "We can have a bite at the compound."

The road curved and lifted its way along a gentle hillside, leaving the town and the people behind. Then night closed in around them. A pair of children passed, holding hands, eyes wide with fear until Rebecca sang out a greeting. Then the children beamed and raced over to hug the missionary's legs. Dottie did not understand a word they spoke. The missionary stood there with the children clinging to her, talking softly, taking all the time in the world. Finally they released one another and the flashlight pointed out the way. "Not long now."

"Was that English you were speaking?"

"Island patois. You pick it up; you have to. The children don't speak anything else." Rebecca pushed through a pair of tall, rusted gates. They followed a graveled track up the hillside. Dottie was puffing hard when she crested the rise and found herself surrounded by light and buildings. Rebecca said, "Welcome to Island Outreach."

The buildings were all of a uniform structure, heavy timbered and single story. The verandas were as broad as the rooms behind. Rebecca pointed out various buildings as they walked—clinic, school, dorm, kitchen, chapel, storage, director's house. Only from the orphanage and the staff dorms came the sound of people. Rebecca led Dottie around the side of the clinic to a small alcove at the back. "These are my quarters."

"You're a doctor?"

"Nurse. But the lines tend to blur down here. The nearest doctor is on Saint Thomas. I've had some further medical training, enough to see me through an emergency. I've stitched up wounds, removed a few inflamed appendixes, even made a Caesarean delivery. That's how I met Matthew. I saved his wife's life. She had a breech birth, and the Saint Thomas doctor was away at another emergency."

Rebecca dropped Dottie's bag by the apartment's only bed, a thin mattress slung upon a leather-strap frame. "I know you're tired and hungry, but let me show you one thing more."

Together they walked down a long path that followed a stream until they came to a second clearing up close to the cliffside. A pair of old trucks stood sentry in a parking area. The place smelled of clay and fresh-cut lumber. Rebecca fished out a great ring of keys from her purse and opened the painted steel door. She used her flashlight to scan a vast expanse of machinery. "This is our pride and joy. The factory run by Miller Kedrick."

Dottie found herself studying Rebecca as much as the factory. The missionary did not sound joyful. She sounded resigned. Rebecca continued, "It's so hard to set up a successful project like this, you just can't imagine. This has been in operation for nine years, and until Miller took it over we lost money steadily. The only reason we kept it up was because it gave jobs and a more meaningful life to some of the locals.

"Six months after Miller arrived, the project started showing its very first profit. Employment has grown to just under forty people. Every dollar made from selling the pots and the furniture and the woven products comes back to Island Outreach. This funds our orphanage, our clinic, our school, everything. It has freed us from the constant need to beg money from churches and relief organizations. Now all our donations can go to outreach projects or expand our programs on other poor islands. In just four years we have gone from a tiny two-building church and school compound to eleven full-time missionaries working on three islands."

But the longer Rebecca spoke, the sadder she became. Dottie asked, "What's the matter with what I'm seeing?"

Rebecca stepped back through the door. The swinging flashlight illuminated features that looked close to weeping. "We'll find out tomorrow."

THIRTY-FIVE

It seemed that Dottie had scarcely laid down her head before Rebecca was shaking her softly. The missionary had slept on a pallet upon the floor. By the time they had finished their cold dinner of bread and cheese and fruit, Dottie had lost interest in anything save going to sleep.

The night still surrounded them with utterly alien sounds and smells. Dottie slipped from beneath the mosquito net and accepted a steaming mug of coffee. Rebecca moved about with a single candle for light. Dottie asked, "Do you have electricity?"

"The compound has its own generator." She spoke barely above a whisper. "But we need to leave undetected. I'm not due back until this afternoon."

"The other people here don't know about what you want to show me?"

Rebecca avoided her gaze as she sorted through a pile of clean clothes. "The director has built his entire career upon the status quo."

"Which is?"

"Here, these are the smallest clothes I have." Rebecca handed over a faded long-sleeved T-shirt and lightweight khaki slacks. "It would be better if you wore these. They're clean. Do you mind changing?"

"No." Clearly she was not going to receive any further information. Dottie slipped into the clothes and cinched the slacks tight with a frayed canvas belt. As soon as she was dressed, Rebecca picked up the overnight bag, waited for Dottie to retrieve her briefcase, then blew out the candle. She opened the outer door, then motioned Dottie forward.

They crossed the silent compound and passed through the tall steel gates. Outside waited an ancient wooden cart. A lantern glowed on the seat beside the driver, revealing the most unattractive horse Dottie had ever seen. The broad back was deeply swayed, tufts of hair sprouted like gray bushes around the worn leather harness, and the neck was so slumped the nose grazed the road.

"Hurry, climb up the back, you."

Only then did Dottie realize the driver was Matthew, the pilot. Now he wore a threadbare shirt, shorts, and woven leather sandals. A sweat-stained reed hat drooped over the upper half of his face. She turned from his anxious glare and followed Rebecca around to the back. They slid in and took seats facing one another, the hard wooden benches cushioned by burlap sacks. Matthew flicked the reins and clicked softly. The nag raised its head and began plodding along. The wagon's rubber car-tires rolled softly over the uneven pavement. The constant potholes soon had the cart pitching like a boat in heavy seas.

Dawn began streaking the eastern horizon. Overhead, palm fronds looked cut from shadow-paper. Parrots sang their raucous laughter to the new day. The air was sweetly scented with flowers and the sea and wood smoke. They passed a cluster of young girls carrying plastic water jugs and chiming words made musical by the patois and the morning. The road climbed steadily. Rebecca reached into her shoulder bag and pulled out a thermos and plastic bag. She handed out big sandwiches of bread and butter and cheese. She filled the thermos top and passed over strong black tea sweetened with pineapple juice. Matthew accepted his sandwich and drink without a word. Dottie did not ask why Rebecca took nothing for herself. The strengthening light revealed a very worried, frightened woman.

Rebecca handed Dottie a scarf and pulled out another for herself, then showed by example how to tie it with a lip far out over her forehead. With the strengthening sun and her hands hidden, it was no longer possible to see the pale tone of her skin.

High in the hills they passed through another small village, this one impossibly poor. Shanties lined both sides of the road. None of them had glass in the windows, few even had doors. Children sat and stared listlessly at their passage. The few adults Dottie saw ignored the cart, keeping their faces turned down like mourners. When they emerged from the town's other side, Rebecca said merely, "Banana plantation town."

The road climbed farther still, until Dottie could look back and see four other islands settled like green jewels upon the blue-blue sea. The heat strengthened with the day. There was little wind. Banana trees stretched out in orderly rows, as far in every direction as Dottie could see. Occasionally trucks passed them, and a few cars, but most of the road traffic was either on foot or horse cart.

They reached a gently sloping ridgeline and immediately began descending into a vast green bowl. The entire center of the island was one immense valley, a prehistoric volcanic crater now covered by lush jungle. The banana groves were less visible here. Rebecca explained that this part of the island had very little water. Even so, the surrounding jungle seemed impossibly thick. Up ahead, Dottie could see where the central island's only road rose and crested the valley's opposite side.

They descended into the valley's heat trap. The air grew very close, the jungle fragrances cloying and thick. Heat shimmered off the road's surface. The T-shirt, which had seemed too thin when Dottie had donned it, was now sweat stained and glued to her back. When they began the ascent up the valley's other side, faint puffs of wind offered the illusion of coolness. Neither Rebecca nor Matthew gave any indication that they noticed the heat at all. Dottie pulled the scarf farther out over her eyes and endured.

Toward the other rim, Matthew halted the cart and slid down from the bench. He gripped the horse's headstall and pulled the wagon off the road and into the underbrush. Rebecca cast tight-eyed glances in both directions, but the road remained clear. They continued into the jungle until the road was no longer visible. Matthew tethered the horse to a tree, then walked back and said simply, "We go."

Rebecca pulled the scarf from her head, stuffed it with Dottie's back in her purse, then asked Dottie, "Do you have a camera?"

"Not with me, no."

"Here." She handed over a pocket Minolta. "Do you know how to operate this?"

The automatic flash had been punctured, the bulb shattered. "Sure."

"I broke the flash; I didn't know any other way to make absolutely sure it wouldn't go off. This button here operates the zoom lens. It's very quiet. I've put in a new roll." She drew a bulky envelope from her bag and handed it over as well. "These are pictures of the compound, the project, the children, the products we ship to America, the factory, everything."

Once Dottie had stowed away the envelope, Matthew shoved Dottie's briefcase and overnight bag beneath the burlap sacks. Rebecca did the same with her shoulder bag. By the time they started back toward the road, Dottie's heart was thundering a frantic pace. They walked up the ridgeline, first Matthew, then Dottie, and finally Rebecca. They kept to the shadows of the first line of trees. Twice they heard voices and slipped into the trees, waiting until the horse carts had passed and disappeared. Once they left the road for a truck. By the time they crested the rise, Dottie was streaming sweat, and not just from the heat.

On the ridgeline's other side, Matthew cut off the road and started down a trail. The jungle and the heat closed in tightly. The path narrowed as it started around a cliff face. The rock protruded from the jungle wall, then in a matter of just a few paces the green disappeared entirely. One moment they were surrounded by fetid steaming growth, and the next they were utterly exposed. On one side was a dusty gray stone wall, rising up a hundred feet and more. On the other side, the narrow trail dropped off like it had been cut with a razor. Dottie's one outward glance revealed a drop of several hundred feet, then a wide swath of green, then the sea. Dottie walked sideways, one hand resting on the rock and the other dangling out over a void. From somewhere below them, an eagle cried. Dottie kept her eyes directed at her feet and struggled not to look out and down.

At the cliff's other side, Matthew used hand motions to plaster them to the rockface. He proceeded on around the bend alone. Then came back, hissed once, and motioned them forward.

On the cliff's other side was a broad plateau, spreading back inland like a gouge into the higher ridge. It was utterly invisible both from the road and the sea. Matthew led them through the ring of trees, moving in a crouch. Up ahead Dottie heard the rumble of a generator and the tinny sounds of a radio, and conversation. They continued silently through the trees, rounding first one wooden shanty, then another. At the third, when they were closest to the chugging generator, Matthew stopped and squatted, motioning them down beside him.

Up ahead, Dottie saw a group of people working in a dusty clearing. Some turned lathes, others molded clay upon a wheel, still others wove reeds. A few young men loitered around the perimeter, armed with automatic weapons. The two groups, workers and guards, said nothing to one another. The generator chugged too loudly for Dottie to make out what was being said. It did not matter. The activity was perfectly clear.

Two men turned over a coffee table identical to the one Dottie had seen in the Orlando church shopping arcade. One of the guards broke away, walked into the nearby hut, and emerged carrying plastic bags containing white powder. The workers waited while the bags were fitted inside the table's hollow legs. Then the workers moved forward and sealed the legs.

Dottie began taking pictures. She photographed the guards loading more bags into the padded seat of a cane chair. She then shot pictures of further bags being stuffed inside a broad-necked clay vase, then of the workers sealing the bags in place with wax. She photographed the amphibious plane waiting at the end of an airstrip carved down the center of the plateau, and the workers stowing the finished goods in its hold.

While the guards and workers were loading the plane, Matthew motioned again. Dottie nodded agreement. She had seen more than enough.

THIRTY-SIX

The sun glowed hard and hot above the western sea when they returned to the harbor. The world was split into light and shadow. Silhouettes of a harbor mouth and crumbling houses and slow-moving people rose off to Dottie's left. She was so tired, she sat with her head as bowed as the horse's while Rebecca walked over and talked to a fisherman about transport. More than just the story was clear to her now. She understood on some deep level why the people here walked with heads slumped downward. She understood why Matthew remained so silent. She understood why, the entire way back from the central highlands, Rebecca had wept occasional tears.

"All right." Rebecca's voice was a whisper of sound, like the gentle waves lapping the rocks beyond the harbor wall. "I know this man. He will see you safely back to Saint Thomas."

"You're not coming?"

"No. No. My place is here." The words left her broken. She looked back down the road toward the unseen compound, and added, "If there's any place for me, after news of this breaks."

"You did the right thing," Dottie said.

"I had no choice." She turned as Matthew slid from the cart and came walking over. He slipped his hat from his head, revealing a face clenched tight as a dark fist. "Thank you, brother."

Matthew stared at the ground between them. "The Master Lord Jesus," he said softly. "He will now forgive me?"

Rebecca smiled with a world of sadness. "Friend, He already has."

Matthew nodded once, slipped on his hat, and walked to the front of the cart. "I go."

Rebecca asked, "Where are you headed?"

"The wife and child, they are already in Panama." He gripped the headstall and began leading the horse away. "From there, someplace far."

Rebecca stood and watched until the man and the cart disappeared from view. Only then did she turn back, the sun reflected upon the wetness on her cheeks. "Remember what I asked."

"Don't worry," Dottie assured her. "I'll go straight from the Orlando airport to Reverend Innes."

Rebecca nodded, defeated by their success. She helped Dottie down into the boat, lowered her overnight bag and briefcase, and said, "Go with God."

THIRTY-SEVEN

The Orlando church receptionist was suitably startled when Dottie walked in the next morning. "Can I help you?"

Dottie knew exactly what the woman was seeing. All the Saint Thomas hotels near to the airport and the harbor had been full. She had slept across three seats in the Saint Thomas terminal. The next set of chairs had been taken by an old man who had snored horribly. Across from her had been a young mother whose baby had lain upon a blanket between them and squalled all night.

That morning Dottie had cleaned up in the airport washroom, changing out of Rebecca's sweat-stained clothes and back into her own business suit. But there was nothing she could do about the matted hair or the sunburned cheeks or the red-rimmed eyes. She knew she looked an absolute mess. And she did not care.

Dottie told the receptionist, "I need to speak with Reverend Innes."

"D-do you have an appointment?"

"No."

"I'm very sorry." She was young and she was trying hard to be friendly. But Dottie's presence clearly unnerved her. "But the pastor is extremely busy today. Perhaps someone else—"

"Is Dr. Innes in this morning?"

"Yes, but—"

"Call him. Now." Dottie leaned across the counter, revealing a hint of what lay behind her fatigue. "Tell him the *Newsday* reporter he met with is about to blow this church right out of the water."

The receptionist scrambled to her feet and backed from the room. "Wait right . . . Just a moment."

Dottie eyed the sofa, but pushed the desire aside. She was afraid if she sat on anything that comfortable looking she would never get up.

She had landed in Miami the hour after dawn. While waiting for her connection to Orlando, she had called Ben. The man had heard her out in silence, then said words she would take with her to the grave, "Dottie, you are carrying a miracle with you."

"What?"

"I don't know what else to call it. We've been scrambling like mad around here, trying to find some way to uncover the principal source the FBI's using to attack us. All I managed to find out is that it was linked to that Orlando church."

"Wait, wait," Dottie had tried to shut out the Miami airport clamor—the voices yammering in a half-dozen tongues, the children and the babies and the adults all caterwauling, the PA system blaring a constant stream of announcements so loud she could not make out the words. "I was telling you about people using a church project to ship drugs into the United States."

"It's more than that, Dottie. A whole universe more." Ben was trying hard to clamp down on his excitement, but he was not succeeding. "This is solid gold, sweetheart."

"But . . ." She felt so shattered and weary, the word bounced around her head like a Ping-Pong ball in a moving crate. *Sweetheart.* "Ben, I don't understand."

"The Lord is at work here." The normally stoic man sounded positively exultant. "I've never said that before. But I've also never been more certain about anything in my entire life."

A single announcement filtered through the clamor and her fatigue. "They're calling my flight."

"Where are you going?"

"Orlando."

"To the church? Are you sure that's wise?"

"I have no choice. Rebecca specifically asked me to tell the pastor first."

"Rebecca, the missionary on the scene?"

"That's right."

Ben was silent a long moment, then said, "There's something you could do for me."

She listened to his request, wishing she could have him say that word one more time. "I can do that."

"Thank you, Dottie. It would help us tremendously." He sounded like a man making notes in his head. "I've got a contact down 'n the Miami bureau office I can trust, I'll put him onto the Saint Catherine operation today. I'll arrange for somebody to get to Orlando as quickly as I can. Give me the church's address, please."

She read the street and phone number from her notes. Hearing his strength and his confidence left her able to confess, "Ben, I'm so tired."

"You take care, and hurry back up to North Carolina. Call me on my mobile. I'll meet you at the airport with a blanket, a cup of hot chocolate, and a backrub."

She smiled for the first time since this journey had started. "You sure know the way to a girl's heart."

Ben's voice gentled. "You remember when the pastor said he felt God's hand upon this? I wonder if maybe he was also talking about you and me."

"I'll call you as soon as I get through at the church." She hung up the phone, and felt his voice still stroke her heart.

"Ms. Betham, do I remember that correctly?" The pastor's secretary appeared in the back doorway. The receptionist peeped nervously from behind her. The secretary was older and far more experienced. "Are you all right?"

"No. Can the pastor see me?"

"Wouldn't you first like to stop by a hotel and have a little—"

"No. I don't have time." She forced herself erect. "And neither does the pastor."

"Well, I suppose . . . " She gave a practiced smile. "Dr. Innes can certainly spare you a few minutes."

"That's more than enough."

Dottie followed the secretary down the hall and into the pastor's outer office. The secretary pointed toward a comfortable corner chair. "Won't you have a seat?"

"I'd better not."

"Can I get you anything? Coffee, a soft drink?"

"Coffee. Black."

The secretary returned swiftly and set the cup and saucer down on the table by the chair. "Please sit down, Ms. Betham. You look about ready to fall over."

"I can't. I'll never get up." Dottie picked up the coffee cup, tried to control her trembling hand, took a sip. She tasted little beyond that it was bitter and hot. Her eye was held by the cup, fine porcelain with a blue rim. For some reason it brought to mind the island compound and the abject poverty. That led to thoughts of Rebecca watching as Dottie's boat pulled away from the harbor wall, the missionary's shoulders bowed like those of a frail old woman. Dottie blinked back tears. She was so tired.

The door leading to the pastor's office opened, and three men in jackets and ties and two gray-haired women walked out. The pastor was patting one man on the shoulder. "You'll make sure they'll have the roofing bids in before this afternoon?"

"I told you I would."

Dottie realized with a chilling start that the man was Miller Kedrick. He had a wrestler's compact build and seemed to radiate menace. Dottie dropped her eyes to the cup, saw the black surface shimmer with her trembling fingers. She could feel the man's eyes rake her. She had stood up to hundreds of hostile interviewees, from Central American dictators to bank directors caught with their hands in the till. But this was something different. Dottie kept her gaze downward and tried to convince herself that it was only because she was so weary.

Before the pastor could walk out with the others, the secretary said, "Ms. Betham is here to see you, Pastor. She says it's urgent."

It was Miller Kedrick who first turned her way. Dottie forced her face into a blank mask and focused upon the pastor. Reverend Innes said, "I read your article about the community, Ms. Betham. I found it factual but rather harsh."

"We need to talk," she replied.

"I really don't have anything further to say."

"Now," Dottie insisted quietly. "Alone."

Miller Kedrick glared at her as he urged, "The rest of the finance committee has already gathered. We've got six months' worth of budget items to cover."

"I won't take long," Dottie said, maintaining a calm she knew was an utter lie. "But this really can't wait."

"Thurgood," Kedrick growled. "Why don't you let me take care of the reporter, you go on in—"

"No, no." Something in Dottie's flat, tired gaze seemed to shake the pastor's composure. "I suppose I can spare you a couple of minutes, Ms. Betham."

"This is crazy," Kedrick snarled. "She can't just show up and take over."

Thurgood Innes turned to stare at the shorter man. "I said I'd take care of this, Miller."

"Look at her," Kedrick snapped. "She's clearly out of it."

But the man's growing hostility only hardened the pastor's resolve. He walked to his inner door and held it open for Dottie. "Please come in."

"You saw her article," Miller Kedrick protested. "She's just another liberal journalist who'll slant anything you say, turn it into an attack—"

Thurgood shut the door. "Please have a seat."

"No thank you."

He stopped in the process of moving around his desk. "I'm sorry things are so busy today—"

"Miller Kedrick is your chief of finance, is that correct?"

"He is the elder responsible for church finances, yes."

"I have some bad news."

The pastor's hands danced over the papers upon his desk. "Really, Ms. Betham, I don't care to hear anything further about the cult community up in—"

"It's not about Kingdom Come, not directly. And it's not a cult."

That raised his eyebrows. "A strange thing for you to say, after that article you wrote."

Dottie refused to be diverted, though the accusation scalded like acid. "Maybe you'd better sit down."

The pastor's hands danced faster, from the desk to his tie to the lobe of his right ear. "I'm not certain I am—"

"I have just returned from your mission outreach project on Saint Catherine." Perhaps if she wasn't so tired she would find a better way to say this. But right now she could find nothing to ease the news. "The project and the factory and the import system are all a front."

"A . . ."

"A front," she repeated. "They're all being used to cover up a drug-smuggling racket. A big one."

The pastor dropped into his chair as though he had been poleaxed.

But she saw something unexpected in his gaze. A hint of something more than desperation. Despite her fatigue, Dottie found herself resuming the professional interviewer's mode. She continued, "I have seen the process firsthand. I also have pictures. There is a second factory, concealed in the highlands. They are making copies of the furniture and pots produced in your mission project's factory. These copies are stuffed with cocaine."

"No." Despite the moaned protest, Dottie realized that Innes may not have known, but he had suspected. "No."

"The products containing drugs are carried by seaplane. In the channel between the islands, they link up with the boat ferrying the wares from Saint Catherine to the larger freight harbor at Saint Thomas. They are stowed together with your legitimate products, and then shipped to the United States." Suddenly Dottie's legs would no longer support her. She collapsed into the chair opposite the pastor. "I've spent the entire journey back going over this. When I was here the first time, the kid working in the curio shop said something about how Kedrick's construction business went through a very rough patch a few years back. But somehow he survived, and now he's flourishing."

Innes leaned forward, placed his elbows on his desk, and buried his face in his hands. He shook his head, slowly, back and forth, the motion rocking his entire upper body.

"Was it about that time that Kedrick became so interested in your mission project, Reverend Innes?"

"I . . . " He lifted his head at the knock on his door.

The secretary opened it far enough to poke her head through. "I'm sorry, Pastor. But the finance board is all waiting for you."

Reverend Innes looked absolutely stricken. "Find Jim. Have him cover—"

"No," Dottie interrupted. She followed the line Ben had laid down in his request. "Please, sir. It's vital you don't do anything out of the ordinary."

He turned an astonished eye toward her. "You expect me—"

"Just until things can be set in place." Dottie tilted her head a fraction of an inch toward where the secretary stood and listened. "Please."

Thurgood Innes straightened. He turned to the door and said, "Tell them I'll be with them shortly."

"Are you all right, Pastor?"

"Fine. Fine. It's just . . . Three minutes and I'll join them."

When the door had closed, he said quietly, "The police will be called in?"

"The FBI."

He winced and lifted one hand to massage his chest. "I'm not as totally surprised as I should be."

"There's something I need to ask you, sir," Dottie continued, following Ben's line. If she was certain the pastor was not involved in the project, Ben had said, ask him this: "Could you please tell me who is the primary source for the information the FBI is using against the Kingdom Come community?"

If anything, the creases in Reverend Innes's face deepened. "What?"

"The primary source. We know it is someone inside this church. If I could please have the name. Was it you?"

"Me? No. I was . . ." The pastor looked ready to weep. "I was used."

Dottie wished she could take out her notebook, but did not dare break the moment. "Excuse me?"

"My ambition . . . I let myself be used, just like a puppet on a string. Pride and selfish ambition are my downfall."

"Sir, are we talking about the community or the drugs?"

"Both," Innes groaned. "They're one and the same."

Dottie rocked back in her seat. "Miller Kedrick."

"He was vicious in his opposition to the community." The pastor turned toward the window. "He said I didn't get it. Brother, did he ever have that one right." He turned back from the window. "I'm surprised to find you so concerned about who's slandered the community, after what you wrote."

"You weren't the only one taken in by outside forces," Dottie replied.

Innes inspected her. "It's not a cult, is it?"

"No."

A moment's pause, then, "Is there a revival going on up there?"

"Yes." No question, no hesitation. "There is."

Innes pushed himself out of his seat. "I better go see to my committee. How long will it take for the authorities to arrive?"

"I'm not sure. Not long."

"All right. Are you going back to Carolina?"

"Straight from here to the airport and the first flight back to Charlotte." Her heart leapt at the thought of seeing Ben.

Thurgood Innes straightened his shoulders and moved toward the door. "Would you give Chuck Griffin a message for me?"

"Of course."

"I'll travel up to Kingdom Come just as soon as the authorities arrive and I can break free here." He opened the door and held it for her. "Tell him I'm sorry. Everything else can wait until I speak with him personally."

✠ ✠

Thurgood Innes sat at the head of the conference table and pretended to listen as one member of his finance committee after another made their reports. He held himself erect, nodded occasionally, thanked each speaker, and gently urged them along. He had no choice. Though he felt like he was dying inside, he kept it well hidden. Miller

Kedrick was watching him intently. The man had blocked the door to the conference room and demanded to know what the woman reporter had wanted.

Thurgood's pretense at weariness had only been half feigned. "They're preparing another attack against the enemy."

Miller had hesitated, wanting to accept this as reassurance. "They're going after the cult again?"

Anger had glowed from the ashes in his heart. "They *are* the enemy, aren't they, Miller?"

The man's gaze had flickered about the hall. "Why're you asking me that? You spearheaded their ouster."

"That's right. I did." Thurgood pushed past the man and entered the conference room.

Now, two hours later, his mind continued to busily sort the news. Strange how it seemed that on one level he had known it all along. This was impossible, of course, but still he could not shake the impression. He had always guessed Chuck's movement was genuine. Why had he objected so? And he had never carefully investigated Miller's background. Why had he ignored repeated hunches of some illegal activity? The answer was clear enough. Ambition. His own selfish desire to move ahead had blinded him. He had been unable to see beyond his own desire to rise within the earthly ranks.

The foul brew of shame and dread swirled about his gut. He was going to be demolished by this. He would probably lose the church. It did not matter that he was innocent. He had let it happen. Thurgood dragged one hand across his forehead, then wiped it on his trouser legs, up and down his thighs, trying to dry off the dampness. A sudden thought occurred to him. One of his parishioners was a retired director of a federal prison. Over dinner one night he had said that every prisoner always declared his innocence. And the truth was, many of them were not totally guilty of the offense they were charged with. What often happened was, a culprit would be brought in, and a charge would be fashioned around the case the prosecutor thought he could win, not always precisely the crime the person had committed. Thurgood nodded as though agreeing with a point made farther along the table. That was certainly the case with him. He was utterly innocent of the charges the world would see, but guilty just the same. Oh yes. As guilty as they came.

Finally it was over. He knew because one by one the people were beginning to close their notebooks and look his way. He had no idea what they had last been speaking about, but he had to close the meeting. A prayer, he had to say a prayer. Thurgood rose to his feet, and for a moment he thought he was going to topple over. He braced himself against the table, bowed over, and planted both fists on his papers. "Heavenly Father," he said, and his voice sounded alien to his own ears. More a groan than a voice at all. "You give us so much, yet all we ever seem to bring to You are requests for more. And what You give us, we don't use properly. Forgive us, Father, for being such poor servants. Forgive us for all the things we do so badly, for the loathsome way we behave, and pretend it is for You. Forgive us. Forgive *me*. Forgive . . ."

He could say no more. He ignored the astounded glances about the table as he turned and left the room.

THIRTY-EIGHT

Carolisa hated her brother.

"Dwayne!" She hated her voice as well, how it broke and sounded like a whiny little kid. "You better wait for me!"

Her brother had the same coloring as she, identical reddish blond curls and a face full of freckles. Only on Dwayne it looked fine, and on her it looked icky. Dwayne turned around, a lithe figure who bounced along the trail like he'd known it all his life and had not just arrived the month before. He shouted back. "I told you, Carolisa, go on home!"

"I don't want to!" Home meant a cramped apartment just inside the compound fencing while they waited for their new house to be finished. There was nobody at home. All the people they had met at Kingdom Come were nice, but they were *old*. At least twenty. Carolisa's only friend her age was her brother, Dwayne. And Dwayne was scampering away. "Mama told you to let me come!"

Dwayne only ran faster. He said something to the two boys with him, and their laughter pealed through the forest. They were laughing at her. She hated that. She hated them all. But she was lonely. She didn't know any girls her age. There was only Dwayne. They were twelve and twins. They used to be very close. But the older Dwayne grew, the more they grew apart. Dwayne had been friendly enough with her when they had first arrived at Kingdom Come. But like Mama said, drop Dwayne down in a tribe in the middle of Africa, and

293

he'd make friends. That was just his way. Carolisa wanted friends too. But Dwayne's friends weren't hers anymore, and the boys seemed to find fun in shutting her out.

"Dwayne!"

Up ahead she could hear their laughter. But the forest was thick here. The trail was hooded by huge branches and walled by dense shrubs and weeds. She picked her way carefully over the fallen logs and gnarled roots. "Dwayne, you wait for me or I'll tell Mama!"

But he was far enough ahead now to claim he hadn't heard her. Carolisa tried to fight down her rising fear, and she picked up her pace. She came around a bend, only to find that the path split. The boys' voices seemed to come from both directions. "Dwayne, which way do I go?"

Then there were no voices at all. All she could hear was the pounding of her own heart. Overhead a very big animal scampered down a limb. Or maybe it was just the wind. But standing there all by herself, she couldn't help but worry. Maybe it was a raccoon. Did raccoons bite? Or a big snake. Or maybe a tiger had escaped from the circus and was hungry. Carolisa chose the right-hand path and flew.

She tripped over a root and went down hard. That only made her get up and run faster. She didn't care that she was crying tears of fear. She wanted to scream, but she couldn't draw enough breath.

The path jinked hard to the right, and she almost slammed into a big metal pipe fastened to a squat metal stand. Underneath the pipe ran a little stream. But it wasn't water. It was some thick black liquid that flowed like glue and stunk horribly. Carolisa ran faster still, her breath coming in little gasping cries.

Then she heard the voice up ahead. It was Dwayne. It had to be. She stopped and leaned against a sapling. When her breath had eased and her legs weren't trembling so, she used her shirttail to clear the tears from her face. No way was her brother going to see she had gotten so scared. Then she started walking calmly on down the trail.

She was halfway around the bend when she realized that it wasn't Dwayne at all.

A man in a strange yellow suit like a raincoat with legs was struggling with a valve and cursing hard. On his feet were yellow boots, and the boots were fastened to the trousers and the trousers to the jacket. He wore yellow gloves as well, and there was a yellow hood, but it was thrown back to reveal his pockmarked face. Carolisa was pretty certain this man wasn't part of the community. She'd never heard language like what he was saying since they had arrived at Kingdom Come. The man cursed and struggled with a big metal wheel, like a faucet handle but bigger. As big as the steering wheel on their car.

There was a tap just below the faucet. It was gushing out that foul black goo she had seen running along under the pipe. The stuff was coming out so fast it sounded like a roaring motor. It shot out straight four or five feet, then splashed down but didn't really splash at all. Carolisa stood and watched and thought how strange it was. The stuff ran like hot molasses. But it smelled like it was burning her nostrils. No wonder the man was talking such bad language. He stood in the middle of a huge collection of pipes and valves and metal vats, all of it on a flat concrete platform surrounded by a high metal fence. The door to the fence was open, and the goo shot out the opening and ran down alongside the pipe. Beyond the collection of pipes and concrete stood a little pond, and this was also surrounded by a fence. Beyond the pond and a stand of trees she could just make out the corner of a very big building.

Carolisa realized she was looking at the textile mill where her father and mother worked. She had seen it from the other side one Saturday when all the children of the employees had been invited in. She had walked down the long lines of clattering machines, fascinated by the speed and the precision. Her father was called a shop foreman and was responsible for seven lines of machines. Her mother was a bookkeeper. Both her parents called the work a godsend. Carolisa had no idea what they meant by that, but she had been very proud of her daddy keeping all those machines working so fast.

Something about the way this man kept attacking the big faucet left her pretty sure he was not supposed to be there. Finally the man picked up a big wrench, fitted it into the spokes of the wheel, and yanked the wheel over. The foul black goo stopped flowing so hard. Another cursing tug on the big wheel, and the goo slowed further. Carolisa knew she had to get out of there before he cut off the flow and looked up. She backed around the bend, then turned on her heels and ran.

This time, as she jinked down the other path, she heard the boys up ahead. Only now they weren't laughing. Carolisa was running so hard she couldn't completely stop when the fence rose up in front of her. She snagged a couple of the metal links to keep from falling. A sign above her head read, "Hamlin Reservoir. Keep out."

Beyond the fence rose a thin stand of young pines. Beyond that was a little muddy beach, then water. Three boys sprawled in the mud and moaned.

"Dwayne!" Carolisa frantically searched up and down the line of fencing until she saw where rain had washed out a small gully. She scrambled under and hurried over.

All three of the boys had been retching their guts out. Dwayne looked up at her and mouthed a word, but she couldn't make out what he said. She didn't need to. The boys were slick with water and mud, and there were crawl marks where they had pulled themselves out of the water. At least they hadn't drowned.

Carolisa looked around and saw immediately what had happened. Farther up to her right, the stinking black goo flowed under the fence. Its entry into the lake was masked by the pines growing near the lake's edge. But she knew what she was looking at, and recognized the inky black stain spreading out over the water.

One of the boys was sprawled right at the lake's edge. He had scooped out the mud with his writhing, and his face was now drenched with the muck. Carolisa grabbed one arm and tried to pull him farther up. She slipped in the mud and went down hard. She rose back up and shrilled, "You've got to help me!"

The boy groaned and feebly kicked his feet, his other arm wrapped tight to his belly. Carolisa managed to drag him up another three feet, then went back over to her brother and said, "I'll go get help!"

She scrambled under the fence, and as she raced back along the path she realized it would be faster to go to the textile plant than all the way back home. If only she could keep from running into that strange bad man.

THIRTY-NINE

Dottie's next call came from the back of a taxi speeding her toward the Orlando airport. When they finished talking, Ben clicked off his mobile phone and reached for his coat. His heart surged as much over the thought of seeing Dottie again as with the news. Miller Kedrick. The name meant nothing to him, but Dottie sounded adamant that the same man behind the cocaine smuggling was also the FBI's chief source. He had his hand on the doorknob when a thought struck him, one so powerful he knew it came from beyond himself.

He picked up his phone again, conscious of how remarkable it was that such thoughts could feel so normal now. Divine intervention, personal guidance from above, an intimate connection with the will of God—he would previously have dismissed such notions out of hand. Ben punched in the number from memory, reflecting on how much had changed over the past few weeks. Especially inside himself.

But it was not Evan Hawkins's deadpan secretary who answered the phone. Instead a strange young voice said, "Justin Ball's office."

Ben froze. Justin Ball was Theron Head's personal assistant. Which could only mean one thing.

"Hello?"

"Oh, excuse me." He opted for a nasal whine, seeking to mask his voice. "I was after the deputy assistant director's office."

"That is correct. Justin Ball is acting DAD."

"And, ah, I'm sorry, I had been given another name, wait, I have it somewhere. Here it is, Evan Hawkins."

"Mr. Hawkins is on leave. Who is calling?"

"Thank you, I'll call back later." Ben hung up. He stood there, his mind racing, running, finally arriving at the only possible conclusion. He dialed Evan's home number. When his former boss answered, Ben asked, "Is this line secure?"

"It doesn't matter any more." Evan sounded more than dispirited. He sounded vacant, as though the man Ben knew was no longer there. "I took the case before the director of the FBI. Right to the top. Dumbest thing I've ever done in my life."

"No it wasn't."

"The director brought in Theron. The man had obviously been preparing for this option. He had a file ready, every slip I've ever made, all painted to reveal an agent slowly losing control."

"Evan, hold on a minute."

"I've been put on indefinite leave, pending a full disciplinary hearing." The man's voice broke. "I'm as good as dead."

"Just listen to me, will you? Going to the director has probably saved your hide."

"What are you talking about?"

"I don't have time to tell you everything right now. Can you come down here?"

"Get real, Ben. Traveling down to the cult right now would be like shooting myself through the heart."

"It's not a cult." But he said it without heat. "And you know this as well as I do, or you wouldn't have taken it to the director."

"I don't know what I think any more."

"You did the right thing, believe me. And I'm asking you down here because we're about ready to light a fire under Theron Head and his gang. Get down to North Carolina in time and you can strike the match yourself."

Evan Hawkins emerged from the plane and entered the Charlotte airport terminal a tired old man. The power and confidence Ben knew so well was gone. For the first time since the attack had been leveled against Lando Buhler, and through him against the community, Ben found himself growing angry. He walked over and gripped Evan's hand, willing the man to accept his own strength, his own confidence. "It's good to see you, Evan."

"I wish I knew why I was here." The man's head was bowed, his forehead creased like a fresh-plowed field. "I move from one gigantic mistake to another these days."

"No you don't." Ben extracted the duffel bag from the man's limp fingers. "You were right when you went to the director, and you were right to come down here now."

Evan put up no resistance as Ben guided him toward the exit. "All I can say for certain is, I couldn't live with myself. Why, I don't know. But there wasn't enough evidence to warrant the kind of attack Theron is planning."

"Not planning," Ben corrected grimly. "Implementing."

"It's already started?"

"He thinks it has." Ben pushed through the outer doors and directed Evan toward the spot reserved for police vehicles. "But he's wrong."

Evan surveyed the Douglas sheriff's car with dismay. "Don't tell me you've joined them."

Ben opened the trunk, stowed Evan's bag, then pointed him to the passenger seat. "There's so much to tell you, I don't know where to start."

But once they were seated, Ben found himself unwilling to speak. Instead his mind was caught by another image. That of his own arrival, and the way he had seen things so differently from the outside. It was only now, he realized, that he had witnessed God's hand within the community that he could understand. Or at least begin to.

Evan asked impatiently, "Are you going to keep me completely in the dark?"

"Sorry." It was impossible, Ben realized, to describe accurately his own personal transformation. So he would need to stow that away and hope that with time Evan would be as touched as he had been himself. And pray. Pray hard for his friend. In the meantime, all he could speak about were the barest facts. "It looks like we're about to arrest Theron's chief source on charges of smuggling cocaine."

Evan's jaw hit his chest. "What?"

Swiftly Ben recounted what little he knew. He finished with, "I've been in touch with Glen Winters down in our Miami office. He's coordinating the investigation. No contact with Washington until we get things tied down. He's coloring outside the lines until he hears back from us."

Evan worked swiftly through the news and came up with, "You were right all along, then."

"Looks that way."

"Is it a cult at all?"

"No." Definite about this. "Not now, not ever."

Whatever Evan found in Ben's features, it was enough to cause him to turn away, shake his head, and sigh quietly. "Why are we sitting here?"

"I have a friend coming in from Orlando. A reporter. She's the one who broke the story about the Caribbean smuggling operation."

"You can trust her?"

"Absolutely." Ben checked his watch and opened his door. "You just sit tight and relax. I'll be back as soon as I can."

It was good he moved when he did, for as he entered the airport he heard the announcement that Dottie's plane was landing fifteen minutes early. He sprinted through the terminal, flashing his badge at the security checkpoint, racing down the long connecting passage. He rounded the corner and spotted her standing there with her weary face and her bags hanging slack. She gave a little cry, dropped her cases, and rushed toward him. Ben felt his heart clench up tight at the way she sped forward, her arms outstretched, her face tight with need. He gripped her and held her with a fierce desire never to let her go. Not ever again.

Their reunion was cut short, however, by the pinging of Ben's mobile phone. He groaned, "I should have left that thing in the car."

But Dottie was already loosening her embrace. Reluctantly she allowed, "Maybe you'd better answer."

Ben flipped open the phone and said, "This better be important."

"Ben?" Hal Drew's voice was pushed a full octave higher. "Where are you?"

"Charlotte airport."

"You hightail it back up here, you hear what I'm saying?" There was the sound of caterwauling and chaos in the background. "We got us a full-blown crisis here!"

Ben was already moving for the door, drawing Dottie along with him. "What's the matter?"

"Man, we got us a war on our hands!" Hal's accent was thickened by panic and anger both. "They done gone after our children!"

FORTY

Ben made the trip back to Douglas in record time. Once he cleared
Charlotte's traffic-clogged downtown, he cut off the siren. Dottie
sat beside him, tightly grabbing the door and the central console,
describing in detail first her journey to the Caribbean and then her
confrontation with the Reverend Thurgood Innes. Evan sat in the
backseat absorbing everything. Ben found it remarkable that the
speeding car and the tensely told story only seemed to increase his
clarity. He listened and at the same time he thought ahead. Hal called
twice more, giving details of the drama unfolding at Kingdom Come.
This did not add to the confusion at all. Instead, the closer they drew
to the community, the clearer became the course of action.

As they crested the final rise and the fence came into view, Ben
handed Dottie his phone. "Call the *Charlotte Observer*. Ask for the
managing editor of the news department. I forget her name. She was
going to send a reporter up here. Find out his mobile number and
where he is."

Evan protested, "Bringing the press into an investigation without
authorization is a serious offense."

"I didn't step over the line here," Ben replied. "Theron Head's little
gang has been climbing all over the media." When Evan did not
protest further, Ben continued to Dottie, "Ask if they'll send up a photographer."

She was already through to the woman and talking hurriedly when Ben pulled up in front of the Kingdom Come medical clinic. As he opened his door she grabbed his arm and said, "She wants to know what's going on."

"Tell her everything," he said. "Long as she promises not to break the Florida story until our Miami people have a chance to move in."

Dottie handed him the note she had just scribbled. "The reporter is supposed to be somewhere around Hamlin."

"Good." To Evan he said, "Let's go."

Hal stood in the clinic entrance waving them forward. "You believe this mess?"

"Absolutely." Ben handed him Dottie's note. "This is a reporter from the *Observer*. He's nosing around somewhere by Hamlin. Track him down and bring him here."

Hal took one look at Ben's face and stowed away all his further questions. "The girl's name is Carolisa. She and her folks are in the waiting room."

"How are the boys?"

"Doc's not certain yet, but he thinks they'll all pull through okay." Hal made a noose out of his two ham-size fists. "Would I ever like to get my hands on them who did this."

"If we're lucky," Ben replied, moving for the door, "that's exactly what will happen."

FORTY-ONE

Wayne Oates made easier going of the path than the two EPA men. They stumbled and cursed sleepily on behind him, making more noise than a herd of elephants. Which only made Wayne more pleased he had insisted on their getting an early start.

The EPA boys had whined and moaned over being woken while it was still dark. There was nothing in their training that had prepared them for a dawn raid. They were regular Washington nine-to-fivers, comfortable with their clean government labs and their careful little routines. Yet here they were, slogging through a mist-draped pine forest. Under other circumstances, Wayne would have loved the hike. His few fond memories of childhood all were of dawn hunts, the coon dogs racing ahead while he and his father and brother marched in a quiet line. Now the first birds chirped sleepily, the trees gave off the sparkling scent of rising pine sap, and the mist glowed softly with the strengthening light. But there was no peace to the day, not for Wayne. Only determination, slow anger, and worry.

He had not been able to raise Theron Head. Or his assistant, Justin Ball. Which was a huge perplexity, seeing as how Justin was now Wayne's acting superior. Normally Wayne's phone calls were responded to instantly. Theron had taken to calling him twice a day, mornings and evenings, pressing him to find the key and turn it. Which was exactly what he had done.

Sabotaging the textile company's processing system had been a stroke of genius. Even Theron himself had said so. Wayne had made the suggestion, and Theron had pulled the strings of his incredible network. Like a spider seated at the center of a great Washington web, Theron had come back with EPA-registered blueprints of the textile company's system. Someone on the staff had identified the flow valve for the very worst of the chemicals, the ones used to color the fabrics and seal the dyes. Arsenic, zinc, lead—they were all in the runoff. The processing plant used the latest system on the market, and was so clean there had been no problem with their drawing cooling water from the town's reservoir. There was a separate pond for the runoff, and an underground collecting point for the processed chemicals. But there was also an emergency flow valve, there had to be. It was perfect.

So where was Theron?

Wayne stepped into the clearing that surrounded the pumping station. He checked the ground, seeing nothing but the softly drifting mist, hearing nothing but the EPA scientists' grumbling and stomping feet. "This way."

He led them around the fenced-in area to where the cooling pipe ran up from the reservoir. He pointed at the ground. "See that?"

The two scientists were suitably horrified. "Is that what I think it is?"

"Unprocessed dyes and finishing chemicals," Wayne agreed. He pointed to his left. "The town's water supply is right down there about two hundred yards."

"Let's get a sample and move on down to the lake," the scientist said.

The mist seemed to congeal, not into people, but into Wayne's worst nightmares. "Hold it right there!" A grim and angry Ben Atkins stepped forward and announced, "You men are all under arrest. Hal, read them their rights."

"Get these cuffs off me!"

Ben ignored Wayne Oates's furious protest. He kept a firm hand on the older of the two EPA scientists, who were too shocked and horrified to do more than complain weakly. Clearly the scientists had no idea what was going on. Evan Hawkins held grimly to the struggling Wayne Oates. Color and fury were back in the deputy assistant director's features. He held the writhing agent with an iron grip.

Wayne shouted, "I *demand* to know what's going on here!"

To Ben's vast satisfaction, the reporter and photographer had remained where he had ordered, back by the patrol cars, next to Dottie and the pastor. The photographer was busy snapping pictures as they approached. When Wayne realized he was being captured on film, he struggled harder still. "You're in big trouble, Atkins! You're *finished*!"

Ben halted a few paces from the first car, keeping his little surprise concealed. "Wayne Oates, you are hereby charged with subverting the course of justice and tampering with evidence in a federal case."

The agent's face was gripped with a frenzied rage. "Do you have any notion just how crazy you sound?"

"You are also charged with assault and intentional infliction of grievous bodily harm."

"What!" The agent's shout was overloud for the quietly strengthening day. "On who?"

"On Dwayne Verrin, Tom Simmons, and Barry Elgin."

"I don't have any idea who you're talking about!"

"You deny coming here yesterday and opening the release valve, thereby dumping untreated industrial chemicals directly into the town's water supply?"

Wayne froze, captured momentarily like a deer in the headlights of an oncoming train. "What?"

"I asked you a simple question. Do you deny dumping those chemicals?"

He swallowed his fear and wrestled against the cuffs and Evan's grip. "I demand that you release me!"

"Do you deny the charges?"

"Of course I do! This whole charade is nothing but your own funeral, Atkins! Soon as word gets back to Washington, you're the one who'll be wearing chains!"

Ben turned back to where the pastor and Dottie stood. "Bring Carolisa on around."

Wayne stopped struggling as the slender girl with the mop of strawberry blond curls was brought into view. He squinted, but clearly did not recognize her.

The girl, however, watched him with great solemn eyes. Ben asked quietly, "Do you recognize this man?"

"Yes sir, Mr. Atkins." She nodded up and down, once, twice, three times. "This is the man."

"Who *is* this girl?"

"Quiet," Ben said, releasing only a trace of his fury. Even so, it was enough to back the girl closer to Dottie. He forced himself to calm down, and said, "You're absolutely positive?"

"He wore a funny yellow suit," the girl replied. "Gloves and boots and everything. But he didn't have on his hat. I saw his face real good." She nodded again. "That's him all right."

Ben shot a glance at Wayne, who was watching the girl with wide-eyed horror. Ben demanded, "You actually saw him turning the valve?"

"It was stuck. He had to use the wrench to get it shut." She used the hand not clinging to Dottie to clear the curls from her forehead. "That's the man who made Dwayne sick, all right."

FORTY-TWO

Ben had his feet propped on the desk and his hands laced behind his head when the pastor entered the Kingdom Come police station. Chuck Griffin smiled down at him and said, "You look to me like a man who's made himself at home."

"That's exactly how I feel." He was finding it increasingly easy to admit, even to himself. "What can I do for you?"

"Take a turn with me, will you?"

Ben checked his watch. He wasn't due to pick up Dottie for another half-hour. "A quick one."

"That's fine." They returned to the outer office, where Jeff was talking on the phone. Ben told him, "I better just go ahead and check out now."

"Hold just one minute please, Mrs. Blake." The young man cupped the receiver. "It's aliens this time. They landed in her back garden last night and they stomped down all her runner-beans."

"Not a chance," Ben said. "I'm all done for the day."

Outside they were greeted by a sweet-scented afternoon. The magnolia across the street was bowed down with blossoms the size of dinner plates. Ben took a deep breath, and said, "Hard to believe we're almost back to normal."

Chuck pointed them away from city hall. "For now."

Ben groaned, "Don't tell me there's more."

"No, not at the moment. And I don't have any prophetic word either. Call it a pastor's hunch."

"Then I don't want to hear about it." Ben waved it away. "Not for a few days, anyway."

Chuck greeted a passing car. "Have you seen the papers?"

"Done my best to avoid them."

"Dottie's entire story was run by the *Charlotte Observer*. Along with an editorial by that tight-faced managing editor. She was remarkably up front in what she had to say. How the press tended to paint all evangelists with an extremist's brush, trying to color them all as lunatics. And how this time they themselves had been stained."

"That was brave of her."

"Exactly what Dottie said when she dropped the piece by. She also says she's received her final check and severance notice from *Newsday*. Apparently they did not take kindly to her attacking them in another newspaper."

"They are the ones who twisted her words."

Chuck waved that aside. "That's not what I wanted to talk with you about. Hear anything from Washington?"

"Theron Head is under formal investigation. And Evan Hawkins has been reinstated," Ben replied, as proud of the news as he had been of anything in a long time. "I'm trying to get him down here for a long vacation. I want him to experience this place for himself. He's promised to get back next month."

Chuck covered a half-block in contemplative silence before saying, "Don't be too disappointed if Evan doesn't find the same sense of calling as you have."

"He was down for the bust, he should—"

"Even so, what he sees and what you have had *revealed* to you are very different things."

Ben found a bit of the day's spice diminished. "That what you wanted to see me about?"

"No." Chuck stopped and faced him. "Ben, I want you to consider becoming mayor of Kingdom Come."

That rocked him back on his heels. "What?"

"Call it city manager if you like, although I'd prefer to see you take on an official role that requires the people voting you in. The thing is, I'm being called away more and more frequently. We're having new communities springing up all over the place, and they all want me to come around. I can't do that and be in charge of day-to-day matters here." When Ben did not respond, Chuck added, "The land of Israel saw fit to divide matters of the temple from matters of the temporal. I need someone here whom I can trust."

"B-but . . ." Ben tried to find an excuse, but could only come up with, "I had sort of figured my work here was done."

Chuck smiled. "Is that what you want?"

He searched up and down the street, but all he saw was a mother waving at them and sunlight off a passing car. "I gotta tell you, Chuck, I was feeling pretty good about myself and the day until you showed up."

Chuck patted his arm. "Just pray on it, will you? That's all I ask."

ABOUT THE AUTHORS

LARRY BURKETT is co-CEO and chairman of the board of directors of Crown Financial Ministries, an organization formed from the September 2000 merger of two Christian ministries, Christian Financial Concepts and Crown Ministries. Crown Financial Ministries is a nonprofit organization dedicated to teaching biblical principles of money management. Its four radio programs, "Money Matters," "How to Manage Your Money," "Money*Watch*," and "A Money Minute," are carried on more than 2,000 radio outlets worldwide.

Larry is the author of more than fifty books, including the bestselling novels *The Illuminati* and *The THOR Conspiracy*. Larry and his wife, Judy, have four grown children and nine grandchildren; they live in Gainesville, Georgia.

Before becoming an award-winning author, T. DAVIS BUNN earned a master's degree in international finance and worked as a business executive in Europe, Africa, and the Middle East. He has written fifty books, including such bestsellers as *The Great Divide, The Book of Hours, Tidings of Comfort and Joy, One Shenandoah Winter, The Warning,* and *The Ultimatum.* In July 2000 his novel *The Meeting Place* (coauthored with Janette Oke) won the Christy Award for Fiction. Davis and his wife, Isabella, live in Oxfordshire, England.

The THOR Conspiracy

BY LARRY BURKETT

A staged accident in New Mexico's Alamogordo missile test facility kills two men who know the ugly truth about the United States' nuclear program . . . A network of armed environmental "regulators" blankets the U.S., ready to deal with any citizen who interferes with its nefarious missions . . .

It begins in the 1960s—an unimaginable series of political machinations leading to one act of greed and destruction after another—until in the twenty-first century the world faces a single global dictator. Behind the takeover is an odd, yet frighteningly effective alliance of international governments and inner-city gangs.

Lining up against the tyrannical forces are three men, each committed to exposing the fifty-year-old conspiracy, and together capable of mounting a formidable resistance. Combining insider savvy, media firepower, and a genius's computer skills, Dale Crawford, Thomas Galt, and Jeff Wells are about to take on the most malevolent superpower the world has ever known. If they succeed, the world has a chance. If they fail, the world is doomed to the prospect of a "Fourth Reich." The key to the world's future is the THOR conspiracy.

ISBN 0-7852-7200-3 • Trade Paperback • 336 pages

The Book of Hours

BY T. DAVIS BUNN

After his wife's death, Brian Blackstone's days became a meaningless blur. But now, recovering from a tropical fever, he finally arrives in the English village of Knightsbridge to confront the inheritance he doesn't want to claim. His wife had insisted that Castle Keep was a place of enchantment and urged him to hold on to the crumbling property. Impoverished and alone, Brian feels only the despair of trying to honor his wife's dying wish.

Then a mysterious letter sends Brian on a search to find the secrets of the ancient estate. The local doctor, Cecilia Lyons, though suspicious at first, soon becomes an ally in the fight to save Castle Keep before it can be auctioned off to the highest bidder.

Before he comes to the end of his quest, Brian will learn that the power of prayer can reach through the centuries in a surprising and wonderful way. Will he find renewal for his spirit and healing for his broken heart?

ISBN 0-7852-7088-4 • Trade Paperback • 324 pages